CW00501466

"With the war still young, there are many battles and struggles ahead, there were times that I was unsure if I could go on, but not him, he never lost his way, on and on he marched, the hope of peace burning bright in his eyes, and our dreams rested solely on his shoulders, I feared what might happen in the battles to come, but he always stood up to the challenge with courage and distinction, let us continue the story."

~ Amelia Phoenix ~

Prologue

The continent of Jarvlan, once a peaceful and serene landscape. The army of demons led by Shiento has now shattered that peace, the landscape now littered with ash and dead bodies, the once luscious, green fields of Selania are now painted red. The once harmonious and silent mountain regions, now full of hissing and infested with demons.

On the other side of the continent, on the western mountain ranges lies the free mechanical city of Qurendia, a scientific wonder, completely unrivalled and unprecedented. The city is slightly south of a large metallic mountain, the city was mechanical and levitated over the mountain region below, the city was held down by a series of gigantic chains that were embedded into the mountains below.

On the southern edge of Jarvlan, lies the ruined structure of Shiento's Black Fortress. Shiento was treading over the crumbled heap, scouring for something. Lady Drask stood under the ruined archway where the front gate once stood watching her master. The sea around them lapping onto the shore, the sun climbing into the sky over the ocean.

Chapter 1: Plotting Revenge

Shiento began to move bits of rubble from an area near the east wall, Lady Drask began to walk over as Shiento threw a large boulder over his shoulder. Shiento then looked down into a gaping hole, at the bottom Shiento and Lady Drask could see two metal spikes sticking out of the ground, the tips glinting in the late morning sun.

"There they are," hissed Shiento.
"What exactly are they, my Lord?" asked Lady Drask.
"My old dragon sabres," answered Shiento.
"Why would you need them?" queried Lady Drask.
"Because I intend to face Silus head on, and this time he will learn that his skill and power will count for nothing," replied Shiento.
"You intend to take on a human form, but why?" questioned Lady Drask.
"Perhaps because I will face Silus on a level playing field," stated Shiento, "maybe because I can use multiple forms of attack at once, or perhaps to fool Silus by approaching him looking like I am no threat."
"I... I think I understand my Lord," stammered Lady Drask.
"Never mind that Lady Drask, how is your wound healing?" asked Shiento.
"It has mostly healed," responded Lady Drask.

Shiento smiled at Lady Drask, the huge dragon then shook its body and dust flew off. Lady Drask jumped backwards to avoid the dust, she then watched as Shiento's body became engulfed in black flames. The huge dark inferno formed an enormous orb around Shiento's body, the orb slowly began to shrink down to match the same height as Lady Drask.

"Lord Shiento?" said Lady Drask, bewitched by the black flames dancing around.

As the flames died down, Lady Drask looked to the body in the void between the dying flames. Shiento then stomped his left foot on the ground to disperse the last of the flames. Shiento stood in his human form, medium length black hair that was swept backwards, he had an average build, he wore a white long sleeve shirt, white trousers and boots, his eyes were a dark hazel colour, and over his right eye was a large scar.

"My Lord... you look magnificent," stammered Lady Drask.
"That is very kind of you, Lady Drask," replied Shiento, "it is the first time I have ever transformed into this body."
"So, what do you intend to do my Lord?" asked Lady Drask.
"Well there are several options of how we can proceed," answered Shiento, "but we shall worry about that a little later, for now I must retrieve my swords."

"That is simple, they are only at the bottom of the hole," replied Lady Drask, "I could retrieve them for you my Lord."

"I am afraid that will not work," responded Shiento.

"What do you mean my Lord?" questioned Lady Drask.

"When I placed those swords in a secret vault, I placed a security enchantment on the vault so that the swords will defend themselves with the magic imbedded within their blades," explained Shiento, "knowing that, would you still be willing to offer to retrieve my weapons?"

"I... I concede your point... my Lord," stammered Lady Drask, "so the blades will not react to you?"

"They will, but seeing as the blades are imbedded with my magic, I can reabsorb the magic as it attacks me," replied Shiento.

Shiento smiled at Lady Drask before walking to stand at the edge of the hole, Lady Drask watched as Shiento stared down into the deep hole. Shiento kicked a small stone into the hole, the sound of the stone hitting the walls echoed back up to reach Shiento and Lady Drask ears.

"Gather half a dozen of the strongest demons you can find, they will be our new Generals," ordered Shiento, as he looked up at Lady Drask.

"As you wish my Lord," answered Lady Drask, "any deployment orders my Lord?"

"No, not yet, I still want to consider possible attack options," replied Shiento.

"Very well, I shall go choose the candidates, as per your instructions my Lord," stated Lady Drask.
"I will be back in a short while," said Shiento as he hopped into the hole.

Lady Drask turned and walked towards the ruined front gate, behind her the sound of lightning crackling began to echo out of the hole, Lady Drask then unveiled her dragon wings and flapped her wings heavily, Lady Drask hovered in the air slightly before flying towards the cliffs, as she neared the cliff face she flapped her wings faster to gain attitude. Atop the cliffs, the plains beyond the cliff were covered with demons, demons of varying size and characteristics, Lady Drask hovered above the edge of the cliff.

"Warriors of Shiento, hear me!" shouted Lady Drask, "our Lord and master requires new Commanders to lead the rest into battle, who among you will answer the call, who dares to stand above the rest?"

The demons began to shout and roar, Lady Drask watched as some groups of demons began to push and shove each other, some titan size demons roared, and the demons began to settle down. After a while a large group of demons began to push their way to the front of the cliff, Lady Drask then landed on the very edge of the cliff as the demons stood before her.

"Well, well, it is pleasant to see so many eager to take command," smirked Lady Drask, "however our Lord and master has asked for only six Commanders, and I count a full dozen here, so let us take account of who is truly worthy."

Lady Drask walked down to the left end of the line, she then turned to look at the first demon, he carried a bow but was quite thin, Lady Drask smiled then pushed him out of the line, the demon fell backwards and the demons around him laughed.

"I asked for Commanders, not scraps of meat," snorted Lady Drask.

The second demon was a six-and-a-half-foot tall demon in heavy plate armour, he had a large battle-axe slung across its back and held a massive two handed sword in its right hand, Lady Drask smiled at the demon then proceeded to stand in front of a female demon who was the same height as her, the demon wore snakeskin leather clothing.

"You do not carry a weapon, that is a rather interesting choice my dear," said Lady Drask.
"I do not require a blade to kill my foe, Lady Drask, you should understand that looks alone can kill any man," hissed the demon.
"I like your confidence, what is your name?" asked Lady Drask.
"They call me Servana," answered Servana.
"And, why might I ask, do you stand before me when all the others all bring weapons and strength?" queried Lady Drask.

"Because these guys are all dim-witted, they believe strength alone will win a battle," explained Servana, "but I would argue, if strength was everything, then Silus would be dead, and Selania and indeed the rest of the world would be burnt to ash by now."

"True, very true my dear," agreed Lady Drask, "however, what skills do you have to convince me of your worthiness of leadership?"

"That is simple my dear, I command a legion of reptiles, they can spy, attack, assassinate or even torture our enemy," replied Servana, "and the fact that most of our enemies are men, and men are dogs when it comes to women, I can alter my appearance to tease any man, would you like a demonstration?"

"No, not necessary, very well Servana, you are officially a Commander of the dread one's army," said Lady Drask.

"I will not disappoint milady," replied Servana.

"We shall see, when our master reveals his plans," chuckled Lady Drask.

Lady Drask smiled then looked to the forth demon, then the fifth, as she looked to the sixth her smile faded, she stood in front of the three demons and with a snap of her fingers three large vines, sprouted out of the ground in front of them. The vines lashed around and sent the demons flying overhead into the middle of the assembled forces.

"You three are a waste of time," hissed Lady Drask.

As Lady Drask approached the seventh demon, a smile returned to her face, the demon had four arms, each wielding a crude looking black sword, Lady Drask then moved on to the next demon, who was in the line but instead of standing to attention and facing forward like the rest, this demon was sat on the ground preparing arrows from a quiver on his back, the demon did not look up at Lady Drask, but was focused on mixing powders and pastes before applying the mixture to its arrow tips.

"And what concoctions are we brewing?" asked Lady Drask.
"Well you see milady, no demon here has the knowledge to forge dragon's bane, but I have found a concoction that at least temporarily paralyzes a dragon, but is potent enough to kill humans, elves or dwarves almost instantly," answered the demon.
"Interesting, well you are an intriguing sort," laughed Lady Drask, "you are the first demon I have met, that is actually interested in alchemy."
"No disrespect milady, but I would not classify it as an interest," said the demon humbly.
"Then what would you classify it as?" asked Lady Drask.
"Alchemy for us, should be a necessity, anything that can weaken or instantly kill an enemy should be an option that is compulsory among this army," explained the demon.
"You only say that because you lack the strength and courage to face the enemy head on," spat the demon to the archer's right.

"You should hold your tongue!" shouted Lady Drask angrily, "do not speak unless spoken to, now get out of my sight, you growling mongrel."

"But... milady," stammered the demon.

"I said out of my sight! Or do you prefer I kill you now!" shouted Lady Drask.

The demon started mumbling as it turned to walk back into the rest of the group. Before the demon could join the rest of the demons, the demon roared in pain as he suddenly burst into flames. The demons looked up to see that Lady Drask had cast a spell.

"Let that be a warning to all of you!" shouted Lady Drask, "I will not tolerate insubordination, and neither will Lord Shiento!"

The demons all grunted in acknowledgment, Lady Drask then looked down to the archer demon as he finished applying his poison to his arrows.

"I like your initiative," said Lady Drask, "if you fight Silus or anyone from Urendos, then make doubly sure your arrows fly true."

"I swear it will be done milady," answered the demon.

"Excellent, carry on," smirked Lady Drask.

The tenth demon looked like it had climbed into a bale of hay, it was a tower of fur standing seven feet tall. Lady Drask quickly moved past and with a wave of her hand, a huge vine sprouted out of the ground, and slammed the demon across the chest. The eleventh demon was a five foot, eleven inches' tall demon that had two legs but two torsos back to back, two heads and four arms, the demon had a goofy smile and eyes like a fly.

"Are you sure you are ready to command demons?" asked Lady Drask.

The demon began hissing back at Lady Drask, the last demon was a tall female who had two spears strapped across her back and a large scythe in her left hand. The scythe stretched out the side of the pole the blade was crude and jagged. Lady Drask then turned back to the fly eyed demon and shooed him back out of the line.

"How disappointing," said Lady Drask, "twelve of you stepped forward, and only five are truly worthy of being a Commander, is there no one else?"

Lady Drask then walked behind the line of demons towards a rather small demon who was crouched down sharpening a series of daggers and swords. As Lady Drask approached the demon, it dropped its dagger and stood to attention.

"You carry all these blades?" asked Lady Drask as she looked down at the blades on the floor and on the demon's body.
"I do milady," answered the demon.
"Do you not consider yourself a worthy candidate?" asked Lady Drask.

"I am only good with my blades milady, I have no authority to boast and my skills are best suited in the heat of battle," replied the demon humbly.

"Well then, you better buck up your ideas," chuckled Lady Drask, "because you are going to be the sixth Commander."

"As you… as you wish, milady," stammered the demon.

"Excellent, now grab your blades and follow me," ordered Lady Drask, "and you five, follow me too."

The small demon quickly grabbed his blades and placed them in various sheathes around his body, before hurrying to catch up to the other demons and Lady Drask. The group of demons walked down a very narrow path down the side of the cliff, the rest of the demons stood still for a moment before turning to start fires or brawls amongst them.

~

In the hole, Shiento had landed at the bottom of the hole, as he went to grab the swords, they began to glow a bright crimson red. The light continued to glow brighter and caused Shiento to close his eyes and rise his left arm to block out the light. Suddenly the light faded, as Shiento lowered his arm and opened his eyes, he saw that he was standing on a large stone platform that appeared to be floating amongst the clouds.

"Oh joy," said Shiento, "my magic has deemed an illusion as its form of defence."
"Ye whom disturbs my form, stand fast, you face the shade of Shiento," growled a voice.
"I am Shiento and you will submit to my will once more," growled Shiento.
"Ye whom disturbs my form, stand fast, you face the shade of Shiento," growled the voice.
"Show yourself sentinel!" ordered Shiento.

As Shiento gazed around he saw a stone statue stand in front of him, the statue looked like a dragon, with its wings folded against its back and its legs stretched to the ground like the statue was standing guard.

"I do not wish to waste time here," growled Shiento, "let me pass sentinel, I am the owner of these blades."
"As per my creation, should anyone try to take the blades, I am to defend them until my destruction," answered the sentinel.
"Then face me already so I can get on with more important matters!" demanded Shiento.

The statue began to crack as Shiento spoke, the statue then stood up on its four legs, its wings broke apart but the fragments of wings levitated in the air above the stone dragon's body, and the head began to smoke as the statue breathed heavily. Its eyes glowed bright crimson red, Shiento raised his right hand towards the statue.

"Pythlon baz!" shouted Shiento.

A huge black lightning bolt shot from Shiento's hand, the bolt hit the stone beast directly on the head. Shiento watched in shock as the demon shook its head briefly, before staring at Shiento and letting out an ear bursting shriek.

"Interesting, you have adopted magical resistances," said Shiento in admiration.

The stone beast then began to charge at Shiento. Shiento dropped to his left knee, as the beast leapt at Shiento, he rolled back and kicked the stone beast over him.

"Frustus!" shouted Shiento as he rolled to his feet.

Shiento watched as several spikes of ice erupted out of the ground, the stone beast landed on the spikes. Shiento smiled as the ice pierced through the stone beast's body, the beast groaned as it wriggled unable to free itself from its impalement.

"Looks like I win," said Shiento.
"Defence protocols failed," groaned the stone beast, "the dragon sabres are yours, my master."

Shiento watched as the stone beast's body began to crumble to small stone fragments, Shiento then turned to face a large boulder that appeared in the middle of the stone platform. On top of the boulder laid Shiento's dragon sabres, Shiento approached the boulder the air humming with energy.

"Long time no see," sighed Shiento, "now we have got work to do."

Shiento placed his hand over the sword handles, as he wrapped his fingers around the handle, he watched as the blades became engulfed in a hurricane of black fire. Shiento then looked around to see the edge of the platform crumbling away, as the fire around Shiento's dragon sabres began to fade away, so did the platform arena around him.

~

Outside the ruins of the Black Fortress, Lady Drask and the six demons had reached the beach, as they walked towards the stone bridge that stood in front of the ruins. As they approached the bridge, a large black flash erupted from the fortress. Lady Drask lined the demons up at the bottom of the bridge, before proceeding up the bridge to stand in the void where the front gate once stood. As Lady Drask stood in the gateway, Shiento climbed out of the hole and immediately walked over to Lady Drask.

"My Lord, it is good to see you safely retrieved your dragon sabres," said Lady Drask.
"Thank you, Lady Drask," replied Shiento, "and how has your assignment gone?"

"Well I wish I could say it was easy or simple," explained Lady Drask, "however twelve demons stepped forward and seven of them I would not trust to steal candy from an infant."

"So, you only have five Commanders?" asked Shiento.

"No, I would not have disobeyed your orders," answered Lady Drask, "I then spotted a very promising, knife wielding demon, who is filling the sixth slot that you asked for."

"Superb, I knew I could rely on you, even if I cannot rely on the demons," smiled Shiento.

"They are simple creatures my Lord," whispered Lady Drask.

"Indeed, well let me inspect your recruits," said Shiento.

"Of course, they await at the bottom of the bridge," replied Lady Drask waving her right hand to point down the bridge.

Lady Drask led Shiento down the stone bridge, at the bottom the six demons stood to attention. As Shiento stepped off the bridge, the demons all bowed to Shiento.

"Greetings friends, you know why you have been brought here, to stand before me that is," said Shiento, "I am in need of new Commanders, seeing as my previous Generals were slain on their assignment to destroy Urendos."

"Merely give an order my Lord, and we will be happy to kill any and all you wish," hissed Servana.

"Ahh... Servana, it would seem you finally found the opportunity to step up," stated Shiento.

"Yes milord," hissed Servana, as she bowed again, "but I assure you milord, I am here to serve."

"We shall see, but your loyalty is not what I ask," explained Shiento, "I just need your help to bring down Silus, without losing all of the army to his magic."

"Sounds like a promising assignment my Lord," said the archer demon, "it will give me a chance to see Silus squirm in agony at the hands of my poisons."

"Take it easy friends," replied Shiento calmly, "Silus is not your immediate target, I have a far more interesting series of tasks for you to complete first."

"Ahh, so what would you ask of us my Lord?" asked the scythe demon.

"Well seeing as I have an alchemist and archer before me," explained Shiento, "I would deem your abilities fit to assassinate the Duke of Qurendia, while Servana you can head for Selania in disguise."

"Am I to kill the King?" asked Servana.

"Not at first, my dear," answered Shiento, "initially I want you to spy on them, find out what their plans are and if Silus, Celestia or anyone of significant importance shows up then you must publicly assassinate the King of Selania, but do not engage Silus or anyone else for that matter, do you understand?"

"Yes master," answered Servana as she bowed to Shiento, "and what a glorious task you have handed to me, but if Silus shows up in Selania, I will not be able to stop myself from engaging him."

"Yes, but so long as you understand what actions I am sanctioning for you to do," replied Shiento, "the last four, you will be marching up the spine of Jarvlan, your target is the Dark Forest, eradicate any and all life you find there."

"As you wish my Lord," answered the scythe demon.

"And before you ask," interrupted Shiento, "I will send four battalions and some titans with you, now all of you, you have your assignments, now go!"

"Yes, Lord Shiento," chanted the six demons.

The archer demon conjured a large black wolf to ride across the beach, Servana transformed into a large black and green viper before disappearing up the side of the cliff. The remaining four demons marched to the top of the cliff, Shiento then turned his head to see Lady Drask staring at him.

"What seems to be bothering you my dear?" asked Shiento.

"Do you even intend on them returning?" queried Lady Drask.

"If they wish to rise to be in command, then they must prove they can fulfil my wishes," answered Shiento.

"So only if they pass this trial of yours, do they earn the black armour?" asked Lady Drask.

"That is correct," answered Shiento, "I do not suppose you will accept my gift of the Black Steel armour now?"

"I would rather not have that armour bound to my form, my Lord," replied Lady Drask, "no disrespect of course."
"None taken my darling," said Shiento humbly, "it would ruin your stunning visage."
"Was that a compliment?" asked Lady Drask, "seems rather out of character for the demonic Lord of the demon army, would you not agree?"

Shiento and Lady Drask began smiling at each other, Shiento then grabbed Lady Drask's right arm with his left hand and pulled her in close. As Lady Drask wrapped her arms around Shiento's neck, the two stared into each other's eyes.

"It has been a while since we have embraced each other like this," stated Shiento.
"Far too long, my love," said Lady Drask.

They tilted their heads to the side and as their lips met, a gentle gust of wind blew across the beach, the waves lapping upon the shore. When Shiento and Lady Drask stepped apart, Shiento turned to face the ruined fortress.

"The gate is destroyed, there is nothing to be done about that," sighed Shiento, "but our home can still be resurrected."
"Indeed, let us get to work," said Lady Drask.

The two stood on either side of the stone bridge, they looked at each other and nodded. In unison they raised their hands and the ruined mess of the fortress began to tremble. Shiento and Lady Drask closed their eyes and lifted their hands higher, as they did the stones levitated into the air. The stones began circling each other, Lady Drask and Shiento then lowered their left hands, and the stones began to slam into the ground, forming a small castle where the fortress once stood.

"You know, it is all well and good us rebuilding our home," said Lady Drask, "but if Silus..."
"Silus has no reason to return here," interrupted Shiento, "he has already destroyed the Akaloth Gate, there is nothing left here to attract his attention."
"You are assuming Silus begins focusing on the rest of the continent?" asked Lady Drask.
"I am not assuming anything," answered Shiento, "I know he will change his focus."

Shiento then looked down at the stone bridge, his breath was heavy, like he had been running. Lady Drask turned to look at Shiento.

"What is bothering you darling?" asked Lady Drask.
"I asked you if Silus knew of our prisoner," answered Shiento, "I believe you were right that before the attack, he did not know for certainty that Fiona Wythernspine was here."
"But?" asked Lady Drask.
"But I have not been able to sense any organic life force below the surface," answered Shiento, "there is a faint aroma of dragon blood, meaning either Silus

or Celestia suffered a wound or two, but I am sure Fiona is not buried down there."

"Meaning Silus found her," said Lady Drask, "how bad can that really be, she went down without a fight, when they invaded our home all those years ago."

"True, but she was not focused then, she was worried that Silus was not allowed to fight at her side," responded Shiento, "but I know Silus trained her, I saw how she fought, her style is similar to Silus', with Silus at her side, you can be sure that she will be a much more difficult adversary the next time you meet."

"Understood," said Lady Drask, "what are the remainder of our forces going to do my Lord?"

"For now, I only want the new commanders and any force assigned to them to mobilise," answered Shiento, "we must strike at Silus's potential allies and therefore weaken him, then we will make a final strike against his life."

"Sounds devious, I love it," chuckled Lady Drask.

"It does, does it not," smirked Shiento, "Silus you will fall to me, sooner or later you will fall."

Lady Drask and Shiento began laughing manically, their laughs echoing across the beach. The demons on the cliff began cheering and roaring to the sky, the sun had soared into the sky, turning the orange sky a pale blue. Shiento then turned to look at the demons standing near the edge of the cliff.

"Silus! We are going to rip you apart piece by blood-soaked piece!" shouted Shiento.

The demons continued to roar and cheer as their voices echoed across the land, the wind began howling forcefully as it rushed through the mountain regions around Flammehelm heading north. Shiento took a deep breath before unleashing a loud roar, the roar exploded from Shiento with such force that the waves were pushed away from the shore, and the cliffs began to tremble.

Chapter 2: The Past Bites Back

Silus awoke suddenly, he was gasping for breath as if waking from a nightmare. Silus looked around to see he was in the war room, he was sat in a chair in front of the war table. As Silus tried to catch his breath, he could hear someone grunting outside the war room door.

"Alright Shiento, you want to divide us, and I am in a playful mood to play along to your little game," Silus whispered to himself.

Silus stood up from the chair and looked down at the war table, he placed several black markers on the spine of the world map, and a black marker on Qurendia and Selania. Silus then walked around the table and headed for the door. Silus opened the door slowly and silently as he gazed out into the great hall, he could see Fiona practising with two dragon sabres, similar to Silus' but the blades had a tint of red glyphs etched into the metal. Silus stepped out of the doorway and quietly leant against the nearest stone column. Fiona continued practising her manoeuvres, not noticing Silus's appearance, as Fiona swung her right sword across her body, she stood still a moment.

"You still favouring your right side," commented Silus.
"Silus," gasped Fiona in surprise, "I did not here you come in, have you been in the war room all night?"

"I kind of fell asleep in there," chuckled Silus.

"As usual, you get far too engaged in your thoughts," laughed Fiona.

"Maybe, but I also remember teaching you to dual wield those swords but using them equally," replied Silus, "favouring one side may not make much of a difference in one on one combat, but in the battles that we will get into, it will leave your left flank exposed to attack."

"Silus stop, I am not a little girl who needs schooling on how to use my blades anymore," said Fiona.

"You may not feel you need to be taught anything," replied Silus stepping away from the column, "but it is clear to me, that you require more training, I cannot in good conscious, let you step onto a battlefield, especially when you leave yourself exposed to the hordes of demons that we will have to face."

"Well then, mentor," grinned Fiona sarcastically, as she turned to face Silus, "I would say now is the best time for that lesson."

"Gladly," smiled Silus, "just do not cry on me when I prove my point."

"Oh please, I am not a kid anymore Silus," sighed Fiona, "now, enguard!"

Fiona darted towards Silus, both swords poised for an upward slash at Silus' torso, Silus conjured a dragon sabre into his left hand and raised it to block Fiona's swords as they crossed in front of him. Fiona grunted as she pushed her swords to make Silus step back.

"Not bad," whispered Silus.

Fiona then began to jab her right hand sword at Silus repeatedly, Silus dodged each jab, while conjuring his other dragon sabre into his right hand. Silus then ducked and tried sweeping at Fiona's feet with his right hand dragon sabre, Fiona jumped over the attack but before she could land, Silus quickly stood up and spun around and kicked Fiona in the stomach with his left leg. Fiona fell backwards and landed on her back, before rolling back to her feet.

"As I said, you are favouring your right, leaves you exposed to counter attacks," explained Silus.
"You are gloating already?" scoffed Fiona, "we have just started my dear."
"You could spar with me a hundred times, and each time I will best you," replied Silus, "when I taught you, you said you prefer dual wielding weapons because it gave you more freedom to position yourself for attack and defence."
"Good memory," sighed Fiona.
"Thank you, but the question is, do you remember what I told you, in response to that statement?" asked Silus.
"You told me that dual wielding may present freedom," answered Fiona, "but dual wielding is about balance, not going all in with attacks or defence."
"Well, well... It seems I am not the only one with a good memory," said Silus, "however it would seem you have not taken my lesson to heart."

On the upper level of the great hall, Amelia had emerged from her room to gaze over the balcony to see Silus and Fiona circling each other, Fiona's swords raised ready to attack, while Silus' were down at his side, Silus looked calm and relaxed, while Fiona seemed agitated.

"If you insist on continuing the lesson, then allow me to show you the balance of dual wielding," instructed Silus as he darted toward Fiona.

Amelia watched on as Silus then leapt into the air, and brought his right dragon sabre down at Fiona, Fiona raised both her swords to block Silus' attack, Silus then rolled over the top of Fiona before raising his left dragon sabre to jab at Fiona. Fiona then rolled forward to avoid Silus's attack, before standing up to face Silus.

"Are these two serious?" Amelia asked herself quietly.

Fiona then charged at Silus with both her dragon sabres on her right side, as she neared she began swinging both swords in unison, Silus stood with his left side facing Fiona, raising his left dragon sabre to block, Fiona then attempted to sweep at Silus's left foot with her right leg, Silus lifted his left foot to avoid the attack. Fiona then spun around bringing her left sword at chest level to slash at Silus, Silus rested both swords across his back as he jumped into the air, his body rolling over Fiona's sword, with their blades clashing in mid-air. Silus landed on both feet, Fiona still in mid spin, Silus then kicked out Fiona's legs with his left foot, as Fiona fell backwards, she let go of her swords. Silus' left dragon sabre vanished in a quick burst of flame as he caught Fiona.

"Ok, I concede your point Silus," sighed Fiona.

Silus chuckled briefly before helping Fiona back to her feet, his right dragon sabre vanishing in a puff of smoke. The two stood facing each other, as their eyes met the two fighters began to laugh. Suddenly the hall echoed with the sound of slow clapping, Silus and Fiona both turned to look at the top of the staircase, to see Celestia slowly walking down the stairs clapping her hands.

"I see you two wasted no time in getting back to trying to kill each other," laughed Celestia.
"Silus was just…" Fiona began to explain.
"Teaching you a lesson in swordplay?" interrupted Celestia, "you two really have not grown up in the slightest, have you?"
"Being locked up in a demon dungeon for several centuries will have that effect on people," scoffed Fiona.
"That I can understand," answered Celestia, "but you Silus, I would expect better."
"Come on Celestia, do not start talking down to me just because I was sparring with Fiona and not you," laughed Silus.

"If you are implying that I am jealous Lord Silus," said Celestia, "then I suggest you get that out of your head right now."

"Ok, ok, I see I hit a sore nerve," replied Silus.

"Come on Celestia, you cannot expect me to sit by and watch ever battle from a distance," interrupted Fiona.

"That is not what I am talking about," said Celestia with a heavy sigh.

"Then what are you talking about, spit it out 'Cely'," replied Fiona spitefully.

"Fiona a word in private please," sighed Celestia as she glanced at Amelia.

"Fine," scoffed Fiona as she turned to walk into the war room.

Celestia looked at Silus, Silus bowed briefly as Celestia walked past him. Silus watched as Celestia closed the door to the war room behind her, Silus then glanced up at Amelia and shrugged his shoulders. Amelia smiled back at Silus, Silus then ran up the stairs to meet Amelia at the top of the staircase. As they met the two wrapped their arms around the other.

"I do not understand what Celestia was on about," said Amelia as she stood back from Silus, "the fight was dazzling, and it seemed that you two were dancing rather than fighting."

"Well, I did train the Wythernspine sisters," sighed Silus, "so I do not see why Celestia would be so harsh in criticizing us."

"Do you really think she was jealous that you two were having fun and she was not included?" asked Amelia.

"Who can tell," answered Silus, "I have known those two for most of their lives, to be honest it still feels weird to know they are both younger than I."

"By how much?" questioned Amelia.

"Oh... about six hundred years younger," answered Silus, "they were born a few hundred years before I bested Shiento."

"During the fight, you both mentioned that it was you who trained Fiona, is that true?" asked Amelia.

"After the fall of Selania all those years ago, I sought the elders of the elemental dragons," explained Silus, "their father, King Dracum Wythernspine was the elder for the deity elements, being the oldest and wisest of any celestial dragon, so in exchange for him training my magic, I was to act as a bodyguard and friend to his daughters."

"And so, you trained them to fight?" asked Amelia.

"In part, I trained them to fight, to use alchemy, magic, I basically taught them everything they know," answered Silus, "however I was still childish back then, so I did tend to play pranks with them, and get into a lot of trouble because of it."

"Celestia did tell me about those days before," stated Amelia, "she also mentioned, how you and Fiona were almost inseparable."

"Indeed we were," sighed Silus, "I would wait in the courtyard at night, she would sneak out her bedroom window and the two of us would sneak out into the city and fly across the land, we trained, we fought, we made a lot of mischief."

"Sounds like you two shared something special," said Amelia, "it makes me feel envious of you two."

"This was a long time ago Amelia," replied Silus softly, "things are different now."

"But you still care for her?" queried Amelia.

"I do, in the same way I care for you, Celestia and the rest of the free world," answered Silus.

Silus let out a heavy sigh and then stared into Amelia's eyes.

"As much as I do have feelings for you, I have to prioritize the safety of the world and the destruction of Shiento and his demon forces," continued Silus, "until he is defeated, I fear there will be no life for me, at least not a life where I am free to do as I please, to be who I please, and who I wish to be with."

"You do not have to sacrifice your freedom and freewill for everyone," said Amelia.

"Unfortunately I do, as a born celestial dragon, I have no choice but to follow the entirety of the dragon's law, to fulfil an obligation that not many others have to," explained Silus, "until I fulfil my duties, to slay Shiento and create peace amongst dragons and non-dragon races, my life is not of my own making."

Silus sighed heavily and leant against the balcony railing, Amelia looked down into the lower hall to see Celestia and Fiona emerge from the war room, and head across the hall into the dining room. Amelia then looked up at Silus, who was staring blankly up at the top of the wall.

"You really do not choose what you are doing?" asked Amelia.
"I have no choice about the destination of my life," answered Silus, "but I get to choose how I get there, that is the only freedom that I truly possess."
"And are you not happy with how your life is?" asked Amelia.
"I will be happier when I slay Shiento once and for all," answered Silus, "until then, I must stumble from one battle to the next until the darkness that plagues this land, has been completely lifted, once that is done, I can be whoever I want to be, I can be with whoever I want to."

Amelia rested her hands on the balcony railing, Silus took a deep breath before standing up and turning to Amelia, who was staring blankly into the lower hall.

"You should not worry yourself with my duties," said Silus, "I accepted long ago that no matter how hard or far I ran, this is who I am supposed to be."
"That does not mean that it is fair for you to stand alone," replied Amelia.
"And as for your comment about standing alone, I am never alone, I have you to keep me company," smiled Silus.

Silus smiled and then wrapped his arms around Amelia and kissed her on the forehead, Amelia slowly placed her arm around Silus' waist before taking a deep breath and closing her eyes. The two stood motionless for a moment before Amelia pushed her way out of Silus' arm.

 "If slaying Shiento is the only way for you to gain some freedom then we should just go slay him now," said Amelia forcefully.
"Amelia," sighed Silus.
"You said so yourself, until you fulfil your duties you have no freedom to be who you want to be," interrupted Amelia, "so we should just go…"
"Amelia, stop!" shouted Silus, "you are not thinking straight."
"If you are afraid to face Shiento now, then just say so!" screamed Amelia, "but if you are the person I think you are, then let us go and butcher Shiento!"
"Amelia, Shiento will not die until he is at his weakest," said Silus calmly.
"I see, so you are just a coward," replied Amelia angrily, "fine then I will slay him myself.

Amelia went to walk past Silus, as she did Silus grabbed Amelia's left wrist. Celestia and Fiona walked out of the dining room to gaze up at Silus and Amelia arguing, Fiona went to push past Celestia but Celestia raised her left arm to stop Fiona.

"It is not our place to intervene," said Celestia calmly.

Amelia tried to wriggle her arm from Silus's grip, Silus then pulled Amelia in close and the two stared into each other's eyes.

"If you chose to face Shiento now, then you will have to do it alone," said Silus, "I have lost enough loved ones to that monster, but I will not face him until he is in a state, where I can land a final fateful blow."
"Let go of my arm Silus," warned Amelia.
"Think about this please," said Silus, "do not throw your life away for this, not for my duties, not for me."

Silus let go of Amelia's arm, Amelia stumbled backwards slightly. The two looked at each other for a moment before Amelia turned and ran down the staircase, Celestia and Fiona watched on in stunned silence. Silus stood still on the balcony, not turning his head to watch Amelia as she ran across the great hall towards the palace doors.

"Amelia!" shouted Silus.

Amelia stopped in the palace doorway, she turned to look up at Silus, who still had not moved or turned to face her.

"I will not try to change your mind!" called out Silus, "but if this is the path you choose, then I wish you all the best of luck."

Amelia took a deep breath before turning to look out the door, her body stunned with hesitation. Amelia sighed before walking out the door and disappearing from view. Fiona then ran up the stairs to stand in front of Silus, her eyes piercing with anger.

"What do you think you are doing Silus!" shouted Fiona, "you need to go and stop her, before she gets herself killed."
"I have no right to stop her from doing what she wants," sighed Silus, "and if that is truly what she wants, then I must trust her to know what she is doing, and respect that she has made this decision."
"If she fights Shiento she will die, or worse be possessed by a demon!" screamed Fiona.

Celestia slowly walked to the staircase, as Fiona's temper began to flare up, she climbed the stairs slowly, the sound of Silus and Fiona arguing filling her ears.

"By dragon's law, 'I cannot force a soul to go against their own freewill, but instead must respect their decision and if proven wrong, allow them to realise they were mistaken and guide them back onto the right path'," replied Silus calmly, "and if you think I just let her walk away without trying to change her mind, you are dead wrong."
"And here Celestia was explaining that you cared for her," said Fiona angrily, as she slapped Silus across is left cheek with her right hand, "guess she was wrong, or you have become a cold, heartless monster in the last few hundred years."

"I do care for her, but I do not own her," answered Silus, "she is her own being, she is allowed to make her own decisions, and I must respect that fact."
"Fiona," interrupted Celestia.

Fiona looked around to see Celestia standing behind her. Her eyes were closed as she took a deep breath, Fiona then took a deep breath and looked at Silus.

"I... I am sorry Silus," apologised Fiona.
"Do not worry" said Silus calmly, "I should try stopping her, but I told her that I am bound by duty to slay Shiento and all those who follow him, I cannot appear hypocritical by breaking our laws to chase after her."
"I... I understand," stammered Fiona.
"Do you really think she will go all the way to face Shiento?" asked Celestia.
"I have a feeling that she would, if her rage does not settle soon," answered Silus, "but I hope she reconsiders before it is too late."

~

Outside the palace, Amelia was sat against the wall to the barracks, to the right of the palace doors. Her eyes full of tears, her breath quivering in a mix of anger and sadness. She looked up to notice the streets were quiet, the sound of pots and pans clanging together as people woke up for breakfast. Amelia grunted before forcing herself to her feet.

"To hell with it," grunted Amelia angrily, "if Silus will not face Shiento, then I will."

Amelia walked across the courtyard to the stables, inside she picked out a black mare that had a saddle already on, the horse seemed uneasy as she approached, but Amelia held out her right hand and the horse began to settle down as Amelia began stroking the horse with her left hand. Amelia climbed onto the horse's back and as she did the horse neighed quietly.

"Sorry, but I need your help to get to the southern reaches," whispered Amelia.

The horse nodded its head, Amelia then lightly kicked her heels into the horse's side, and the horse began to trot out of the stables. Amelia then directed the horse for a gate on the south eastern side of the city. The air was still as the horse walked towards the gate. The gate began to open as their approached, once the gate had opened Amelia squeezed the horse's sides with her legs and the horse began to canter into the tunnel.

"There we go," whispered Amelia.

~

In the palace, Silus, Celestia and Fiona were sitting in the dining room. As they ate their food, a maid entered the room and stood at the far end of the table and bowed.

"Yes?" asked Fiona.

"Pardon the interruption your graces," answered the maid, "but it would seem that Lady Amelia has left the city on horseback."

"Thank you for letting us know," replied Silus.

"Of course, my Lord, now if you will excuse me, I must return to my duties," pleaded the maid.

"You are excused," said Celestia.

The maid bowed and then turned and left the room quickly, Silus placed his cutlery on his plate. Silus rested his elbows on the table and placed his head in his hands.

"So, what are we going to do about Amelia?" asked Celestia, "or more accurately, what do you intend to do Silus?"

"As I said earlier," answered Silus, "Amelia is acting upon what she believes is right, and we should not stop her, this is her choice."

"Very well," replied Celestia.

"So, what will we do?" queried Fiona.

"Now that is just the problem I have been considering," sighed Silus.

"What do you mean?" asked Celestia.

"Well, you know this scar forms a link between me and Shiento?" questioned Silus as he held his side.

"Yes, you mentioned that before," answered Celestia.

"Last night, as I slept, I had a link to Shiento, I could only see through his eyes and hear through his ears," explained Silus, "but it seems he has assigned six

Commanders to three tasks, an archer is to assassinate the Duke of Qurendia, four Commanders and a large contingent is to wipe out the Dark Forest and its inhabitants, while a serpent type demon is to assassinate the King of Selania."

"What?" shouted Celestia and Fiona in outrage.

"I know," responded Silus.

"Well... what are we going to do?" asked Fiona.

"What can we do?" queried Silus, "if we go Selania, Qurendia and the forest will fall, if we go Qurendia, Selania will lose its King and the forest will still be destroyed."

"And should we try to defend the forest, we would risk a large battle and the two cities will lose their rulers," interrupted Celestia.

"Precisely," agreed Silus, "even if we tried splitting up, the best we can hope for is saving the King and the Duke."

"You could help the elves destroy the demons," said Celestia.

"That would be at the discretion of Lady Fiona," replied Silus, "after all, she asked I accompany her to Selania."

"Well Fiona, what will it be?" asked Celestia.

"I... I do not know," stammered Fiona, "does Shiento know that I was rescued?"

"He seems to recognise that there is nothing buried under his fortress, so I would assume he does know of your survival," answered Silus.

"Then I must insist that Silus stay with me, at least for now," replied Fiona, "if I run into Shiento, I cannot even hope to survive."

"You should recognise that as a dragon, your life is no more important than those we are charged with protecting," said Celestia.

"Celestia, with all due respect your majesty," said Silus, "we have only just got Fiona back, would you wish her death so quickly?"

"Well... no, it is just..." stammered Celestia.

"Listen, we can send Randalene to her people with a portal," explained Silus, "and the three of us can venture to Selania."

"And what of Qurendia?" asked Celestia, "Do you intend to let the innocent people of the free city suffer?"

"Of course not, I do not intend to leave them to fend for themselves," answered Silus, "but only from Selania can we get to Qurendia quickly."

"We can teleport to Qurendia, just as easy as we could to Selania," stated Celestia.

"I am afraid teleporting to Qurendia is out of the question, same for Selania," replied Silus, "you see, the demons will know of our movements if we teleported, with Randalene its fine, she can at least ready her people for an attack or order an evacuation."

"Someone mention evacuation?" asked Randalene from the doorway.

Silus, Celestia and Fiona looked around to see Randalene standing in the doorway. Randalene walked into the room and sat down at the table next to Silus.

"What is this about an evacuation?" asked Randalene. "Shiento has dispatched four Commanders and a large contingent to eradicate all of the Dark Forest," explained Silus.

"What? How could you know this?" questioned Randalene.

"I had a vision last night of what Shiento is doing," answered Silus.

"So, what are we going to do?" asked Randalene.

"See, that is the dilemma we have just be debating," stated Silus.

"Why are you debating?" queried Randalene in outrage, "we must save my people."

"If only that were our only problem," replied Fiona.

"What do you mean?" asked Randalene, looking to Silus.

Silus let out a heavy sigh, as he sat back in his chair.

"Shiento has also sent assassins, to take out the Duke of Qurendia and the King of Selania," stated Silus.

"Oh... I... see," stammered Randalene.

"At the best of times, this is a bad situation, for the time being we can make two moves," explained Silus, "we teleport you back to your people, to either evacuate them or lead them into battle, and the three of us will go re-join the dragonkin forces in Selania, from there we can redeploy them as we need to."

"You talk as if they are your troops Silus," said Celestia.

"Lady Celestia please, can we not argue this now?" asked Silus, "yes they are not my troops, but I am in this war just as much as they are."

"He is right Celestia," agreed Fiona, "Randalene, once we teleport you home, what will you do?"

"How many and what type of demons has Shiento sent?" Randalene asked Silus.

"A couple of titan demons, along with at least three battalions of regular demons and four Commanders," answered Silus.

"Anything you can tell us of these Commanders?" questioned Celestia, "all six of them, I mean?"

"The assassin heading to Qurendia is an archer, he dabbles in poisons and ointments," explained Silus, "the Selanian assassin is a serpent type demon, and she will have a venomous nature."

"Save the jokes for another time please," interrupted Celestia.

"As you wish," answered Silus.

"What of those headed for my home?" asked Randalene.

Silus took a deep breath, he then raised his goblet and took a sip of water. Silus then gazed down into the water, his reflection showing his dragon eyes in the rippled surface.

"There is a scythe and spear wielding she-devil, a large brute carrying a bastard sword and battle axe," explained Silus, "another carries an assortment of daggers and short swords, the last one is what I believe is referred to as a Mogata."

"A multi-limbed demon?" stated Randalene in disbelief.

"Four arms, two legs," detailed Silus, "all of them are rearing to kill something."

"By the gods," sighed Randalene as she slumped back in her chair, "then there is no hope for my people."

"That is why we need to divide and conquer," explained Silus, "but sending any one of us to Qurendia alone would be a dramatic error."

"So, you intend to make for Selania and send a squad with someone?" asked Fiona.

"There is a problem with my plan," said Silus.

"What do you mean?" questioned Celestia.

"The person I would preferably have sent to Qurendia... she just left the city," answered Silus.

"Amelia?" asked Fiona in disbelief, "then we..."

"We need to let her make her own choices," interrupted Silus.

Silus stood up and walked to the side of the room where a jug was standing on top of a table, Silus poured water from the jug into his goblet before turning to face the others. Fiona and Celestia looked at each other than to Randalene. Silus drank his goblet of water.

"Anyway, enough debating," stated Silus as he placed his goblet on the table, "we need to start moving, the demons may take a little while to mobilize, but we need to get a move on, if we are to have a hope of stopping them."

"I... I suppose you are right," agreed Celestia.

"Then let us get moving," said Fiona.

"I will meet you all in the courtyard, when you are all ready, meet me out there," explained Silus as he quickly walked out of the room.

"To think the demons are mobilizing so quickly after the blow we dealt them yesterday," sighed Randalene.

"Silus predicted that our attack would anger Shiento," replied Celestia, "were you expecting him to go into mourning?"

"No, it is just, that I hoped he would have taken longer to plan a comeback," answered Randalene.

"Then let us hope, that these attacks are rash and lacking thought," responded Fiona, "it will mean Shiento has made a grave mistake, one that will bring us closer to defeating him."

Fiona and Celestia left the room without another word, Randalene sat still for a moment before taking a deep breath and standing up. As Randalene left the dining room, she could hear horses neighing outside the palace doors. Randalene followed Celestia and Fiona up the stairs to the upper floor, where they all split to enter different rooms.

"Right, let us see if Legolas has rested," Silus said to himself.

Outside in the courtyard, Silus had put his armour back on, as well as a hood and scarf, Silus lowered the hood from his head as he entered the stables, after a short while Silus began leading Legolas and a restless black stallion out of the stables, as they reached the middle of the courtyard, the black stallion began to settle down a bit, Silus then began checking the saddles of Legolas and the stallion. Eventually, Celestia and Fiona emerged from the palace doors with Randalene following behind them. Celestia was wearing a long white dress with her hair tied into a long-plaited ponytail. Fiona was wearing a long ocean blue dress, her hair was left untied and free flowing down her back. Randalene had put her armour on and carried her helmet under her right arm.

"So, are we ready to go Silus?" asked Fiona.
"Of course, Randalene I will open a portal for you to get home quickly," replied Silus.
"Thank you Silus," said Randalene.

Silus let go of the horse's reins, and stepped to the right of the courtyard, Celestia climbed onto the black stallion's back and sat side saddled, as Silus began chanting quietly. Fiona stroked Legolas' neck, the Pegasus turned its head as if surprised by Fiona's presence. Eventually a large black and orange portal opened in front of Silus, Randalene walked over and stood in front of the portal.

"Silus," said Randalene.
"Yes?" asked Silus.
"When you arrive in Selania, can you please tell Gilnur to begin marching my troops home," requested Randalene, "and please inform them of the demons, so they understand the importance of my orders."

"Of course, good luck Queen Randalene," replied Silus, "may Halandra favour you in the battle to come."

"You never cease to surprise me Silus, I hope Halandra is watching over you, and guiding you on your path," said Randalene, "and I hope we will meet again, hopefully in a brighter time."

"As do I, but I assure you, I will not leave you to fend for yourselves." replied Silus.

"Thank you, Lord Silus," sighed Randalene.

Randalene entered the portal, Silus turned to look at Fiona and smiled. Silus then turned back to look at the portal and with a quick wave of his right hand, the portal faded away. Silus then turned and walked over to Celestia and Fiona.

"You have knowledge of the elven gods?" asked Celestia.

"I told you before, I worked with Randalene and her elves to destroy Akaloth Gates," answered Silus, "I did spend a few years with them, and so it was hard not to pick up on their customs and deities."

"Fair enough," replied Celestia, "shall we make our way to Selania then?"

"Yes, we should get moving," said Silus.

"One last thing Silus?" queried Celestia.

"What is it?" asked Silus.

"Have you been truly honest with us about these demons?" questioned Celestia.

"I have told you all I know," answered Silus.

"No, that is not what I was asking," replied Celestia, "we know you have lived in every nation for a period of time, that you ran from Shiento, then fought Shiento, and even slayed Shiento once... My question is, have you been fully honest with us about everything?"

"If there is something that I have not mentioned, then it is something that is properly worth forgetting, my Lady," explained Silus, "is that all, should we get going?"

"Take care with how you proceed Silus," urged Fiona, "what happens in the darkness, is always revealed in the light."

"I shall bear that in mind, milady," said Silus.

Silus climbed onto Legolas' back, Legolas moved about seeming unsettled, Silus then patted Legolas on the neck. Fiona then approached Legolas, the Pegasus neighed quietly before turning his head to watch Fiona approach his side. Silus held out his right hand and lifted Fiona so she could sit side saddled in front of Silus. Legolas began shifting about restlessly again.

"Easy Legolas, easy," said Silus.
"What is wrong?" asked Fiona.
"Not too sure, I have never seen him this agitated before," answered Silus, "Legolas, relax already."

The Pegasus began pawing the ground with his right hoof, Silus looked down and noticed a small piece of metal sticking out of the ground, Silus held out his right hand and the metal object broke free of the ground. As the object floated in the air, Silus became worried.

"What is that?" asked Celestia.
"It looks like," answered Fiona, "is that what I think it is Silus?"
"I would say so, this looks like a piece of dragon's bane," answered Silus, "but what is it doing here in Urendos."
"Just destroy it and let us get moving," ordered Fiona.
"Agreed," replied Silus, "sazarach!"

The fragment of dragon's bane burst into flames, the metal boiling down to a liquid before evaporating. Legolas then settled down, Silus and Celestia squeezed the sides of their mounts, the stallion and the Pegasus set off. Fiona lent her head against Silus' chest. Celestia rode alongside Silus' right side and stared at Fiona.

"So, should I even ask what is going on between you two?" asked Silus.
"You mean you are not just going to read our minds?" asked Celestia.
"I only read peoples mind's if it comes to telling if they are lying," answered Silus, "and I do not intend to read either of your minds, my ladies."

Celestia looked at Silus, Silus looked from Fiona to Celestia. Celestia then took a deep breath.

"You remember earlier, when I was giving you both a hard time about training together?" asked Celestia.

"Hard to forget, it was only two hours ago," answered Silus.

"Well you know how I went to speak with Fiona shortly after that?" queried Celestia, "well I was arguing with Fiona, how the two of you were acting like you used to, with the glances and such."

"So, what am I missing here?" asked Silus.

"I just thought you were romancing together, Amelia was watching your sparring match after all," answered Celestia.

"Ahh... I see now, you thought I was falling for Amelia and Fiona at the same time, correct?" questioned Silus.

"Do not misunderstand Silus," replied Celestia, "but Amelia is a fragile girl, her sister has not been seen in years, and she's recently lost her mother, I just do not think she is as strong as she makes herself out to be, and I do not want to see her get hurt."

"I guess you were right to worry," sighed Silus, "but I assure you, I would never cause harm to her, physical or emotional, and she knows how I feel for her."

"Are you actually admitting you love her?" queried Celestia, "because you have never admitted it before now?"

"Yes, I do love her, but," answered Silus, "but, I am confused on how I should act."

"What do you mean?" asked Fiona.

"Well, all eyes are on me to defeat Shiento, and I know I must defeat him," explained Silus, "but I also want to show her how I feel, but doing so would make her a new target for Shiento to get at me."

"I understand your concerns Silus, but you are going to have to come out and be honest about everything sooner or later, preferably sooner rather than later," said Celestia.

"Celestia is right Silus," agreed Fiona, "as much as I wish the two of us can go back in time, I also understand that I have been gone a while and must accept the changes, in which I have returned to."

As the trio neared a gate on the northern side of the city, a dragonkin guard approached them, Silus and Celestia pulled back on the reins slightly to bring their mounts to a halt.

"Your majesties, surely it is not necessary for both of you to leave now?" asked the guard.

"We have no choice, we are needed in Selania, the King of Selania and our troops expect us soon," answered Celestia.

"I understand milady," replied the guard.

The dragonkin guard then bowed and signalled a guard near a lever to open the gate. As the gates opened, Silus and Celestia squeezed their mounts sides to get them moving again. The horses walked through the gates, the tunnels ahead were large and lit by thousands of tiny glowing crystals. As the city gates closed behind them, Silus and Celestia lightly kicked their heels into their steeds, the mounts then began to canter along the tunnel.

~

Amelia slowed her horse to a trot because the tunnel had become a ramp into the ceiling. Amelia looked around to see a small lever hidden behind a stalagmite, Amelia got off her horse to go and activate the lever. As Amelia pulled on the lever, the ceiling at the top of the ramp began to open up. Amelia climbed back onto the horses back, the horse was unsettled but Amelia squeezed its sides and the horse began to walk up the ramp. Outside the tunnel, Amelia had arrived at a large clearing overlooking a forest, and behind her was a large open field of luscious green grass. Amelia looked up at the sky to notice the black clouds were still a fair distance to the south.

"Well at least the black clouds are still quite far away," said Amelia.

The wind then began to blow heavily from the north, Amelia's horse became nervous and unsettled, Amelia looked north to see smoke rising from near Selania. The smell of smoke filled the air.

"Easy girl, it is just the wind," said Amelia calmly as she stroked the horse's neck.

The horse then stopped shuffling about, and pointed to face north, Amelia tried to direct her horse to face south again, but the horse would not move. Amelia then looked around and noticed a small shadow wriggle across the valley floor. A shadow that had no form, no figure for light to cast it, but there it was.

"What is that?" Amelia asked herself.

The air began to echo with the faint sound of hissing, Amelia then pulled on the left rein to turn the horse onto a path that lead around the field. With a double squeeze of her legs the horse began to canter down the path.

"I need to warn the others," said Amelia, "how foolish to come all this way, and realise my mistake."

~

Silus, Celestia and Fiona had travelled a long way from Urendos, they were nearing a small junction in the tunnel where the path split, one heading west the other continuing straight on, Silus steered Legolas straight on, Celestia followed behind Silus. The two steeds continuing their canter along the tunnel.

"We should reach the end of the tunnel soon," said Silus.
"That is good, but where will this tunnel end?" asked Celestia.
"This is the passage Sergeant Drake took to bring the troops to Selania," answered Silus, "so the exit will be in a small woodland to the west of the city, once we are out of the tunnel, it will be a short journey to the city gates."

"Then we need to keep moving, the sooner we reach Selania the better," stated Fiona.

"Agreed," replied Silus.

The tunnel was quiet, the only sound coming from the horse's hooves clapping against the tunnel floor. Eventually they reached a small ramp that lead into the ceiling, Silus waved his right hand towards a long stalagmite and there was a loud click as the ceiling began to open up.

"Here we go," said Silus as he steered Legolas to climb the slope.

As they exited the tunnel the warm glow of the late morning sun greeted them, a cool gentle breeze blew in from the northern ocean. As the trio continued down the path towards Selania, Silus looked to the right to see how far away the black clouds were to the south.

"Well at least those demonic clouds are at a distance now," said Silus.

"Yes, but we should not let ourselves get distracted Silus," replied Celestia, "We need to re-join the troops."

"Agreed," answered Silus.

A little while later, Silus, Fiona and Celestia neared Selania, Silus raised his hood and scarf to cover his face, the fields surrounding Selania were a wash of bodies being cremated or wounded soldiers being brought back to Selania, as they approached the city gates, a soldier approached them and halted them.

"What business do you have in Selania?" asked the soldier.

"Queen's Fiona and Celestia of Urendos, we are here to speak with King Jacob and their troops," answered Silus.

"And who would that make you?" queried the soldier.

"I am their bodyguard," answered Silus, "seeing as all their soldiers are here, they need at least one bodyguard."

"Very well, you may all pass," said the solider, "open the gate!"

"You could have been honest with your answer," whispered Fiona.

"Like I said, I do not like the idea of announcing my return to this city," answered Silus quietly, "they would sooner execute me, then accept any help from me."

"Given what they have just gone through," whispered Fiona, "do you really think they will rather execute you than let you help?"

"To Selania, I am a criminal of desertion, they take stuff like that very seriously," answered Silus quietly.

Once the gate had been fully opened Celestia led the way into the city, as they passed through the gates. The site of hundreds of soldiers receiving medical treatment greeted them, the once bustling marketplace, now a make shift infirmary. Sergeant Drake was standing with King Jacob near the back of the market square, as Celestia and Silus rode closer to them, Sergeant Drake stepped forward and knelt down. The remaining dragonkin and phoenix soldiers around also knelt down as Celestia halted her horse.

"All hail, Queen Celestia, ruler of Urendos," called out Sergeant Drake.
"Hail Queen Celestia!" shouted the soldiers.
"No need to stand on ceremony here!" shouted Celestia, "return to your duties!"

The dragonkin and phoenix guards stood up and continued lending aid to the wounded. Commander Hawke walked over from the city wall to stand with Sergeant Drake. Celestia dismounted from her horse to stand in front of Sergeant Drake.

"It was a lovely greeting, but I think you missed someone," said Celestia pointing towards Fiona.
"Lady Fiona," gasped Sergeant Drake, "please forgive me, my Queen."
"Do not worry Sergeant, you have not offended me, I understand how strange the circumstances may seem to you," answered Fiona as Silus helped her down from Legolas' back, before dismounting himself.
"So finally, you take time to come and see us," scoffed King Jacob, "and who are..."

King Jacob walked past Celestia and began approaching Silus, as he neared Silus he drew his sword into his right hand and held it to Silus's right shoulder.

"Remove your hood!" ordered King Jacob.

"Stand down King Jacob, Silus is not here to fight," instructed Fiona.

"You will not order me about in my city, now step away, this is Selanian business," ordered King Jacob angrily.

"You best change that tone Jacob," growled Silus as he removed his hood and scarf, "you keep that attitude up and I will make you regret it."

"You dare to threaten me, your head is for the executioner's axe already," scoffed King Jacob.

"If you even dare to harm Silus, then Urendos will be forced to declare war on Selania," advised Celestia.

"What?" asked King Jacob in outrage.

"Silus Drago, led the attack on Shiento's fortress, rescuing me in the process, not to mention forcing Shiento to call off his attack here," explained Fiona, "Silus is my bodyguard, and so harming him is a threat against me, one which honour would demand that I retaliate against you."

"Defend him as you may, but this boy is a Selanian citizen and must answer for his crimes," insisted King Jacob.

"Wrong, Selania is a city of humans, Silus is a born dragon," explained Celestia, "therefore in accordance to the ancient treaties, and he cannot be held as a criminal to any law except the draconian law."

"I do not care for your traditions," scoffed King Jacob, "and I will not have two pathetic rulers who are worthless and..."

Silus quickly grabbed King Jacobs's outstretched arm with his left hand and then kicked out the King's feet from under him with his right leg. As King Jacob fell to the floor, he let go of his sword and Silus drew his left dragon sabre into his right hand. King Jacob then crashed on the floor and looked up to see Silus holding both swords at the King's neck.

"You can insult me all you like, but if you intend to threaten or insult either Lady Fiona or Celestia again, then you will have me to contend with," threatened Silus as his dragon eyes appeared, "do I make myself clear?"

"I... well..." stammered King Jacob.

"Answer me!" shouted Silus.

"Yes, you have made you intention clear!" screamed King Jacob.

"Excellent, glad we are on the same page," said Silus as he stabbed Jacob's sword into the ground, "now stand up and let us try to get along."

"You are still not excused of your crimes boy," grunted King Jacob as he climbed to his feet, "one day I will have your head in retaliation for what you did."

"You believe whatever you have to, but I had my reasons for abandoning Selania back then," replied Silus, "one reason that has led me to this point."

"Nonsense, the whole world knows you fled in cowardice!" shouted King Jacob.

"I will not argue facts and rumours with a pathetic bureaucrat like you," spat Silus, "you are so narrow minded you cannot see what is going on around you."

King Jacob looked around to see all the dragonkin guards standing and brandishing their weapons. Commander Hawke also drew his sword. King Jacob then looked back to Silus.

"Listen, yes I ran from Shiento before, but like I said, I have a reason," said Silus calmly, "one I would love to explain to you, but now is not the best time."
"And why is that?" asked King Jacob.
"Because Shiento has sent an assassin to take your head, another assassin to kill the Duke of Qurendia and a large force to eradicate all life the Dark Forest," answered Celestia, "so if you are done being a screaming cry baby, perhaps we can move onto more important matters?"
"I am inclined to agree with you, Lady Celestia," replied King Jacob.
"We had best move this away from the ears of the people," suggested Silus.

The King nodded and beckoned everyone to follow him. King Jacob led the group across the market square and around the arena towards the palace. As they entered the palace courtyard, Silus looked around to see several guards placing their hands on their swords. As the group neared the palace, Silus looked to the right of the door and in an enclosed garden, Silus saw a statue of a former King holding his sword high above his head. Silus then stopped to stare at the statue, Fiona turned to look at Silus then stopped to look at the statue too.

"Silus… is something wrong?" asked Fiona.

"I knew coming back was a bad idea," answered Silus quietly.

"What do you mean?" queried Fiona.

"There are just too many bad memories here," replied Silus, "ones I was hoping to avoid."

"You lived here for a while before this war started, did you not?" asked Fiona.

"I did, but I did not come into this courtyard or anywhere that inflicted me with these bad memories," answered Silus.

"Come on Silus, we should catch up with the others," replied Fiona.

Silus let out a heavy sigh, before nodding and following Fiona into the palace. Inside the palace, Silus looked around to see that the floor and columns were decorated with gems and gold, the walls decorated with bright red tapestries, and large portraits of Kings and their families and wars that have long since passed.

"I see King Jacob has been kind enough to leave these halls unchanged," scoffed Silus sarcastically, "apart from his blatant disregard of maintaining a somewhat humble appearance."

"What do you mean?" asked Fiona.

"Look at all these gems, they were not here before," answered Silus, "he has turned these halls into a shambled state, and it is truly disgusting."

"Each to their own Silus," said Fiona.

"Selania was never a city that would use gemstones like this, it was never a city that would fail to aid others," replied Silus, "the honour of Selania is stained by the rule of this wannabe King."

Silus and Fiona continued walking forward to a large staircase that stood on the opposite side of the hall. At the top of the stairs was a large open room, at the end of this room was a large throne, gilded in jewels and gold. In the centre of the room a large table had been laid out with a map and several markers placed across it, around the table was King Jacob, Commander Hawke, Sergeant Drake and Celestia. As Silus and Fiona neared the table, Silus turned and walked to the edge of the room and knelt on the ground.

"Silus? Do you not wish to have a say on what we are discussing?" asked Celestia.
"It is not my place, I am here only as a bodyguard," answered Silus, "nothing more, and nothing less."
"Like Selania could put their trust in this boy anyway," scoffed King Jacob.
"It is due to Silus's plan that Selania is still standing," explained Celestia, "Silus planned to attack Shiento's fortress and protect Selania at the same time, and now look, the fortress and the Akaloth Gate within, have been destroyed, and Selania was successfully defended, can you not accept that?"
"I refuse to accept that this boy had a hand in it," replied King Jacob, "this boy does not care for the

world, he will watch us all crawl in the dirt, before he is satisfied."

Fiona walked around the table her fists clenched tightly, as she neared the King, Celestia turned and wrapped her arms around Fiona, stopping her from throwing a punch.

"Let go of me Celestia," grunted Fiona angrily. "We are here to join together with Selania against Shiento, not to fight each other!" shouted Celestia, "Silus, a little assistance would be appreciated." "Draconom sen'tu tumpra," whispered Silus.

As Silus whispered the incantation, Fiona's body slowly stopped struggling in Celestia's arms. As Celestia let go, Fiona stood still, her eyes still staring at the King and filled with rage. Sergeant Drake and Commander Hawke then left the room and exited the palace.

"Where are they going?" asked King Jacob. "To help the troops and get ready for deployment," answered Silus. "You have no right to speak or even be here boy," scoffed King Jacob, "so hold your tongue." "If you are unable to accept that Silus is trying to help you, then perhaps we should all leave you to the demons," grunted Fiona. "As much as I just stopped Fiona from punching you, I agree with her, this relentless hatred and disregard for Silus, it needs to come to an end," said Celestia, "as King you should be focused on your enemies, not your allies."

"Silus let hundreds die!" shouted King Jacob, "I cannot! I will not tolerate that!"

"So, you are saying that because hundreds of humans died a few hundred years ago, I should be held accountable, correct?" asked Silus.

"Do you accept that charge?" responded King Jacob.

"Fine, I will accept it so long as you accept the failings of yourself and your bloodline's failure to help the smaller villages that fall in your domain," answered Silus as he clenched his hands into tight fists.

"What the devil are you talking about?" scoffed King Jacob.

Silus stood up and began to walk across the room towards King Jacob, his arms swinging naturally by his side.

"Fifty years ago, Selania failed to go to the aid of a village called Fordas, south-east of here, the whole village destroyed by bandits," explained Silus.

"That has nothing to do with Selania," responded King Jacob.

"Wrong, Fordas was a village that fell under Selanian protection," explained Silus, "your predecessor failed to act ninety-four years ago when demons were rampaging through the southern Selanian territory, attacking merchants, patrols and attacked several small settlements."

"Our men would not have been able to get there in time," answered King Jacob.

"Those attacks lasted for five weeks!" shouted Silus, "and you are going to try and defend your honour by saying your troops could not make a journey to try and prevent loss of life and property!"

The lanterns and torches around the room began to burn brighter, the flames jumping between the lanterns and torches. Fiona quickly ran to Silus and tugged on his right arm heavily. Silus's arm shaking as his anger continued to make the lanterns and torches burn bigger and brighter.

"Silus, that is enough, you have made your point," said Fiona nervously.

Silus's arm stopped shaking, Silus took a step backwards and took a deep breath, as he did the lanterns and torches returned to their original state. Silus then looked around to meet Fiona's eyes, Silus then looked around to Celestia then King Jacob.

"My apologies," said Silus, "my point is, King Jacob, that if I am to be held accountable for the lives lost because of my inadequacy, then Selania and its rulers should be held accountable for their failings too."
"So, you do care?" pondered King Jacob, "so, Lord Silus, do you intend to see this war through to its bitter end, regardless of whether you win or lose?"
"If I lose, Shiento destroys everything," answered Silus, "so you best not be considering a negative outcome."

~

Amelia was racing through a woodland area south of Selania, her horse panting heavily from fatigue.

"Hang on, we are almost at Selania," said Amelia looking ahead as the tree line began to fade, "what in the heavens?"

As Amelia and her horse emerged from the trees, Amelia looked out across the fields outside Selania, to see the ground charred black with ash, in the distance she could see soldiers' settings pyres alight to burn the dead.

"I had no idea the scale of this battle was like this," sighed Amelia, "Silus, I hope you are here, and I hope you can forgive me, come on a little further and we will get to Selania."

Amelia lightly squeezed her heels into the horse's side, the horse neighed before cantering across the field towards Selania. The wind blowing lightly as they made their way across the field. As they neared the city the sound of the pyres crackling away, and the sight of so many dead soldiers filled Amelia with sorrow.

"You all fought bravely, be proud that you stood against this tide of darkness and gave it everything you had, rest in peace," whispered Amelia as she watched the pyres burn.

"Halt!" shouted a Selanian guard as Amelia approached the gates.

Amelia pulled back on the reins and her horse stopped a few paces from the guard. Amelia looked at the guard as he approached.

"Selania is in full lockdown, there is no entry to those who are foreign to us," informed the guard.
"My name is Amelia phoenix, I am the ruler of Flammehelm, I am looking for Silus Drago, who is accompanying Queen Celestia and Fiona Wythernspine to Selania," answered Amelia.
"Lady Amelia?" called a low voice.

Amelia looked up to see Sergeant Drake walking out the gate. The guard turned to face Sergeant Drake.

"You know this woman?" asked the guard.
"Yes, she is who she claims to be, after Cynthia Phoenix's tragic death, Lady Amelia became the Queen of Flammehelm," answered Sergeant Drake, "you are looking for Silus, are you not milady?"
"Yes, is he here Sergeant?" questioned Amelia.
"He is, along with Lady Celestia and Lady Fiona, they are currently talking with King Jacob to discuss how we proceed from here," answered Sergeant Drake, "Guardsman, I can vouch for Lady Amelia's credentials, please allow her entry to Selania."
"I guess you can enter my Lady," responded the guardsman, "however, I would not expect a very warm welcome your highness, our people are in

mourning, and we are preoccupied with preparing for another attack."

"I understand, then I shall not keep you from your duties," answered Amelia.

Amelia lightly squeezed her horse's sides and the horse slowly walked through the gates, Sergeant Drake walked beside Amelia and explained that her horse will have to wait in the main square, she would have to go to the palace on the other side of the city by foot. Amelia dismounted and left her horse with Sergeant Drake, she then ran across the main square heading towards the arena.

~

Silus turned to look at the palace doors, Fiona looked up from the map on the table to see Silus.

"What is wrong Silus?" asked Fiona.
"It would seem Amelia has arrived in the city," answered Silus.
"How can you be so sure?" queried Celestia.
"I can sense her magic, there is no denying it," responded Silus.
"Who is this Amelia?" questioned King Jacob.
"Queen Amelia Phoenix recently appointed ruler of Flammehelm, after Lady Cynthia's tragic and unfortunate death," explained Fiona.
"If you will excuse me, I should see Amelia," said Silus.
"Of course, Silus," replied Fiona.

"This is a slightly weird request, but when Amelia gets here and sees you, could you tell her to meet me where we first met?" asked Silus.

"You are not going straight to Amelia?" queried Celestia.

"I think it would be best for us to talk somewhere familiar to both of us," answered Silus, "do not worry she will understand the request, that and it will keep our conversation in an area where no one would normally venture."

"And where is that precisely?" questioned King Jacob.

"Some questions are best left unanswered," answered Silus.

"But…" stammered King Jacob.

"Get going Silus, otherwise she will be here before you even leave," said Fiona.

"As you wish my Lady," replied Silus as he bowed to Fiona and Celestia before running towards the palace door.

As Silus emerged into the palace courtyard, his dragon wings stretched out from his back and he took to the sky and flew straight for the arena. In the distance, he could see the black clouds spreading across to the west. Silus flew over the top of the arena walls before descending into a viewing area on the eastern side of the arena. As Silus landed his wings disappeared. Silus looked around quickly before walking to a staircase at the back of the viewing area.

~

Amelia reached the edge of the courtyard to the palace, painting heavily as she stopped to look around at the arena, before turning back to face the palace. She began walking across the courtyard trying to catch her breath.

"Silus, where are you?" asked Amelia.

As Amelia reached the palace doors, a member of the royal guard pointed towards the staircase that led up to the throne room. Amelia nodded and began walking towards the staircase. As she reached the top, she looked across to see Celestia, Fiona and Jacob standing around the table.

"Celestia, Fiona!" called out Amelia as she ran to greet them.
"Amelia, it is good to see you safe," said Fiona as she turned to hug Amelia.
"I hope you do not think less of me for rushing off like I did?" asked Amelia.
"Of course not Amelia, Silus explained everything to us," answered Celestia as she walked around the table to hug Amelia, "thank the gods you made it here safely."
"So, you are the new Queen to Flammehelm?" queried King Jacob.
"Yes, I am Queen Amelia Phoenix of Flammehelm, you are King Jacob, correct?" replied Amelia.
"I am indeed, I am sorry to hear of your mother's unfortunate fate, you have my condolences,"

answered King Jacob as he held out his right hand to Amelia.

"Thank you, your highness," said Amelia as she reached for Jacob's hand.

As they shook hands, Amelia looked around trying to spot Silus, King Jacob smiled and turned to face the table once more.

"You are looking for Silus, I presume?" asked King Jacob.

"Yes, I just assumed he travelled here with Celestia and Fiona?" queried Amelia.

"He did, however he just left the palace, because he sensed you had entered the city," answered King Jacob, "he asked that we relay a message to you."

"A... message?" stammered Amelia.

"Do not fret, he merely requests that you meet him, where you two first met," explained Fiona.

"Where we first met?" asked Amelia, "why?"

"He understands you wish to speak with him, so he wants to talk in a location you both know, and away from anyone else."

"I... I think I understand," said Amelia, "well, I should not keep him waiting, so if you will excuse me?"

"Of course," answered King Jacob, "it was nice to meet you, my Lady."

"Same to you, King Jacob," replied Amelia, "Celestia, Fiona I will see you later."

"Take care Amelia," responded Celestia and Fiona together.

Amelia turned and ran towards the palace doors. Celestia and Fiona smiled as they watched Amelia go. King Jacob cracked a smile as Amelia disappeared from view.

"Ah, I see now," said King Jacob.
"See what?" asked Fiona.
"Him... her... though Silus is what I would consider old, they are both still young when you consider the aging rate for dragons and phoenixes," explained King Jacob, "love is certainly something to fight for, I think I understand why Silus has made such a change to his view on this war."
"Love is why he fights so hard," explained Celestia, "but Silus also has a score to settle with Shiento, and his honour to restore among dragons."
"Fair enough," replied King Jacob, "so let us continue our discussion on how we shall all proceed."
"Agreed, we have to conclude on how to keep you safe, and save the Duke of Qurendia, while hopefully not abandoning the elves as well," responded Fiona.

~

Amelia emerged into the courtyard, as she stood in the centre of the courtyard, she looked up to the arena, Fiona's words echoing in her mind.

"Where we first met," whispered Amelia.

Amelia stood looking up at the arena, her feathered wings slowly stretched out from her back. With a heavy flap she took off into the sky, as Amelia soared over the top of the arena wall, the memories of her battle with Silus began flooding into her mind. Amelia landed in the viewing area on the east side of the arena, then immediately began running for the staircase at the back of the viewing area, as Amelia ran up the stairs she could hear the wind rushing through the windows on the side of the staircase. As Amelia reached the top of the stairs she looked across the room to see Silus standing in the middle of the room. As his eyes met hers, she smiled.

"Silus," panted Amelia.
"It is good to see you too, Amelia," smiled Silus, "though you did not have to rush all the way here, I was not exactly going anywhere."

Amelia began to chuckle before darting across the room to hug Silus. As Amelia wrapped her arms around Silus, Silus rested his head on hers then wrapped his arms around her.

"It is good to see you safe Amelia," said Silus, "I am glad you did not go charging after Shiento after all."
"I realised the mistake I made when I got to the surface," replied Amelia as she looked up to look at Silus, "but I came to warn you, I saw a large force of demons moving west."
"I know, Shiento has ordered the mobilization of a large force to destroy the elven home in the Dark Forest, along with assassins sent alone to kill the King

of Selania and the Duke of Qurendia," explained Silus.

"What are we going to do?" asked Amelia.

"I intend to send Sergeant Drake, Commander Hawke and their troops to the Dark Forest to bolster their forces and give the elven civilians a chase to flee to Selania," answered Silus, "at the same time, I intend to ask you and Fiona to go to Qurendia to help there as best you can."

"You will not be coming with us?" asked Amelia.

"I will be heading to the Dark Forest to aid the elves, they came to us and aided in my plan to assault the Black Fortress, I owe them my swords, and my aid," answered Silus.

Amelia held Silus tightly, with tears in her eyes she began to cry into Silus's chest. Silus raised his right hand and began to stroke Amelia's head.

"Silus, I do not want to be separated from you again, please let me come with you," cried Amelia.

"Amelia, listen to me," replied Silus, "as the Queen of Flammehelm your duties are different to mine, this does not mean we will never see each other again, it just means we each have our roles to play."

"But you are more capable to stop this assassin then I am," sobbed Amelia.

"As the more capable fighter, I will be of more use fighting the army heading west, Shiento has sent a large force including titan demons and four newly appointed Generals," explained Silus, "that is where I am needed most, besides between your and Fiona's skills and magic, the assassin heading for Qurendia does not stand a chance."

"Please Silus, just stay with me," cried Amelia.

"Hey, why do you keep sounding like this parting will last forever?" asked Silus, "listen the assassin will not reach Qurendia for at least three days, that should be more than enough time for me to help in the Dark Forest and get to Qurendia in time to see you take that monster's head."

"So, you will be going Qurendia?" questioned Amelia.

"Would I send you all that way for no reason?" answered Silus, "besides I will need to speak with the Duke myself, so my arrival will just be slightly delayed, but I promise I will get there, and you know I would not break a promise, especially not to you."

"Ok, just give those demons hell," said Amelia as she closed her eyes and looked out into the arena below.

"With pleasure," chuckled Silus as he looked out into the arena, "seems kind of strange does it not?"

"What do you mean?" asked Amelia.

"The last time the two of us stood here, we fought each other, and now we embrace each other," explained Silus, "this moment could not feel any more different from our first meeting even if we tried."

"Maybe, but this is a good change," said Amelia softly.

Silus and Amelia stood still for a moment, the wind gently blowing across the room as they held each other. Silus then turned to look out across the city. Amelia lifted her head to look at Silus.

"Something wrong?" asked Amelia.

"I am just wondering where the assassin sent to Selania is," answered Silus, "it is certainly within reason to suspect she is already here by now, Selania is a lot closer to the Black Fortress than Qurendia."

"Maybe, but what can we do, it is not like we can sense a demon," replied Amelia, "they do not have souls to react to either of our sensing capabilities."

"That is what worries me, this demon I saw her in my vision, she is called Servana, she can control reptiles and even change her form to resemble another," explained Silus, "she is what you could consider a chameleon, she could blend into any crowd and we would never know she was there."

"Then we best be careful," replied Amelia.

"Agreed," stated Silus, "come on, we best return to Fiona and Celestia."

Silus walked to the edge of the room, overlooking the arena, Amelia stood beside him and without a word they both leant over the edge and in the blink of the eye, their wings had appeared and they took off into the skies above the arena.

~

On the southern edge of Jarvlan, Shiento stood atop his rebuilt castle gazing out across the southern ocean, Lady Drask was standing on the ruined bridge that Silus had created during the battle and the army of demons waited patiently atop the cliffs. Suddenly, the sound of wings flapping echoed in Shiento's ears,

73

as he turned to look into the sky he saw a small winged demon fly towards Lady Drask and land next to her on the bridge, the demon knelt down facing Shiento.

"What news do you bring of our advanced troops?" asked Shiento.

"My Lord," answered the demon, "Servana has entered Selania, and is poised and ready to strike at the King the moment he leaves the palace, as for Groda the archer, he has finally separated from the horde and making his way across the southern mountain range, he is making swift progress towards Qurendia."

"And what of the horde?" queried Shiento.

"They are moving into the Dark Forest as we speak, progress is slow due to the terrain my Lord, but they are in high spirits to slay the elves," replied the demon.

"Of course they are," chuckled Shiento, "the elves have been slaying demons for centuries, it is only natural for a demon to be happy about invading the elven homeland."

"How should we proceed Lord Shiento?" questioned Lady Drask.

"For now, we wait to hear news of the fall of the rulers of Selania and Qurendia," responded Shiento, "once we know the results of our assassins, we can mobilize to annihilate the cities as we see fit."

"Should we not begin mobilizing now then, my Lord?" queried Lady Drask.

"No... no, we wait," answered Shiento, "for you see, my brother has no doubt moved to Selania, and is readying a defence for them as well as sending forces to aid his friends, Silus will undoubtedly head to the Dark Forest, that boy cannot help it, he must fight in the biggest battles he can find."

"If that is true my Lord, then we should split our army and destroy Qurendia and Selania while Silus is in the Dark Forest," said Lady Drask, "the humans will not be able to stand against us if the dragonkins' and phoenixes are not there."

"I do not like repeating myself, Lady Drask," sighed Shiento, "our army will remain here, if the leaders of the cities are killed their societies will fall to chaos, and in that chaos we can then sweep through, however until we know the fates of the Duke of Qurendia and the King of Selania, the army stays here."

"I... I understand my Lord," stammered Lady Drask.

"Do you?" questioned Shiento, "you are rash and impulsive, do you hate the fact that I sent others to assassinate the leaders of the human race instead of you?"

"No, of course not my Lord, I do not mean to question your leadership," replied Lady Drask, "I just, I do not see why our armies cannot move closer to our targets."

Shiento began to chuckle, he then slowly began to walk across the castle courtyard towards Lady Drask. Lady Drask nervously took two steps back, as Shiento approached her, his eyes met hers and he smiled.

"To divide our forces now and move them closer to either city will only help Silus, if our forces are divided he will have less enemies to fight in one go, the boy may seem cocky and brash, but he is actually very cautious and powerful, he alone could stand up to the forces we have here," explained Shiento, "only by being more cautious and more thorough with our planning, can we eventually bring that boy to his end."

"So, you are more focused on ending the life of your brother than conquering the world?" asked Lady Drask.

"Do you not consider him to be the biggest threat to our plans?" queried Shiento.

Lady Drask lowered her head, her mind racing with Shiento's words. She then turned to look at the top of the cliff as the demons up there looked down at her and Shiento. Lady Drask then cleared her throat and looked back to Shiento.

"If he is truly our greatest threat, then allow me to make a suggestion my Lord," said Lady Drask.

"You have a better plan than what I just detailed to you?" asked Shiento as he sat down on a raised piece of rumble, "then by all means my love, please share."

"The phoenix, Amelia Phoenix to be precise," answered Lady Drask, "she is awfully close to Silus, I would even be as bold as to say, that they are in love."

Shiento's face lit up, his mouth stretching from a small grin to a beaming smile. Shiento's eyes changed from their dark hazel colour to his dragon eyes, shining bright yellow in the afternoon light.

"You propose that we utilize the girl to get to Silus?" asked Shiento, "an intriguing plan to say the least, but how?"
"Silus most likely intends to keep their bond secret from you, to avoid you targeting her, and so he will likely send her off to Qurendia while he fights the horde in the Dark Forest," answered Lady Drask, "therefore I intend to go and capture the girl."
"And what would you do once you have her?" asked Shiento.
"Demand Silus to face me on my terms," laughed Lady Drask, "and once he arrives at a location of my choosing, I threaten to kill the girl, and in doing so force Silus to throw down his weapons and sacrifice himself to save her."
"I like this plan," chuckled Shiento, "however there is one fatal flaw I see with your plan."
"And what is that, my Lord?" asked Lady Drask.
"You are pretty much assuming that Silus even leaves Selania without Amelia, what if Amelia stays beside Silus, or even returns to Urendos?" asked Shiento, "if either of those things occur, then you will not be able to get at her."
"Maybe I am," replied Lady Drask, "however you are having to assume, all be it, a more educated presumption of Silus' actions, so are you not doing the exact same as me?"

"Very well," answered Shiento, "I give you leave to go and pursue your own plans."

"Thank you, my Lord," replied Lady Drask as she bowed.

"Be warned, if you get into trouble, no demon will aid you," growled Shiento, "this is your plan and you alone will fulfil it, or fall to the enemy, do you understand?"

"Of course, my Lord, and I would not have it any other way," answered Lady Drask, "I hope this will prove myself to be an equal tactician to you, my Lord."

"We shall see," whispered Shiento as Lady Drask spread her wings and took to the sky.

Lady Drask soared straight into the sky and above the clouds. Shiento began chuckling to himself as Lady Drask disappeared from view, the winged demon looked at Shiento confused. Shiento then stood up and turned to face the southern ocean once more.

"Is something wrong my Lord?" asked the demon.

"No, I knew she would hate my plan to wait until our enemy make their move," chuckled Shiento, "however, Lady Drask must learn where her limits are, I know my brother, that is why I am being patient to fulfilling my goal of a global conquest, while Lady Drask has a personal hatred of Silus, and will not be tied down to one spot for too long."

"With all due respect my Lord," said the demon, "but if no demon will go to her ladyship's aid, do you predict her plan failing?"

"Without a doubt, she underestimates my brother," scoffed Shiento, "the only question is whether she returns wounded, or not at all."

"But my Lord," pleaded the demon.

"Enough!" shouted Shiento, "return to your patrol, do not return here unless the King of Selania is dead."

"As you wish, my Lord," agreed the demon.

Shiento continued to gaze out across the ocean, the demon bowed to Shiento, then it turned and took off and flapped its wings heavily to get above the cliff. The demons atop the cliff then moved away from the edge, before they returned to sharpening their weapons and duelling each other.

~

In Selania, Silus and Amelia had landed in the palace courtyard, just as Celestia, Fiona and Jacob were exiting the palace doors. As Silus and Amelia stood still and waited for Celestia, Fiona and Jacob to reach them, the wind blew heavily across the courtyard, whipping the girls' hair roughly.

"So are the plans set?" asked Silus.

"Do you even know what we agreed on?" responded King Jacob.

"I imagine you are sending two of us, plus either the dragonkin or phoenix guards to Qurendia, while sending another group to the Dark Forest to aid the elves," answered Silus, "and one of us remains within Selania, ready to send word to the others should the demons return, as well as call for reinforcements from Urendos, does that about cover it?"

King Jacob stared at Silus blankly, Silus stood still looking from Celestia and Fiona to King Jacob. The King cleared his throat before taking a breath and looking to Celestia and Fiona.

"Do not worry, Silus is like that sometimes," said Fiona, "though I feel you should apologise Silus, you read our minds without permission."
"Only the King's," responded Silus, "and for that, I am sorry your majesty."
"No that is quite alright," replied King Jacob, "I suppose that saves us the trouble of detailing the plan to you and Amelia."
"Only one thing is missing, which is to say my exact involvement in this plan," stated Silus.
"We thought we would let you decide," replied Celestia.
"It sounds like you do not disagree with us," said Fiona, "however I feel you have specific candidates in mind for each task, am I correct?"
"You know me too well, Lady Fiona," replied Silus, "but she is right, if you want my recommendation, then I would send Amelia and Fiona to Qurendia accompanied by Commander Hawke and his men."
"What of the Dark Forest?" asked Celestia.
"Send me, Sergeant Drake and the dragonkins," replied Silus, "and as for yourself milady and King Jacob, you two should remain here, as well as call for reinforcements from Urendos."

"Well, I do not have any arguments with Silus's recommendations, do you Fiona?" questioned Celestia.

"My only question is, are you so sure to separate you two so quickly after being reunited?" queried Fiona.

"We discussed this already," answered Silus, "if Shiento were to figure out me and Amelia are closer than meets the eye, then she will become a target, a stepping stone to get to me."

"As much as I argued against Silus' idea, at first," said Amelia, "I understand why he chooses to separate us, at least for the time being."

Fiona and Celestia then looked at each other, then both turned to look at the King. All three nodded together before turning back to look at Silus and Amelia.

"Very well," said Celestia, "then we should head for the city gates, Commander Hawke and Sergeant Drake will be waiting for their orders."

Silus and Amelia nodded then began to lead Celestia, Fiona and King Jacob toward the city gates. As they walked the sounds of the city filled the air, the sound of merchants selling their wares, of blacksmiths working at their forges and the children running around playing. As they walked Silus began to smile, Amelia looked at Silus watching the city as they passed by and began to smile herself.

Chapter 3: The Rise and Fall of Friends

As Silus, Amelia, Fiona, Celestia and King Jacob reached the main plaza the sky had begun to change to a grapefruit pink, the plaza was bustling as wounded soldiers were moved to shelters, and weapons and armour being repaired. Sergeant Drake and Commander Hawke were standing near the stables just inside the city gates. Silus looked around to see that despite what the people have gone through, they still hold onto hope.

"Sergeant Drake, Commander Hawke, front and centre please!" called out Celestia.

Sergeant Drake and Commander Hawke stopped talking and immediately began walking towards Celestia. Amelia looked at Silus and could see that the smile on his face had faded.

"What is the matter Silus?" asked Amelia quietly.
"I look around now, and all I see are people grasping to what little hope they have left," whispered Silus, "they wish to see the end of this war, but lack the strength to do it, all they can do is hold onto their hope."
"Not everyone can stand on the battlefield Silus," replied Amelia.
"That is not what I mean, I mean that, how do I explain it..." whispered Silus, "people like us, people

who were born and raised to fight, whose only fear is failing their duties, a war like this is nothing, but to these humans, they fear so much, and all they have to fight that fear, is the hope that they will eventually prevail."

"Humans were not made for this kind of war," said Amelia, "that is why we are here."

"And the sooner we end this, the better," growled Silus.

"Yes, Lady Celestia?" said Sergeant Drake as he approached the group.

Silus and Amelia turned to look at Sergeant Drake and Commander Hawke as they began speaking to Celestia. Fiona looked over to Silus and noticed he was tense.

"We have come to an agreement about how to proceed," said Celestia.

Around the plaza children were running around, laughing and playing with the soldiers. King Jacob was looking around when he spotted a single young girl sat on the floor alone, the girl was wearing rags as clothing, her eyes staring blankly at the ground in front of her.

"Lady's Fiona and Amelia will travel to Qurendia accompanied by Commander Hawke and the phoenix soldiers," explained Celestia, "meanwhile you and the dragonkins will go aid the elves in their homeland of the Dark Forest but, Silus will be the overall commanding officer for this mission, is that alright with you?"

"Of course, my Lady, if not for Silus, Selania would have fallen, I will follow him into battle any day," answered Sergeant Drake.

"Your devotion and loyalty have always been an inspiration, but I do not think a soldier of your stature is honoured by your current rank," said Celestia, "therefore, I now promote you to the rank of Commander."

"I... thank you, my Lady," stuttered Commander Drake.

"I understand this is hardly a worthy promotion ceremony, but under the circumstances, we do not have the luxury of time."

King Jacob quietly walked away from the group and towards the lone girl. As the King neared the girl, he could hear her sobbing quietly.

"Amelia, Fiona, Commander Hawke, gather yourselves and your troops quickly, you must make it to Qurendia with all haste, warn the Duke and protect him," ordered Celestia, "once finished in the Dark Forest, Silus, Commander Drake and the dragonkins will join you."

"Let me quickly gather my men, my Lady," answered Commander Hawke.

Commander Hawke bowed before turning to run towards a shelter on the west side of the plaza. Silus and Amelia hugged briefly before Amelia and Fiona started walking towards the city gates.

"Take care of yourselves," said Silus.
"Just do not keep us waiting Silus," joked Fiona.
"Yeah, yeah, go on get going," smirked Silus.
"Are you not worried about them?" asked Celestia as she crossed her arms.
"Should I be?" queried Silus.
"I cannot speak for Amelia, but Fiona, we both know is hot-headed, it will not take much for her to start a fight," explained Celestia, "and she never was too subtle in her dabbling of politics."
"Is that not why we are sending Amelia too?" questioned Silus.
"You think she is all that it will take to keep Fiona in line?" queried Celestia.
"If Amelia can manage to stop me from losing my cool, then she can handle your sister," laughed Silus.
"Maybe," giggled Celestia.
"It has been a while since I heard you giggle like that," said Silus, "well there they go."

Silus looked up to just above the city gates, Celestia turned to look up to see Amelia and Fiona standing atop the city gates as Commander Hawke and the phoenix troops all took to the skies. Silus and Celestia gave small wave to Amelia and Fiona, who waved back before soaring into the skies after the phoenix troops.

"Well that is step one," sighed Celestia.

"Commander Drake," said Silus.

"My Lord?" answered Commander Drake.

"Gather your men," ordered Silus, "we will head off to the Dark Forest soon, the demons should be arriving there by daybreak tomorrow, and I want to have a defence plan drawn up by then."

"Of course, my Lord," answered Commander Drake.

"Be on your guard my Lady," said Silus, "the assassin sent to kill the King, may try for your life as well."

"I am more than aware of that fact Silus," replied Celestia, "however as a dragon, I am prepared to sacrifice myself for the humans, my only concern is, are you prepared to make that same sacrifice?"

Silus looked at Celestia, before looking around, as the sound of hissing began to echo in Silus' ears, Silus looked around for King Jacob, his heart began racing inside his chest. Suddenly Silus spotted the King kneeling down next to the girl, Silus then began sprinting towards the King.

"King Jacob, get away from her!" shouted Silus.

The King looked up to see Silus, as the kings gaze met Silus', the girl quickly conjured a small black dagger into her hand, and stabbed the dagger into the King's chest. The King's head slowly turned to see the girl grinning. Silus conjured his dragon sabres and shot a fireball at the girl, the King's body slowly began to fall backwards. The girl stood up and jumped into the air to avoid Silus' attack, the people in the plaza turned to see the King's body hit the ground.

"Damn you, there is no need to hide Servana!" shouted Silus angrily.

The little girl began laughing manically as black smoke began to surround her body. The girl's appearance changed to match that of a middle aged woman, her clothing changed from rags to snakeskin, her eyes turned a bright green.

"You failed boy, the King of Selania is dead!" shouted Servana as she continued laughing.
"And you will be too when I am finished with you!" grunted Silus, "Wobattle!"

Silus swung his right hand sword in a downward direction, as the tip of the blade scratched the ground, a huge shockwave caused the ground to form a spike which shot at Servana. Servana continued laughing as she waved her left hand, causing a shockwave that destroyed Silus' stone spike. Celestia ran and knelt beside the King's lifeless body.

"A poisoned dagger?" said Celestia in disbelief.
"Even if that dagger was not poisoned, the King would have died," grunted Silus, "damn this demon, she was able to disguise her demonic presence so we could not tell who she was in a crowded area like this."
"Well I must say my dear Silus, killing the King was fun," chuckled Servana, "but not as satisfying and bringing your severed head to my master."

"You do not have the power to defeat me!" shouted Silus, "do you honestly see this ending in any other way, then me destroying you?"
"Maybe not, but I have abilities that will certainly help me," laughed Servana, "but I will not leave you guessing, now Silus Drago, face your demise!"

Servana held her arms out to her side, and her body became shrouded by black smoke. Silus watched as the black smoke grew in size, until a large scaly foot emerged from the smoke, followed closely by a second. As the smoke faded Silus glanced up to see a giant five headed serpent. All the people in the plaza began screaming and running into the town, the soldiers formed a defensive line separating the people from the main plaza area.

"What... what is that thing?" shouted Celestia.
"she... she... she shape-shifted into a hydra!" stammered Silus, "she chose one of the hardest creatures to kill, so long as one head lives she will not be killed."
"But hydra's can regenerate their heads," replied Celestia.
"Worse, for every head we cut off, two will grow back in its place," grunted Silus.
"What do we do Silus?" asked Celestia.
"I am thinking," growled Silus, "just be careful the middle head..."

Silus jumped backwards, as he did his dragon sabres vanished. Silus quickly picked up Celestia then leapt into the air as a huge fireball landed where they were just standing. Silus landed beside the King's dead body, as he put Celestia down, he conjured his dragon sabres once more.

"Fire?" said Celestia in disbelief, "hydra's can breathe fire?"
"Not quite, Hydra's typically have three or five heads, only the middle head can breathe fire," grunted Silus.
"What is the matter Silus?" asked Servana in a loud feminine voice, "are you realising that you cannot beat me anymore?"
"Silus, how do we fight a hydra?" questioned Celestia.
"I do not know," answered Silus, "I have never encountered a hydra before, I always thought they were a myth."
"Oh I am very real Silus, come test your pitiful might against your myth," hissed Servana.
"As you wish," growled Silus as he darted forward towards Servana.
"Silus wait!" shouted Celestia.

Celestia watched as Silus' body became a blur as his charged towards Servana sped up. As Silus neared Servana, his left dragon sabre began crackling with electricity, Silus then leapt into the air and slashed his dragon sabre at the hydra's middle head. Celestia watched as the beasts head fell to the ground. Silus landed behind the hydra, as he turned to look at the hydra, he heard the sound of laughter.

"Not bad Silus," chuckled Servana, "but that kind of hurt, now I will make you pay!"

Silus watched in horror as the beasts severed head disappeared in a cloud of smoke and the monster grew two new heads in replacement of its severed one. The beast then turned around and raised it left foot to stamp on Silus. Silus jumped to his side and rolled back onto his feet as the beast's foot slammed into the ground.

"Damn, how do you beat something that can survive being decapitated?" grunted Silus, "wo'dren!"

Silus pulled his right hand dragon sabre across his chest, as he did a shockwave of air shot up at the beast. Commander Drake and the dragonkins had assembled and stood near the gate, preparing to stop the beast from fleeing. Silus and Celestia watched as Silus' shockwave cut through all six of the hydra's heads. The beast body then fell to the ground and began wriggling violently. Celestia then gazed at the heads and almost fell into a trance.

"Now stay down," grunted Silus as he began dusting his armour.

Silus then stopped dusting himself as he heard laughter coming from the hydra's body. Silus watched on in horror as all six severed heads disappeared in a puff of smoke, and the beast's body stood back up, each neck regenerating with two heads.

"How can you still be alive?" sighed Silus. "Hydra's may not be a common enemy to face, but they are the most powerful force in this world," chuckled Servana, "aww poor, poor Silus, you thought you had won, but sadly you have only made it worse."

The beast stood tall and as the last of its new heads regenerated, Silus looked up in horror as twelve scaly heads each with two bright yellows eyes staring back at him. Lady Celestia then looked around at the people in the plaza, then began to think, as she did the hydra began shooting fire at Silus again, this time from four heads that all originate from the central neck. Silus used water spells to block the fireballs.

"Look out for the tail!" shouted Commander Drake.

Silus looked around but could not see anything, due to the steam produced by the hydra's fire attacks that clashed with Silus water spells. Suddenly Silus felt his right leg be dragged out from under him. Celestia and Commander Drake watched on as the beast lashed its tail slamming Silus into the ground three times before throwing him at a fountain on the north side of the plaza.

"Silus!" called out Celestia.
"Ok, that one hurt," grunted Silus as he slowly climbed back onto his feet.
"My, my, are you not just determined to go down slowly," admired Servana, "just how much longer do

you expect to last my dear Silus? A few minutes? An hour?"

"I will not go down until all you demon scum are back in hell!" shouted Silus as he raised his right hand dragon sabre at pointed it at the hydra's chest, "Pythlon baz!"

Silus fired a bolt of lightning into the hydra's chest, the beast recoiled violently and the air filled with an ear-piercing scream, as Servana then lunged toward Silus.

~

Amelia and Fiona flew in the middle of the phoenix soldiers, the group being led by Commander Hawke. The group was flying over the Dark Forest which ran up the spine of Jarvlan, below the sound of hammers working metal and orders being shouted back and forth as the elves prepared for battle. Amelia looked over her right shoulder, in the distance she could see flashes of red and white coming from Selania.

"Something wrong Amelia?" asked Fiona.
"Silus is fighting the assassin," answered Amelia.
"How can you tell?" queried Fiona.
"I can see the flashes as he is using his magic, that and I can sense his anger towards the demon," replied Amelia.
"You can sense that from here?" questioned Fiona, "you must have a really strong bond with Silus to be able to sense that from here."

"It is his anger that worries me," said Amelia.

"What do you mean?" asked Fiona.

"Silus' anger is normally only directed at Shiento, but for him to be this angry at this demon means something is wrong," explained Amelia.

"You think that the assassin might have killed the King?" questioned Fiona.

"Maybe, I cannot say for certain, I cannot even sense Lady Celestia," said Amelia, "all I can sense is Silus' anger and his power."

"Well, we cannot worry about that, we have our mission to focus on," replied Fiona.

"I just feel like I should be with him, helping him fight or at least supporting him," mumbled Amelia.

"Do not worry, Silus will kill the assassin," said Fiona as she smiled at Amelia, "if Silus is still the same as I remember, then he will not back down until he has won."

"I know," replied Amelia.

"Anyway, we should focus on our goal, the sun has started to fall, we should get to Qurendia before it sets," said Fiona.

"You are right," agreed Amelia, "Commander, let us pick up the pace!"

"As you wish my Lady," answered Commander Hawke.

The group began flapping their wings faster, as they did they gained some altitude. Amelia glanced over her shoulder once more before, flapping her wings harder to take the lead of the group.

"My Lady, you should remain in the centre to avoid being targeted by any demons out there," suggested Commander Hawke.

"It does not matter, we need to get to Qurendia as soon as possible," answered Amelia.

"Amelia," said Fiona.

Amelia did not answer Fiona, she just continued to fly faster, the phoenix soldiers increased their speed to catch up with Amelia. Fiona flew alongside Commander Hawke.

"Why the sudden urgency?" asked Commander Hawke.

"I guess she is trying to get further away from Selania so she cannot sense the battle going on there," answered Fiona.

"How do we even know there is a battle there?" queried Commander Hawke.

"She told me she could sense Silus' anger at the demon," explained Fiona, "and that is all the validation I need to know what she is saying is true."

"I see, still for her to sense that from this distance..." replied Commander Hawke.

"I know, still we must focus on our mission," said Fiona.

Fiona and Commander Hawke began to flap their wings harder to catch up to the rest of the group. As they caught up to Amelia, they had cleared the Dark Forest and were now flying over a vast mountain range. In the distance they could see a large chuck of land being held down by chains.

"There it is, Qurendia," said Commander Hawke, "we should get there with an hour or two."
"Good," said Fiona, "the sooner we can warn the Duke, the sooner we can make preparations to find and kill this assassin."

Amelia continued flying in silence, her thoughts were focused on how Silus was feeling. She clenched her fists and closed her eyes as she flew. Fiona looked at Amelia and thought about the fight in Selania.

"Is the fight still bothering you?" asked Fiona.
"Silus is having trouble with that assassin," answered Amelia, "he has taken a few hits, and the assassin has shape shifted into a beast of some kind, and it seems to only be getting stronger."
"How could you be sensing so much with any accuracy from here?" thought Commander Hawke to himself.
"Curse it all, we should be fighting with him," grunted Amelia.
"No, we all agreed to this mission, we should continue on as we planned," said Fiona.
"I know!" shouted Amelia, "I know."

Amelia continued flying at the head of the group, the phoenix guards were scanning the area below trying to spot any monsters in the area. Commander Hawke and Fiona looked at each other before flying alongside Amelia. The group continued flying along towards Qurendia, the sound of the wind rushing past their ears as they flew.

~

Silus jumped into the air, diving between the beast necks, as Silus was over the beast's back, he dug his left hand dragon sabre into the hydra's back, Servana screamed in pain as Silus forced his dragon sabre even further into her back.

"Silus, be careful!" shouted Celestia.
"A little late for that," grunted Silus, "Syphdura!"

As Silus spoke the incantation, he flicked his right dragon sabre to his right. Celestia and Commander Drake watched as Silus' right hand dragon sabre changed from a blade to an extending vine. As Silus flicked his dragon sabre around the vine that was once his blade, began stretching around the hydra's necks.

"What are you doing?" shrieked Servana in disbelief, "get off of me, you filthy mongrel."

Celestia looked at Silus and noticed that his leg plate armour had been badly scratched to the point where you can see through the armour, then Celestia caught a glimpse of a scarred area on Silus' right leg.

"Wait that is it," whispered Celestia.

"What is the matter, my Lady?" asked Commander Drake.

Silus pulled his right dragon sabre across his chest to tighten the vine around the hydra's necks. The beast wriggled and screamed trying to free itself from Silus' spell.

"Lady Celestia, what is wrong?" asked Commander Drake.
"That is how we can beat her," said Celestia, "Silus!"

Silus looked over his right shoulder at Celestia, he then removed his left dragon sabre from the Hydra's back and with a mighty tug on his right dragon sabre, and he forced the beast to fall to its left. With its necks still wrapped up, Silus turned to look at Celestia.

"What is it Celestia?" asked Silus.
"I think I have an idea of how to beat her!" shouted Celestia.

Behind Silus, Servana had managed to turn one of heads around to face Silus. Silus turned around in time to see one of the hydra's heads spit acid at him. Silus released his spell from the hydra and tried to duck out of the way but the acid caught his pauldron on his right shoulder. Silus glanced down to see the acid eat through his mithril armour, Silus quickly cut the strap to the pauldron and threw the armour away.

"If you have an idea, then do not hold back!" called out Silus, "because I am about out of ideas at this point."
"Remember that time me, you and Fiona went to train on the southern mountain range?" asked Celestia.
"Is now the best time to reminisce about the past?" asked Silus.
"Just pay attention!" shouted Celestia, "that monster that attacked us, what did you tell me and Fiona to do when you took that hit in the leg?"

Silus looked at the hydra as it got back to its feet, Silus then started diving and rolling repeatedly to the side, as the hydra began spit acid and fire at Silus. Silus then stabbed his dragon sabre into the ground and a huge wall of water appeared in front of him.

"You want to try cauterizing her severed heads?" asked Silus.
"It may be the only way to stop a hydra's head from regenerating," answered Celestia.
"All right, I will cut off a head, you burn the stump," pondered Silus, "sounds like a plan."
"Look out my Lord!" shouted Commander Drake.

Servana stabbed her tail through the wall of water, Celestia and Commander Drake watched as Servana's tail crashed into the ground, the air filled with steam. Servana began laughing manically, as the steam cleared she could see that Silus was not standing where she thought he was.

"What?" shouted Servana in disbelief, "where did you go Silus, I am not done with you yet."
"Same to you!" shouted a voice from above.

Servana, Celestia and Commander Drake looked up to see Silus diving towards Servana, Celestia then began running towards Servana. As the hydra turned to attack Celestia, Silus used a wind spell to cut off two of the beast's heads. Servana screamed as Silus hovered over the broken fountain.

"Now!" shouted Silus.
"Sazarach!" shouted Silus and Celestia together.

Servana continued to roar in pain, as Silus and Celestia fired a stream of fire at the two exposed stumps on the hydras body.

"Now you die whore!" shouted Servana as she lunged at Celestia with one of her heads.

Celestia watched as Servana's head neared her, Celestia fell backwards and landed on the floor, helpless as Servana's jaws were bearing down upon her. But before Celestia could move, Silus appeared in front of her and cut of the beast's extended neck.

"Sazarach!" shouted Silus as he fired a fireball at the freshly made stump on the beast's neck.
"Silus," gasped Celestia.

"Come on, this is not the time to be resting," said Silus as he stabbed his right dragon sabre into the ground and held his hand out to Celestia, "we still have nine more heads to go."

"You bastard!" roared Servana, "I will make you pay for what you have done to me!"

"No Servana, you are finished," said Silus, "you chose a hydra because no one has ever defeated one, but on this day, we will do just that."

"Ha, this fight is not over yet my dear Silus," chuckled Servana.

"Celestia, get the Commander and his men ready to charge," whispered Silus of his shoulder.

"What do you intend to do?" asked Celestia.

"I intend to end this," said Silus as he looked up at the hydra.

As Silus charged at Servana again, Celestia ran towards Commander Drake. Silus was darting from side to side trying to avoid Servana acid and fire attacks, as Celestia reached Commander Drake, she looked around to see Servana whip her tail around, the tail hit Silus across the chest and sent him tumbling backwards across the plaza floor. Celestia turned to look at Commander Drake.

"Commander ready your troops to charge at that demon," ordered Celestia.

"What is Silus planning?" asked Commander Drake.

"I think he intends to cut all of its heads off at once, but not even my power and his combined could seal those wounds, so he needs all of the dragonkins to pitch in and burn the stumps made when that beast loses all nine heads at once," explained Celestia. "Very well," answered Commander Drake, "men be prepared to charge, once Silus cuts of the beast's heads, we charge in and burn that demon."

The dragonkins began cheering as Silus began charging at the hydra once again, his body began crackling with electricity as his speed increased, Servana began spitting fire and acid at Silus as quickly as she could, Silus's body began to blur and it almost looked like his body was a lightning bolt as he dodged the attacks.

"Do it now Silus!" shouted Celestia.

Silus leapt into the air, as Servana lifted her head and spat a fireball at Silus, his body blurred again and he appeared behind the hydra, Silus crossed his dragon sabre across his body. As he did the blades began to glow white.

"Take this demon," said Silus, "wo'dren!"

As Silus shouted the incantation, his slashed his dragon sabres across his chest, as he did two huge shockwaves launched from his sword tips, Servana looked around to see the shockwaves flying towards her, but before she could react, the shockwaves sliced through her nine remaining necks.

"Now!" shouted Silus.

"Charge!" shouted Commander Drake.

The dragonkin soldiers and Celestia began charge at the beast's headless body, and in unison they all began firing torrents of fire at the beast's necks. Silus watched as the hydra's body became enshrouded in smoke, then Servana appeared in her normal form charging for Silus with a long thin black sword clutched tightly in both her hands.

"I will kill you!" screamed Servana.

Servana swung her sword from her right side across to her left shoulder, Silus raised his left hand dragon sabre to knock Servana's blade up, then he spun around and swung his right hand dragon sabre at Servana's neck. Servana stopped running a few paces behind Silus. Celestia, Commander Drake and all the soldiers watched on as Servana dropped to her knees, as she did her head separated from her neck, Servana's headless body then fell to the left and crashed against the ground. Silus turned to see that Servana's severed head was still moving.

"You may have bested me on this day," hissed Servana, "but you cannot hope to best Lord Shiento, he will descend upon you and bring death to those who oppose him."
"Whether it be tomorrow, the next day, or even next month, when I see Shiento, I will end him, just as I have ended you," gasped Silus as he tried to gather his breath.

"Believe what you will, but you are not strong enough to end this," hissed Servana, "sooner or later you will realise that."

"Enough of this," said Celestia, "sazarach."

Silus and Celestia watched as Servana's body and severed head caught fire, Servana closed her eyes and quietly let herself pass. Commander Drake walked across the plaza to pick up the pauldron that Silus discarded, as he walked back towards Celestia and Silus, he examined the armour to see how badly corroded it had become after being hit by the acid.

"Well, we did it," sighed Celestia, "we took down a hydra."

"But at what cost, we failed to save the King," grunted Silus.

"You should not be focusing on the negative, Selania has to continue as it always has," said Celestia.

"That which happens in the past, can haunt your future, only by facing the past, does the future become bright," replied Silus as he walked off towards the stables.

"Lord Silus is being rather harsh about himself, do you not think milady?" asked Commander Drake.

"He is, but I can understand why," answered Celestia.

"What do you mean?" queried Commander Drake.

"Silus never intended to arrive in Selania announced, and if he did, he would wish to make up for his past failings," explained Celestia, "but because Jacob is dead, Silus just sees this battle as a repeat of his own history."

Silus entered the stable and walked straight to the back, where Legolas was standing drinking some water. As Silus approached Legolas lifted his head to look at Silus, Silus began stroking Legolas' neck.

"Well the assassin is dead, but so is the King," whispered Silus, "looks like I failed the people again."

Legolas shook his head and nudged Silus' chest.

"I know, we have to keep moving forward," said Silus, "next we need to help the elves in the Dark Forest, and after that, get to Qurendia."

Legolas began clapping his front left hoof on the floor, then nodded his head, before turning to face the front of the stable.

"I am worried about her too, believe me, I worry more than I show it," said Silus, "but there is nothing I can do at the minute, the demon attack on the elves is more imminent, and as we both know, dragons cannot put their personal feelings above our duties."

Legolas let out a heavy sigh, before nodding his head again. Silus then walked around and picked up Legolas' saddle from the floor and as Silus lifted the saddle onto Legolas' back, Celestia walked into the stables and walked towards Silus. Silus continued fastening Legolas' saddle as Celestia approach.

"Do not worry Celestia," said Silus, "I am going to the Dark Forest."
"I was not doubting that," replied Celestia.

Silus stood up and picked up Legolas' muzzle, as he raised his arms to put the muzzle and reins onto Legolas, Celestia stepped forward and placed her right hand on Silus' right shoulder. Silus stopped moving his arms, Celestia then pulled on Silus's shoulder to turn him around.

"Silus," said Celestia.

As Silus turned around he let his arms drop to his side, still holding Legolas' muzzle, Celestia looked at Silus before stepping forward to wrap her arms around him.

"Silus, the King's death is not your fault," said Celestia, "do not blame yourself for that."
"I do not," whispered Silus as he hugged Celestia back.
"You do not?" asked Celestia, "then what is bothering you?"
"During the fight, I could still sense Amelia's presence, even when she was over the Dark Forest, even now I can sense her," explained Silus as he let go of Celestia and looked out of the stables, "and what is bothering me, is even as far away as she is, I can tell how she is feeling, she is wishing to have stayed and helped fight, and to be honest, I would rather stay with her."

"I can understand that but…" replied Celestia.

"I know, I know, our duties as dragons come first," said Silus, "Celestia."

"Yes Silus?" asked Celestia.

"When I get to the Dark Forest, Randalene will undoubtedly be keeping her people in their homes, she will not abandon her home," explained Silus, "I will convince her not to endanger her people, and send those who are not fighting here to Selania, can you see to it that the elves receive shelter here?"

"Of course," answered Celestia.

"Thank you," said Silus as he attached Legolas' muzzle and reins, "we will be heading off shortly, we will be with the elves by sun set."

"Take care Silus, you may not have received any serious injuries but going from one fight to another without rest can prove fatal," replied Celestia, "even to a seasoned fighter like yourself."

"I know," sighed Silus.

Silus walked Legolas out of the stable, in the plaza Commander Drake had assembled all of his troops, as Silus approached they all bowed to Silus. Silus turned to look at Celestia who was standing in the entrance to the stables.

"Are we ready to move Commander?" asked Silus as he turned back to face the dragonkin's.

"Awaiting your orders my Lord," answered Commander Drake, "each soldier ready to give the demons hell, I have informed them that even with me there, you are the commanding officer."

"We will fight under your command Lord Silus, the demons do not stand a chance against us!" shouted a dragonkin soldier who stood on the front right corner of the squad.

"What is your name?" questioned Silus.

"Foot soldier Scals, my Lord," answered the dragonkin.

"Scals? You are the son of the former General of Urendos, General Vruts, are you not?" queried Silus.

"Yes, my Lord," answered Scals.

"Excellent, then you best be prepared to step up," said Silus.

"My Lord?" responded Scals looking at Silus with a confused expression.

"I now promote you to the rank of Corporal, you best be ready to lead, because I have an idea for how to deal with the demons in the Dark Forest," explained Silus.

"Thank you, my Lord," answered Scals, "I swear on my sword, I will not fail you."

"Good," replied Silus, "alright, we head for the Dark Forest, we will fly to the edge of the forest then make the rest of the way on foot, the elves will be on high alert and will treat any approach as a potential threat, but once they know that we are approaching, they will permit us entry, so keep your weapons sheathed and follow my lead, do you understand?"

Silus watched as all the dragonkins began stamping their spears on the ground in unison, after five stamps they raised their spears up and roared together. Silus smiled then mounted Legolas, as he did the Pegasus spread his wings. The human soldiers in the plaza watched on as Silus and Legolas took off into the sky, followed closely by Commander Drake and the dragonkin soldiers. Celestia watched as Silus and the dragonkins began to shrink into the distance.

"Lady Celestia," said the Guard-Captain as he approached her from the barracks.
"What is it Guard-Captain?" asked Celestia.
"How will Selania go on without a King?" queried the Guard-Captain, "we have no King and no one to succeed him, how will Selania carry on?"
"For now, I will do what I can to help you all, and hopefully we can end this war before too long," explained Celestia, "as for who is elected the new King of Selania, that is not within my power to control nor predict."
"Should we hold an assembly to make a decision?" asked the Guard-Captain.
"That is for you to decide, however I would advise you put the leadership of Selania to the side and instead be preparing for a possible final battle," answered Celestia, "for now the demons may not return for a week or two, however we should prepare for every eventuality."
"Of course," replied the Guard-Captain as he turned to return to the barracks, the Captain turned his head to look at Celestia over his right shoulder, "but, do you propose we should return to the prophecy, and appoint the Dragonborne as our King?"
"That is the decision to be made by the Selanian council, not me," said Celestia.

"As you wish," replied the Guard-Captain.

The Guard-Captain then marched off to the barracks, Celestia looked to the sky once more to see that Silus and the dragonkin soldiers had disappeared from view, as Celestia tried scanning the sky for them she noticed a winged beast hovering over the western side of the city wall. The beast then turned as flew towards the south quickly.

"Now it is your turn, Shiento," whispered Celestia.

~

Silus and the dragonkin soldiers swooped down so they were flying just above a small woodland, just ahead was a deep gorge, and across the gorge was a wooden bridge. Silus directed Legolas to swoop over the bridge and then land just on the other side of the gorge. As they landed Legolas continued forward a few paces into a large forest. Behind them Commander Drake and the dragonkins landed inside the tree line. Silus turned Legolas to face the soldiers.

"Ok, from here we must travel on foot," instructed Silus, "form up into two ranks, keep two paces between you, remember your weapons must stay sheathed, unless a beast comes out and attacks us we keep our weapons sheathed, everyone understand?"

Silus looked over the group as they nodded to agree, Silus then turned Legolas to face the forest before lightly kicking Legolas' sides, Legolas began walking down the pathway. The forest was dark, hardly any light penetrated the treetops, however the forest was lit up by various luminous mushrooms and vines that covered the surrounding ground and tree trunks. Commander Drake walked beside Silus.

"My Lord," said Commander Drake.
"Yes Commander?" asked Silus.
"I have two queries if you will allow me to ask?" queried Commander Drake.
"Speak your mind Commander," answered Silus.
"Well firstly do you expect our forces numbing only to three battalions is enough to tip the tides of the coming battle?" questioned Commander Drake.
"Our presence will have a bigger impact than you think Commander," responded Silus, "what of your second concern?"
"Not to question your judgement, but why promote Scals?" asked Commander Drake, "his service record hardly reflects his rank."
"With all due respect Commander, but the same could be said of your service record, which would only suit you to the rank of Captain?" queried Silus.
"That is true," answered Commander Drake, "you knew the General, did you not?"
"When I resided in Urendos, training under the former King and training up his daughters, I had a few run ins with the General," explained Silus, "but he was a strong fighter, and loyal, when he fell at the Black Fortress all those years ago, I knew that dark times were upon us."

"And now we have you to lead us through them," said Commander Drake.

"Do not be relying solely upon me," replied Silus, "an army is only as strong as its weakest soldier."

Commander Drake looked up at Silus, Silus did not turn his head. Commander Drake then looked back at his soldiers, before turning to face the front. The forest was quiet, not even the wind had a sound. The group continued on marching in silence for a while, until they saw a large hill in the forest floor, the hill had no trees growing on it, but they could see more light shining over the top of the hill. The sound of hammers working metal, and voices calling out orders began to fill the air.

"Ok, we are here, just follow me, no sudden moves they will be suspicious of us as they may think us to be demons in disguise," explained Silus as he spoke over his shoulder.

Silus turned to face the front again, as Legolas reached the bottom of the hill, he let out a neigh and stopped. Silus looked up to see a line of elves standing atop the hill, all of them drawing arrows to their bows readying to fire.

"Easy Legolas," whispered Silus.

"Wod tu suma de'ar?" called out one of the elves.

"Segra Silus Drago, ia dou vitima," replied Silus.

"Did I just hear that right?" called out a female voice.

Silus smiled as Randalene appeared from between two archers. Randalene then raised her left hand and the archers lowered their bows and disappeared from sight, Legolas then began walking up the hill, Randalene greeted Legolas as he reached the top of the hill, Silus then dismounted Legolas and stood facing Randalene.

"What brings you to this neck of the forest, Lord Silus?" asked Randalene.

"You did not think I would just send you home to face the demons along, did you?" queried Silus.

"I kind of thought you had, I am glad I was mistaken," sighed Randalene.

"Well you came and helped me when I needed it," explained Silus, "now it is time I repay the favour, myself and the troops you see before you are ready to bring down some demons."

"Thank you," said Randalene turning to face the dragonkins, "your help is greatly appreciated, on behalf of all my people, I thank you for coming to us in our darkest hour."

"All right men, set your camp up on the southern edge of the city, ready yourselves for tomorrow, if your weapons or armour need tending to speak to one of the many smiths here," ordered Silus, "you are dismissed."

Commander Drake and the dragonkins stood to attention and saluted Silus briefly before breaking formation and climbing the hill. Commander Drake stood with Silus and Randalene at the top of the hill.

The three looked over the city as warriors sharpened their blades and archers practised their shots and healers prepared potions.

"For centuries our people have hunted the demons," sighed Randalene, "it seems fate has turned the hunters into the hunted."

"Fate had nothing to do with it," said Silus, "Shiento is to blame for your predicament."

"True, but we will surely lose a lot of soldiers tomorrow," replied Randalene, "I would not have blamed you if you did not come here, this fight will bring my people to the verge of extinction."

"Which is why Lord Silus would not abandon you," said Commander Drake.

"That and I always repay my debts," added Silus.

"Even knowing that you and your men might die?" asked Randalene.

"We all accept that death is inevitable," said Commander Drake, "the only difference is that we get to choose how we die, whether it be on a battlefield or of old age."

"And to a dragon dying honourably in battle is far more appealing," explained Silus, "do not worry Randalene, I swear, we will find a way to save as many as possible."

"Your confidence is reassuring Silus, but all possible scenarios point to the fact, that my people will nearly be wiped out in the coming battle," replied Randalene.

"That was before we arrived, the tables have turned," said Commander Drake, "but there are so many civilians here."

"Of course, they are here," scoffed Randalene, "this is our home, and I will not abandon it."

"Admirable as that may be," said Silus, "you were sad cause your kind would be wiped out in this battle, yet you will allow the innocent to fall victim to this attack? I do not mean to be rude, but that is rather contradictory, do you not think?"

"What would you have me do Silus?" asked Randalene, "abandon our ancestral home? Send the women, children and craftsmen to their deaths?"

"You do not have to necessarily abandon your home," explained Silus, "just order those who cannot fight to seek shelter in Selania, once this war is over, you and your people can return here."

"No, we will not abandon our homes!" shouted Randalene, "I thought you would have understood my stance on this matter."

"I do understand, but that does not mean I am ready to condone the lives of the innocent and the defenceless, to the brutality of this demonic attack," replied Silus, "why allow your people to suffer at their hands?"

"Because this is where we belong," answered Randalene.

"And I thought dwarves were stubborn," scoffed Silus.

"Do not compare us to the dwarves!" shouted Randalene.

"I am going to be blunt," said Silus, "you are being completely and utterly ridiculous, you would let your people die? Simply because it is where you have always lived? If you let them be sacrificed, then what will be left when this war is over? Your people, your possessions, everything that the elves have ever stood for, your race will disappear, and fade to the pages of history."

Randalene looked at Silus shocked as his eyes turned from his human green eyes to his dragon blue ones. Randalene stared into Silus' eyes, almost mesmerised by them. Randalene then turned and looked across the city, several groups of elves were looking at them.

"Silus, I followed your orders before, and you did not let a single person under your command die," said Randalene, "can you promise me that for as long as you draw breath, you will try to avoid inflicting casualties to my warriors?"
"So long as I draw breath, I will find a solution that will end this fight suffering a minimum number of casualties, and where possible, no loss of life for any elf or dragonkin," replied Silus.
"Then I leave the fate of my people in your hands," said Randalene as she knelt before Silus.
"Then we do this together," replied Silus holding out his right hand.

Randalene looked up at Silus, the glow of his dragon eyes almost like looking into a calm, clear lake on a bright summer's day. Randalene then raised her right hand and took Silus's outstretched hand, Silus helped Randalene to her feet and smiled.

"Right we have not got much time left, but we best get to work," said Silus.
"The war table is in the central plaza," replied Randalene.
"Then let us go," said Silus.

Chapter 4: The Darkened Forest

Silus, Commander Drake and Randalene, descended down the hill into the city. The city was made of homes and buildings built into the trunks of large trees, some being built out of stone. The city lit up by more glowing vegetation, as well as glass balls filled with fireflies. At the war table, Silus could see Gilnur already standing with three other commanders discussing battle plans. One Commander had a large two handed sword across his back, the other two commanders were female, one had a large halberd on her back and a buckler strapped to her left arm, the last Commander had a longbow on her back along with a quiver on her back and one on her left hip. As they approached, Gilnur and the other Commanders bowed to Randalene.

"Welcome to our home Lord Silus," said Gilnur, "and to you Sergeant Drake."
"He is a Commander now," replied Silus.
"My apologies, Commander," said Gilnur.
"No need for formalities, it is good to see you to Gilnur," replied Commander Drake, "how is your shoulder doing?"
"Much better now, thank you," answered Gilnur.
"Commanders, I will tell you now that any and all plans made to defend our homes, now go through Lord Silus," explained Randalene, "I have entrusted our fate to him."

Silus was looking over the drawings and markers on the war table, the elven Commanders looked between themselves, each looking shocked and confused.

"With no disrespect to Lord Silus," said Gilnur, "but you are our Queen."

"Yes, and lack experience in large scale fights," explained Randalene, "whereas Silus has spent most of his life going from battle to battle, if there is someone who has experience planning for a major battle, it is Silus Drago."

"I appreciate the compliment my Lady," said Silus, "but I think your exaggerating a little too much."

"Never the less," said Randalene, "I put my full faith in Silus."

"I suppose there is not anything we can complain about then," said the elven commander who had a large two handed sword across his back.

"So, the demons are coming in from the south, the terrain has given you a fair amount of time to prepare, so what have you currently decided on?" asked Silus.

"We will have the glaive spinners atop the city boundaries, and our forces will be in formation at the base of the wall which will be our holding line," explained Gilnur pointing at various markers on the map, "the civilians will be holed up in the great oak temple."

"Lady Randalene," said Silus.

"I know, you wish me to order an evacuation," replied Randalene.

"Out of the question, we do not have time to get everyone out safely," interrupted a female elven Commander, "the battle will begin before we can get everyone out of the city."

"Then we buy them some time," said Silus, "Commander, find Corporal Scals, and ready a squad of men for a sabotage run."

"At once, my Lord," replied Commander Drake as he turned to run south.

"As for the glaive spinners," said Silus, "I have no issue with their positioning, however I would urge that we avoid using them in the early stages of the battle."

"How would you utilize them Silus?" asked Gilnur.

"I would prefer keeping them poised and ready to shoot the titans that are in this demon attack," answered Silus, "since we cannot truly predict how the demon Commanders will deploy their troops, we should try a strategy that puts more responsibility on the fighting force rather than the artillery."

"I can understand that, but how can we make our fighting force more effective to adhere to that sort of strategy?" queried Gilnur.

"Normally elven strategy is to use a wall of shields and spears, and have archers fire as many volleys as possible before the enemy reaches the wall, correct?" quizzed Silus.

"Indeed," answered the elven Commander with the bow.

"Well instead of the wall, we will have to go with a full frontal charge," explained Silus as he pointed at various markers on the map, "if all troops who are adequate archers fire two or three volleys in quick succession, then all soldiers switch to melee weapons to charge the enemy, we can keep the demons further from the city, and if possible I would also suggest moving this line forward as much as we can without taking the fight too far from the glaive spinners."

"I can see what you are seeing my Lord," said Gilnur, "but you have to understand most elven military are specialized troops, they are either archers or they are warriors."

"I know, but that does not stop them from learning the skills needed to fulfil the other role," answered Silus, "I am not proposing to send every member of your forces into the fray, merely to try and focus the fight further from the city wall, this will create a larger safety area for the last of the civilians to evacuate."

Randalene watched quietly as Silus moved the markers around. Once Silus had finished moving the markers she leant over the table, and examined the new layout.

"All in all Silus, I agree with what you are proposing," said Randalene, "Commanders, what do you think?"

The four Commander studied the map, before looking at each other, and without speaking a word they nodded to each other.

"Very well, if this is to be the plan, we will gladly follow Silus' lead," said Gilnur.

"Thank you," replied Silus, "but I must also ask that some of your troops act as escorts to the civilians."

"Of course," replied Randalene, "Commander Luthia organise twenty troops to be the escorts I will leave it to you to decide how many are archers or warriors."

"At once my Queen," answered Commander Luthia.

"Commander Gilnur, order the evacuation," ordered Randalene.

"Yes, your majesty," answered Gilnur.

Silus and Randalene watched as Commander Gilnur and Luthia bowed before running off to complete their duties.

"Commander Uveal and Nocte, can you continue the preparations as Silus has instructed?" asked Randalene.

"As you wish," answered the Commanders together.

As Commander Uveal and Nocte bowed and turned to run off to ready the elven troops, Commander Drake returned to the table with Corporal Scals. The Corporal bowed to Silus and Randalene then stood up waiting for his orders.

"Corporal, time to prove yourself," said Silus.

"Ask of me what you will, my Lord," answered Corporal Scals.

"Have you got a squad to lead?" asked Silus.

"The Commander has arranged for nine others to follow me on this mission, they are gearing up as we speak," responded Corporal Scals.

"Very well," sighed Silus, "then here are your orders, the demons are to the south, for the moment they should be fairly far off, however we are evacuating any elves that will not be participating in the battle, this is where you and your squad come in, you will scout around the south, once you have their position, you will lay a small ambush for them, but do not engage them directly, a series of magical traps is all you will need, just make sure the traps slow them down even more."

"I understand my Lord," said Corporal Scals, "rest assured, my squad will not fail you."

"Just remember that Lord Silus is not authorising you to take on the demons, Corporal," interrupted Commander Drake, "just set the traps and return."

"I understand Commander," replied Corporal Scals, "very well, I should get to my mission, do not fret Queen Randalene, we will ensure your people have time to evacuate."

"Thank you Corporal," replied Randalene.

Corporal Scals bowed to Silus and Randalene, before turning and running south. Silus looked at Commander Drake who shook his head in disapproval.

"I am still not convinced that Scals is ready to lead a squad, my Lord," said Commander Drake.

"I accept that you have your reticence about it, but he wishes to make his father proud, and I will not deny him that," explained Silus.

"You knew that soldier's father?" asked Randalene.

"You did too," answered Silus, "Scals is the only child to Urendos' former General, General Vruts."

"That was Vruts' only son?" asked Randalene in disbelief, "I think I side with the Commander now Silus."

"You two need to have more faith," said Silus, "the way I see it, the demons may have a forward party, which could spot the squad setting up a trap and might have a small scrap, which will mean it will be a true test of whether or not Scals is ready or not for his new role."

"That is a pretty big risk Silus," said Randalene.

"Agreed," scoffed Commander Drake.

"As much as I agree with what you are saying, we are at war," explained Silus, "we all need to take risks if we wish to see its end."

"You are right," sighed Commander Drake, "as much as I hate to admit it, you have a point my Lord."

"Look let us just focus on our preparations, leave the Corporal to plan out his mission as he needs to," said Silus, "which on the subject of preparations, Randalene who is the best armourer in the city?"

"Armourer?" asked Randalene, "now that you mention it, you do not look quite ready to step onto the battlefield, and might I inquire as to what happened to your mithril set?"

"That is a long story," sighed Silus.

"Has it anything to do with the assassin sent to Selania?" questioned Randalene.

"Commander, can you go inform your troops of the plan for tomorrow?" asked Silus.

"Of course, my Lord," answered Commander Drake.

Commander Drake bowed before turning to walk to the south. Silus and Randalene then began walking towards the eastern side of the city.

"Well as you said, I had mithril armour," explained Silus, "however it seems the assassin sent to kill the King was very cunning, she could spit acid which could melt into mithril armour, hence my lack of a pauldron and leg plates."
"And what of the King?" asked Randalene.

Silus let out a heavy sigh and looked at the ground as they walked. Randalene pointed down a street to let Silus know where the armourer was, as she did she noticed the look on Silus' face.

"I see, that is unfortunate," said Randalene, "the assassin succeeded, where exactly have Lady's Celestia, Fiona and Amelia got to?"
"Fiona and Amelia are about to arrive in Qurendia, Celestia meanwhile is currently helping control Selania in the absence of a ruler," explained Silus.
"I imagine since you brought dragonkins with you, that Lady Celestia will be summoning reinforcements from Urendos?" asked Randalene.
"That is the plan, she will call upon our naval forces," answered Silus, "however, it would seem Selania is becoming a home to all races."
"What do you mean?" queried Randalene.

"Dragons, elves, humans, and soon even the dwarves will have to seek refuge somewhere," explained Silus, "Shiento will not simply ignore them."
"True, in fact, I had a report recently detailing that Urthrad has called for his mountain to empty, all civilians are heading through tunnels to Urendos, while the army and their siege weapons are mobilizing, heading to Selania even as we speak," stated Randalene, "it seems all indications point to a final confrontation happening in Selania.

Silus sighed as Randalene stopped walking, Silus turned to look at the shop she stopped at, the sign was an anvil with two hammers crossed above it. The streets were quiet, a gentle gust of wind swept through the streets.

"Well you wanted the best armourer, this is where you will find her," said Randalene.
"Is that you 'vouching' for her work?" asked Silus.
"What surprises me is that you question if I vouch for her work, rather than questioning the fact that my best armourer is a woman," pondered Randalene.
"I have met several female smiths, some can make truly beautiful pieces, but lack reliability, others have reliability but no style," said Silus, "so what is this armourer like?"
"I think you will like her work," replied Randalene, "I will leave you to get some armour, I should ensure the evacuation is proceeding efficiently."
"Would she not be evacuating too?" asked Silus.

"Even if she was, the soldiers all get their armour made here, so I think she would stick around even if I personally told her to leave," answered Randalene, "trust me, you will find some armour here that I think you can appreciate."

"Thank you Randalene," replied Silus.

"You do not need to thank me," said Randalene, "just as long as you can slay these demons before I lose too many good people."

"You still doubt the plan?" queried Silus.

"No, I trust you," answered Randalene, "it is just that the last time demons invaded our homeland, it was the worst fight ever seen by the elves."

"This time will be slightly easier, that is a promise," said Silus.

"If you say so," replied Randalene.

Randalene turned and started walking back up the street towards the centre of the city. Silus took another look at the shop sign before heading in the door, as Silus stepped into the shop and small chiming sound filled the air. A loud bang came from behind the counter. Silus watched as a young elf with long blonde hair and sky blue eyes stumbled out of the workshop behind the counter, she wore a brown apron, underneath Silus spotted she wore a mithril chainmail cuirass, she had two large brown gloves that stretched to her upper arms.

"Hi, oops sorry, one moment," said the girl cheerfully as she removed her gloves and apron, "I am so sorry, hello, welcome to Cirilla's armoury."

"You must be Cirilla, correct?" asked Silus.

"I am, how I can help you?" queried Cirilla.

"Queen Randalene recommended that I come here to get some new armour, to replace the stuff I used to have," explained Silus.

"The Queen... recommended me..." stammered Cirilla.

"You seem surprised?" asked Silus.

"It is not that I am surprised, more confused," answered Cirilla.

"Confused about what?" queried Silus, "if you have a reputation for making reliable armour, should you not take pride in your work?"

"I do, it is just with the evacuation going on, I was working as hard as I could to make armour ready for the battle," explained Cirilla, "I did not think anyone would come here for armour, more to tell me to leave."

"You work alone?" questioned Silus, "no apprentices, no one else?"

"Yup, being surrounded by people makes me nervous, and even now, you are a stranger, I do not understand why Randalene would send you to me," answered Cirilla.

"Oh, sorry I should introduce myself," said Silus, "my name is Silus Drago, it is a pleasure to meet you."

Silus held out his right hand across the counter. Cirilla looked at Silus in shock, Silus looked at Cirilla as she began to blush.

"By the gods, your Silus Drago?" asked Cirilla as she quickly shook Silus' hand, "this is so amazing, I would be glad to make you some armour."

"There is no need to freshly forge anything, I just need a pauldron for my right shoulder and some leg plates," said Silus.

"Well I normally do not keep armour on a shelf, I forge everything fresh, that way people can be assured that my goods are always at their best," explained Cirilla.

"Fair enough, how long would you need to forge my armour?" asked Silus.

"That depends on what type of metal you want," explained Cirilla, "do you want steel, mithril, or would you like to try a new compound I started working with?"

"A new compound?" queried Silus, "I thought elven smiths only used mithril and steel? My experience is that elves hold onto tradition more than anything else."

"Oh, we do, but that does not mean we will not try experimenting," answered Cirilla.

"Well, what is this compound like?" questioned Silus.

"Really, you want to see my new work?" asked Cirilla, "well, if you come into my workshop I could show you."

"Are you sure, I thought most smiths do not let people see their work shop?"

"Oh just come on," said Cirilla excitedly as she grabbed Silus' arm and tugged on his arm to pull him towards the end of the counter.

"Ok, ok, I will come," replied Silus.

Silus followed Cirilla through the door that she had stumbled out of, as Silus looked through the doorway he picked up Cirilla's gloves and apron. The workshop was a bit untidy, previous works left across the floor, and to the left was an unusual forge which was a stone circle with a green ball of fire floating in its centre. Cirilla scrambled through the mess on the floor to a large pile at the back of the workshop, the pile was compiled of freshly made armour.

"Need a hand?" asked Silus.
"No... no... just second," stammered Cirilla.

Silus waved his right hand, then watched as the armour pieces across the floor began to levitate to form neat piles on various shelves around the room. Eventually Cirilla stood up from the pile with a large plate of black metal in her hands, Silus then waved his right hand again as the pile in front of Cirilla began moving and stacking itself on the shelves with similar pieces of armour.

"Did... did you just tidy my shop?" asked Cirilla.
"At least everything is categorised and easier to find," answered Silus, "is that the metal you spoke of?"
"Yeah, I have not quite named it yet, I got the means to make lots more, but not sure if I should," said Cirilla nervously.
"How come?" queried Silus as he approached Cirilla to examine the metal more closely.

"Well just feel it, it looks like it would be heavy, but even someone like me can lift this with ease," explained Cirilla, "and light metal tends to mean it is easier to break."

"Have you not tested it yet?" questioned Silus.

"I... no... not yet," stammered Cirilla.

"Then let us test it out," said Silus.

Cirilla looked at Silus, Silus just smiled and took the plate out the back of the workshop into a small courtyard. Silus fastened the plate to a manikin that was stood at the end of the courtyard. Cirilla stood in the doorway watching Silus, a sense of surprise and confusion filled her.

"Why are you so eager to help me?" whispered Cirilla to herself.

"Do you want me to just use sword blows, or should I use magic too?" asked Silus.

"Huh... oh do whatever you want, I am not too sure how the metal will react," answered Cirilla.

"Ok, if you are sure," said Silus.

Silus conjured a dragon sabre into his left hand, Cirilla admired Silus' sword as it appeared. She then looked confused as the swords appearance resembled the plate of metal. Silus then lunged at the plate of metal, Cirilla watched as Silus' sword bounced off of the metal plate, Silus then spun around to slash at the plate, Silus's dragon crashed into the plate but Cirilla could see that the blade just ran across the surface of the metal.

"Not even made a scratch, so far," said Silus, "now for some magic."

Cirilla watched as Silus' sword began to glow an icy white colour, as Silus slashed at the metal plate, Cirilla saw that the sword became encrusted in ice, as the ice covered sword hit the metal, the ice just shattered. Silus then spun around and lunged at the metal as his sword began to crackle with electricity. The tip of Silus's sword hit the metal plate dead centre, Cirilla watched on as Silus channelled more magic into the attack. Then a small flash of light caused Cirilla to look away. As the light faded Cirilla looked up to see that Silus was now standing near the shop window, his arm crackling with electricity as he gasped for breath.

"You ok?" asked Cirilla.
"Yeah, whatever that metal is, it is certainly nothing to scoff at, it is incredible," answered Silus.
"Aww, you are just saying that," said Cirilla as she began to blush.
"No, I am being completely serious, if I had armour like that I would wear it with pride," replied Silus as he let his dragon sabre fade in a cloud of smoke.
"Really? You think it is that good?" said Cirilla in shock.
"How long would it take for you to make me some armour out of this stuff?" asked Silus.
"Well it can only be forged through a mana forge," explained Cirilla, "but I cannot stoke the fire at the

same time I am working the metal, so it could take a day."

"And if I created and maintained a mana forge for you?" queried Silus.

"You know the spell?" asked Cirilla.

"I did use to live among your people, I learnt a few things," laughed Silus.

"If you were helping with the forge I could have it done by sun rise," said Cirilla excitedly.

"Are you sure you want to work through the night?" questioned Silus.

"Are you kidding, you agreed to use my new material, I would not be able to sleep tonight anyway," said Cirilla as she ran around the shop gather her tools and pieces of metal giggling to herself.

"Alright, I will light the forge then," said Silus.

Silus walked across the room to the stone circle, the green fire that was there before was now a tiny dull flame, Silus waved his right hand to extinguish it. As Silus stood outside the circle, Cirilla was still giggling. Silus smiled then looked at the stone circle, he took a deep breath then began chanting a spell. Cirilla put the various metal pieces near the stone circle and placed her tools across a work bench, as Silus continued chanting a ball of green fire began to appear and grow in size. Cirilla watched as the fire filled the stone circle.

"Wow, you have a better mastery of that spell than me," whispered Cirilla.

Silus stopped chanting just as the ball of fire formed a cylinder inside the stone circle, he turned to Cirilla and smiled.

"There you go, you can start now," said Silus as stepped away from the mana forge.
"Right, now its two pieces of this, one of this and half a piece of this," mumbled Cirilla as she focused on the mana forge."

Silus watched quietly as Cirilla put her gloves back on and pushed her hands into the mana forge. Cirilla began moving her hands around to warp the metal pieces together to form a solid bar. Cirilla continued mumbling to herself. Silus watched as the Cirilla's behaviour changed from being shy and clumsy to focused and passionate. Eventually Cirilla pulled out her right hand to grab a thick metal pole and inserted it into the fire. Cirilla pulled the bar out and at the end was a forged ingot of a dark coloured metal. Cirilla then quickly turned around and grabbed her hammer and moved to her right to start working the metal on the anvil.

"One, two, three, four, flip, one, two, three, four, side," mumbled Cirilla as she began hammering the ingot.
"A combination of passion and precision," whispered Silus, "not many smiths can manage that."

Silus continued to sit out of the way watching as Cirilla worked the metal, returning to the forge after counting twenty hammer blows. Eventually Cirilla had worked the metal into a curved shape, Cirilla then moved to the horn of the anvil and removed the pole, and she began hammering again, Silus watched as Cirilla began counting differently to how she started.

"One, two, three, four, five, six, and rotate, one two, three, four, five, six, and rotate..." mumbled Cirilla.

Silus started chanting again, even from across the room he was able to maintain the mana forge. Cirilla almost seemed like she was in a trance as she moved from finishing the first piece of armour and onto the next. The two continued their work through the evening.

~

Outside, lanterns were being lit through the city, the elven and dragonkin soldiers began to lie down in their camps and barracks, the sound and feel of the wind being the only comforting feeling they had. For tomorrow, they would be thrown into a cauldron of war.

To the south of the city, Corporal Scals and his squad had taken positions near a ridge, even in the dead of night, they could see the demon force marching without hesitation or fatigue. Corporal Scals signalled for six of his squad to begin setting the magic traps, while he and the remaining three keep lookout for any forward parties.

"Why is it, that these demons cannot call it a night like everyone else?" whispered a female dragonkin next to Corporal Scals.
"Because they do not have a soul, Kimberly," answered Corporal Scals.
"So inconsiderate of them," whispered Kimberly, "so how does it feel to be leading a squad?"
"As much as I want to make my father proud, I did not really expect this to happen, perhaps I should not have spoken in Selania," sighed Corporal Scals.
"Well it was certainly a shock to the whole battalion," whispered Kimberly, "but everyone was really impressed that you had the guts to speak up in front of the Commander, the Queen and a very serious looking Silus."
"Thanks," replied Corporal Scals.
"Corporal," whispered a dragonkin soldier.

Corporal Scals crawled backwards off of the ridge, to meet the rest of the squad, at the base of an oak tree.

"These traps are ready yes?" asked Corporal Scals quietly.
"Yes Corporal," whispered the dragonkin soldier.
"Ok, now we will move hundred metres back towards the city, if you two take positions in the trees at this point, and send a signal if the demons get too close, the rest of us will set up as many magical traps as we can then head back," instructed Corporal Scals, "just

remember to space them out, and place a discreet marker so the rest of us know where each trap is."

The dragonkins all nodded in agreement, two dragonkins slowly moved towards two maple trees that were fifty metres apart from one another before flying up to the branches above. Corporal Scals and the rest of the squad took off and flew low back towards the city. Corporal Scals landed while the rest of the squad split up to cover an extended line before a clearing. As they set to creating their traps, the sound of birds chirping filled the air, and twigs being snapped in the distance to the south.

~

On the southern edge of Jarvlan, Shiento was standing atop the cliff. The demons fighting amongst themselves, restless as they have been stationary for over a day. Shiento looked to the sky as the sound of wings flapping reached his ears, the winged demon landed in front of Shiento and bowed.

"So, is it done?" asked Shiento.
"The King of Selania is dead, my Lord," answered the demon, "I also wish to report that a large group of dwarves were heading east from their mountain, I would even dare say Silus will send all the elven people who are not fighting to Selania."
"So, the dwarves wish to aid Selania in an inevitable final battle?" pondered Shiento, "and if the elves

move to Selania, we could take out all our biggest enemies in one fell swoop, how interesting."
"So, we march north?" asked the demon.
"No, not yet, let us give them time to settle in, let them get complacent," chuckled Shiento, "then when we are ready, we will obliterate them all!"

The horde of demons began to cheer with joy, Shiento watched as the demons raised their weapons and heads and cheered into the sky. The winged demon looked at Shiento, as Shiento looked down at the demon he noticed the demon looked a little sad.

"What is it?" asked Shiento.
"My Lord, I am sorry to say, but Servana has been slain," answered the demon.

The horde of demons fell silent at the winged demon's words, Shiento began to grin as he looked at the demon's face.

"And this makes you feel sad?" asked Shiento.
"Forgive me, my Lord, but another demon has fallen to the hands of our enemy, why should we not feel sad?" queried the demon.
"Servana was not going to stop at the King, with his death she would have searched for Silus and tried to kill him," explained Shiento, "her death at his hands was inevitable."
"What are your orders, my Lord?" grumbled a demon in front of the horde.

"You and the horde are to do nothing," said Shiento, "the horde is to remain here, until I return." "Where are you going my Lord?" asked the demon. "I think a trip to see my brother is in order," answered Shiento, "I should congratulate him on surviving this long, and warn him that he will meet his end soon enough." "Does this mean you will force Silus to play along to Lady Drask's plans?" asked the demon. "I think I should give Silus a fair chance to meet his end," chuckled Shiento, "to all demons, wait here until I return, then we shall march to Selania and wipe out all life forms that congregate there."

The demons began to roar with excitement at their master's words. The sound of their weapons stamping the ground echoed into the evening sky, the ground trembling slightly as the repeated impact of tens of thousands of weapons stamped the earth. Shiento's wings stretched out from his back, and with a deep breath Shiento, let himself fall backwards off of the cliff. With a quick turn, he began gliding across the shoreline, the horde watched as he then flapped his wings and soared into the air heading north-west towards the Dark Forest.

~

Fiona, Amelia and Commander Hawke, landed in a hanger on the upper level of Qurendia's city edge, followed closely by the rest of the phoenix soldiers. Amelia looked around at all the metal lanterns, and the metal walls. As their wings folded into their backs, a large group of Qurendian shoulders ran into the hanger and formed a semi-circle around the group and raised their spears and pointed them towards Amelia, Fiona and the phoenix soldiers. All the soldiers wore chainmail cuirasses with a yellow and black tabard, with a crest on the chest.

"Not used to being in a city made entirely metal," said Amelia, "and not entirely liking being surrounded by some angry looking soldiers."

Two of the soldiers stepped aside to allow a man dressed in plate armour, with the crest on a pauldron on his right shoulder. The man looked around the group and spotted Commander Hawke's armour and approached him.

"Are you the Commander of these men?" asked the man.
"I am in charge of the soldier yes, but..." answered Commander Hawke.
"Then tell your men, that you are not welcome here, and must go, now!" interrupted the man.
"I am here under orders from Queen Celestia of Urendos and Lord Silus Drago," said Commander Hawke, "and if you want me to follow an order then you must address your comments to Queen Amelia Phoenix of Flammehelm, who is standing behind you."

"What are you blathering about, the Queen of Flammehelm is Cynthia Phoenix," said the man in disbelief.

"And so she was," answered Fiona, "until the demons attacked Flammehelm and then Urendos, where her ladyship unfortunately died."

"And who are you?" asked the man.

"I am Fiona Wythernspine of Urendos, acting on behalf of my sister Celestia, as we have to split our assets due to the war," explained Fiona.

"There is no war here in Qurendia," said the man, "not unless you bring war to us."

"You know who we are, yet you sir, have failed to introduce yourself to us," replied Amelia.

"I am Guard-Captain Frederick," answered the man, "and I am under strict orders from the Duke to forbid entry to any outsider."

"Well Captain, we are here because Shiento, the..." explained Fiona.

"Do not speak that name in these walls," interrupted Captain Frederick.

"Well we have been told to come here and warn you of an assassin being sent by the demon dragon, to slay the Duke, then we have also been ordered to stay and help protect the Duke as best as we can," explained Amelia.

"Preposterous," scoffed Captain Frederick, "no demon could infiltrate Qurendia and it is not like they can arrive on a gondola either."

"That as it may be Captain, we need to speak with the Duke," said Fiona.

"Out of the question," replied Captain Frederick, "I will allow one of you to speak with the Duke and allow the rest to remain here, until the Duke has made a decision."

Amelia looked at Fiona, the two then nodded to each other. The Captain then approached Amelia.

"Right, then seeing as you are a leader of a state, Lady Phoenix, then you will speak with the Duke," said Captain Frederick.
"If Lady Phoenix or Lady Fiona go then they require an escort," stated Commander Hawke.
"You do not make the rules here," replied Captain Frederick.
"I am not making a rule, Captain, I am stating the rules," said Commander Hawke angrily, "in the same way your Duke will have an escort everywhere he goes, same rule applies to all leaders of state."
"Commander Hawke, stand down," said Amelia calmly.

Captain Frederick stared at Commander Hawke, both had their left hands grasped tightly on their swords. Amelia then stepped between the two and faced Commander Hawke.

"Commander Hawke," said Amelia as she stared into the Commander's eyes.
"As you wish, my Queen," replied Commander Hawke.

Commander Hawke took his hand off his sword and then stepped back a few paces, Amelia then turned to face Captain Frederick. The Captain raised his hand off his sword and held both his hands in front of him as if surrendering to Amelia.

"Very well," said Captain Frederick, "Queen Phoenix, choose a second person to act as your escort."
"You are not going to dictate anything else?" asked Amelia.
"I am going to show a sense of good faith towards you and your troop's presence," answered Captain Frederick.
"Very well, then Lady Fiona will act as my escort," said Amelia.
"My Lady," said Commander Hawke.
"Commander you and the troops will remain here, and try not to cause any more trouble," instructed Amelia.
"I... as you wish, my Queen," stammered Commander Hawke.
"Happy to proceed Captain?" asked Amelia.
"Yes, this way your ladyships," answered Captain Frederick.

Captain Frederick lead Amelia and Fiona followed by five of the soldiers out of the hanger, Commander Hawke and his troops moved to the left hand hanger wall and sat down to rest. Some soldiers left and quickly returned with some water and some food for the phoenix soldiers to eat. As the Captain led Amelia and Fiona into the streets of Qurendia, the smell of coal burning and oil being burnt filled their noses. Amelia struggled to look normal as she walked through the streets, the people in the streets watched cautiously as the Captain led Amelia and Fiona up the street towards a large building at the top of the street.

"Have either of you been to Qurendia before?" asked Captain Frederick.
"Once as a child, visiting with my father and sister," answered Fiona, "I think Silus was there too."
"That would not surprise me, that boy is everywhere, and yet when you look for him, he is gone," chuckled Captain Frederick, "and you Lady Phoenix?"
"This is my first time," answered Amelia.
"And what do you think of our city?" asked Captain Frederick.
"I am not too sure, I did not really know what to expect of it," replied Amelia, "the one thing I will say is that the smell of burning coal and oil is rather pungent."
"Oh it is not so bad," chuckled Captain Frederick, "to us this is normal."
"I mean no offense Captain," said Amelia.
"Do not worry yourself," replied Captain Frederick, "I know our city is vastly different to any other, and certainly the smell can be unnerving to first timers."

As the trio reached the large building at the end of the street, Captain Frederick opened a metal door and invited Amelia and Fiona to step inside. As the girls walked through the door, they saw a large room with two metal lines running parallel along the floor. As

Captain Frederick closed the door behind him, he began to smile.

"Welcome to Qurendia's rail network," said Captain Frederick, "from here we will catch a train towards the keep."
"Keep?" asked Fiona, "is the Duke residency not a palace?"
"Aye, it was once called that," answered Captain Frederick, "but now we call it the Keep, the military barracks is one huge line of buildings running the circumference of the Keep's courtyard, and outside that line is the normal city, but inside our line, it is the Duke's private property."
"From what I have heard of Duke Horacio, he is a friendly man and does not believe in a strict military regime," stated Fiona.
"Aye, he was... once," sighed Captain Frederick, "but you see he lost his son a few decades back when bandits broke into the palace and slaughtered his son, and then again except this time his wife, that was only a decade of so ago."
"Oh, I am sorry to hear that," said Fiona.
"Yeah, since the loss of his son, the Duke has been a different man, and the loss of his wife only made things worse," explained Captain Frederick.
"Are bandits normal for Qurendia?" asked Amelia.
"Unfortunately, they are," answered Captain Frederick, "or they were, I should say, in recent months, the attacks made by bandits have dropped dramatically."

"Then you and your guards are doing well in dealing with them?" queried Fiona.

"That is the thing, we have not done much to deal with them," explained Captain Frederick, "Ahh, here is our train now."

Amelia and Fiona looked to their left to see a large metal object moving into the building. The train was made entirely of metal, a pipe at the front spat out a constant stream of steam, the whole thing rolled along the tracks on eight large wheels. Behind the train were five carriages being towed along by the locomotive. As the train stopped, Captain Frederick gestured to Amelia and Fiona to step into the first carriage. Amelia and Fiona climbed into the carriage, followed by Captain Frederick. Inside the carriage, there were several rows of benches with tables.

"Take a seat, the train will depart soon," said Captain Frederick.

"This is really unusual," said Amelia quietly, "is the train the only way to reach the Keep?"

"It is for now, all the bridges leading to the Keep are heavily fortified," explained Captain Frederick, "the whole train will undergo a strict inspection upon its arrival into the Keep's station, but do not worry about that."

Suddenly the carriage jutted backwards as the train slowly began to pull out of the station. Outside the window the metallic city swept by, Amelia looked out into the darkness as the city became lit by thousands of lanterns. As she watched the city pass by, she almost fell into a trance.

"You can still sense Silus?" asked Fiona.
"Yeah, he is relaxed for the moment, but I can tell he is anxious," answered Amelia, "it seems that Silus convinced Randalene to evacuate her people to Selania."
"Well at least the women and children will be safe there," said Fiona.
"For now," replied Amelia, "Shiento will try to level Selania again, and I have a feeling that it will be sooner than we think."
"If I may, what is Silus to you two?" asked Captain Frederick, "you both speak of him, yet I get the feeling there is more to the story, than what appears on the surface."

Fiona looked from Amelia to Captain Frederick, the Captain looked at Amelia then glanced at Fiona.

"Well Silus was my bodyguard for many years," explained Fiona, "well, I say bodyguard, but he was my friend, he trained me to fight and use my magic, and we fought together a few times, before my father ordered me to go on a mission but forbid Silus from going."
"Why did he do that?" asked Captain Frederick.
"The reason is not important," answered Fiona, "because Silus disobeyed my father and was still there on that mission, even if no one really knew that."

"Fair enough, I will not pry," said Captain Frederick, "and what about you, Lady Phoenix?"

"I was sent to find him, and bring him to Flammehelm," answered Amelia, "but it did not take long for trouble to find us, we fought demons all the way to Flammehelm, and continued fighting them ever since, I make it sound like we were together for years."

"How long have you known Silus?" questioned Captain Frederick.

"Well the truth is he was once my guardian, mine and my sisters, but I do not remember those days," explained Amelia, "but since I was sent to find him, it has been three weeks."

"Three weeks?" said Fiona in astonishment, "I would have thought you two had travelled together for much longer than that, the bond you share to be able to sense each other from here, would indicate you would have been together for years."

"Sorry to disappoint," mumbled Amelia quietly.

"Ok, let us change topics, Lady Phoenix is clearly not up for talking about it," said Captain Frederick, "anyway the next station is the Keep."

The three sat in silence as the train pulled into the station, Amelia stood up and quietly walked to the door. Fiona and Captain Frederick looked at each other before standing up and following Amelia. As they climbed out the carriage, Amelia looked around to see that the sky had turned completely black, no stars, and no moon. Several guards were questioning and searching the train, they avoided Amelia and Fiona as they were standing with Captain Frederick.

"This way your ladyships," said Captain Frederick as he began walking towards a large building that looked like a metallic castle, "I should warn you, the Duke may be a little cold and unwilling to speak."
"That does not change our purpose for speaking with him," replied Fiona.
"As you wish," said Captain Frederick.

As the three walked, Amelia looked around at the courtyard, the only building in it was the Keep, beyond that was just a large ring of buildings linked together. As Amelia looked up at which looked like a church spire, she noticed someone standing there, the person was wearing a large red cloak which waved in the evening breeze.

"Something wrong Amelia?" asked Fiona.
"Huh... sorry... I was... completely spaced out," stammered Amelia.
"Relax will you, I did not mean to interrupt your train of thought," said Fiona.

As the three approached Keep Amelia looked up to see that the Keep was heavily plated with thick sheet steel. The Captain waved his right hand at the guardsmen standing in front of a pair of large doors. The guardsmen then began to pull open the doors, revealing a narrow hallway, at the end was a large portrait of a man standing with a woman and a young boy.

"Ahh Captain Frederick," called out a dull voice from the top of a staircase on the left hand side of the hall, "who are these two?"

Amelia and Fiona looked up to see a man with combed black hair, his eyes were a calm hazel colour, he wore black clothes with red embroidery. Captain Frederick saluted the man before answering.

"Forgive the lateness of this matter, your Excellency," said Captain Frederick, "but about an hour ago, these two landed in the upper hanger along with a small group of troops."
"Landed?" questioned the man, "you mean they did not use the gondola?"
"No sir," answered Captain Frederick.
"Who are these two then? And for what reason have you brought them before me?" asked the man.
"Well your excellency, they are emissaries sent by Queen Celestia Wythernspine of Urendos and the wanderer Silus Drago, they…" explained Captain Frederick.
"Silus? Silus sent you?" interrupted Duke Horacio.
"Him and my sister," answered Fiona.
"Sister, you say?" pondered Duke Horacio, "then that would make you Lady Fiona Wythernspine, correct?"
"Yes, your Excellency," answered Fiona.
"And who is your companion?" asked Duke Horacio.

"I am Amelia Phoenix, recently appointed Queen of Flammehelm," responded Amelia, "it is a pleasure to make your acquaintance, your Excellency, we have..." "Let us take this to my study, standing in this hall will lead to others eavesdropping on us," interrupted Duke Horacio, "Captain, bring them up."
"Yes, your Excellency," replied Captain Frederick.

Captain Frederick beckoned Amelia and Fiona to follow him, as the three begin to climb the stairs, the guards by the doors closed them. The hall was decorated with lots of paintings of various events and times in Qurendia's history. At the top of the stairs Amelia and Fiona could see the Duke walk into a doorway at the end of the balcony.

"I can see what you mean when you warned us the Duke might be cold and unwilling to speak," said Amelia.
"Can you blame him?" asked Captain Frederick, "he lost his family to this city's bandits, he will not take any chances."
"Why does he stay then?" queried Amelia.
"The Dukes family has governed Qurendia for eight generations, he will not be bullied out of his family's home by some low-level thugs," explained Captain Frederick.
"I can understand that, still nothing will change unless the bandits can be dealt with," said Fiona, "but you said their actions have decreased, even without much effort from the guards."

"That is because there is some phantom vigilante scaring the hell out of the bandits," explained Captain Frederick.

"A phantom vigilante?" asked Amelia, "you are trying to say that there is a ghost beating the bandits up at night?"

"I only wish that was the case," answered Captain Frederick.

As Captain Frederick held the door open for Amelia and Fiona to pass through, the sound of an arrow whistling through the air began to fill the air. Inside the room, Amelia could see an arrow hit a wooden board through a slightly open window, the board had several dents in it. The Duke walked over to the board and removed the arrow.

"How curious," said the Duke calmly.

"Are you ok, Duke Horacio?" asked Fiona.

"Not too worry, this is merely a message," answered Duke Horacio.

"A message? From who?" questioned Amelia.

"From the phantom vigilante that the Captain was just telling you about," replied Duke Horacio, "for you see ladies, this vigilante is very real, but lacking a name, though this message does not seem to be for me as they usually are."

"What do you mean your grace?" queried Captain Frederick.

"This letter is addressed to an A.P." explained Duke Horacio, "so I can only assume that the vigilante wishes to tell you something, Lady Phoenix."

"A message... for me?" said Amelia in astonishment.
"So it would seem, here take a look," said Duke
Horacio as he held out a rolled parchment in his right
hand.

Amelia walked across the room and slowly took the
parchment from the Duke. Before she unrolled the
parchment she looked at Fiona.

"Just keep the message to yourself," said the Duke, "I
only receive messages when the vigilante has taken
down a group of bandits, and I order my men to take
them into custody, so if this message is not for me,
then I do not want to hear it."
"I understand your Excellency," replied Amelia, "but
this can wait, we should return to the matter of why
we are are here."
"Ah, yes, I interrupted you in the hallway, how rude
of me," said Duke Horacio, "my apologies Lady
Phoenix, so why have you, Lady Fiona and a small
detachment of troops ventured all the way out here,
you mentioned Silus and Lady Celestia, but for what
reason?"
"Because the demon dragon has sent an assassin to
claim your head, your Excellency," answered Fiona.
"Really?" pondered Duke Horacio, "how can you be
so sure? Demons are not known for being
predictable."
"True, but Shiento is not your typical demon," said
Amelia.

"Indeed, so am I to assume that Silus is busy elsewhere?" asked Duke Horacio, "seeing as you are here in his place?"

"Silus is currently in the Dark Forest preparing to fight a horde of demons with the elves," answered Amelia, "he will be here once he has dealt with that."

"I see, Captain Frederick, allow their troops to move to the courtyard, see that they get a shelter, food and water," said Duke Horacio.

"Forgive my curiosity in this matter, your Excellency," replied Captain Frederick humbly, "but you are not taking what these ladies are saying seriously? No demon has ever infiltrated this city."

"I understand what you are saying Captain," responded Duke Horacio calmly, "but the tables have turned, and I can see that we have kept to ourselves for too long, the enemy is ready to break down our front door and we cannot simply be complacent."

"Very well, your Excellency, I will go and bring the troops here myself," answered Captain Frederick.

"In the meantime," said Duke Horacio as he sat in a chair near the window, "I shall have a maid make up some rooms for you two, if you head back down the balcony the second door is for the dining room, the butler will bring you something to eat, for now I wish to consider this situation carefully."

"Thank you for your hospitality your grace," said Amelia as her and Fiona bowed slightly, "we shall leave you in peace then."

Amelia and Fiona left the room, the Duke remained in his chair, as he turned to look out the window, to see the city, the city only lit by lanterns and street lamps. Beyond the city was just a pitch black blanket. Outside the study, Amelia, Fiona and Captain Frederick were quietly talking before Captain Frederick walked down the stairs to the Keep doors. Amelia and Fiona walked into the dining room, inside was a large round table, the walls decorated with cabinets and tapestries. As they took a seat at the table an elderly, thin man walked into the room, the man wore a tuxedo, he approached Amelia and Fiona and bowed briefly.

"Good evening ladies, as guests of the Duke, I am to offer you some food and drink, so is there anything in particular that you fancy?" explained the man.
"What sort of food is favourable in Qurendia?" asked Amelia.
"Ahh, your first time here, and while I could recommend a hearty stew, using bison as the main ingredient," answered the man, "you could also have a steak with a salad."
"The stew sounds rather interesting," said Fiona.
"Certainly, my Lady," replied the man.
"What type of steak do you serve?" quizzed Amelia.
"At the moment, we have a stock of wyvern steaks," answered the man.
"Lovely, I will have the steak, can I have it cooked, medium-rare?" queried Amelia.
"Of course you can, my Lady," answered the man, "your meals should be ready in twenty minutes, can I offer you any drinks while you wait?"
"Just water for us please," said Amelia.

"As you wish," replied the man.

The man turned around and walked to a cabinet and pulled out mats, cutlery and two glasses. He placed them on the table then left the room briefly before returning with a jug of water. He poured water into both glasses before placing the jug on the table and disappearing from the room again.

"So, what does the message say?" asked Fiona.
"I looked at it briefly before," answered Amelia as she unrolled the parchment, "it reads, 'Dear Amelia, it has been a long time since we have talked, I did not think you would ever venture this far west, when I get the chance, I will message you again telling you where to meet me'."
"Is it signed by anyone?" asked Fiona.
"The only thing at the bottom is the letters C.C." answered Amelia, "the thing is, I do not know anyone by those initials."
"Are you sure?" quizzed Fiona.
"I have been thinking about it and... not a single person comes to mind," answered Amelia.
"Well, I guess we will just have to sit tight until we can figure it out and until then, we try and take down the assassin," said Fiona.
"At this moment, that is all we can do," replied Amelia, "I just hope Silus will get here soon."
"Can you sense anything?" asked Fiona.
"Well since we arrived here, my ability to sense anything has been clouded," answered Amelia, "but

the last I picked up was, Silus using some magic for a forge."

"A forge?" said Fiona in confusion, "well, the elves did develop a spell for something called a mana forge, which they use for forging weapons and arms."

Amelia and Fiona continued talking into the late hours, even when the food arrived, they continued talking. Eventually they had finished eating, then the butler cleared away their plates as they got up to leave, a maid showed them to their rooms, as they went into their separate rooms, they got the feeling that the Duke does not use many of the rooms. As the two laid down in their rooms the air was still, not even a breeze blew through the windows.

Chapter 5: The Struggle Begins

Just after midnight, Silus was examining the pieces of armour made from the strange metal. Cirilla had gone to the corner of the workshop and curled up and fallen asleep. Suddenly the sound of a bell rang from the front of shop, Silus walked to the shop door and looked out of it to see Randalene standing in the shop.

"I thought you would be asleep by now," said Silus.
"I tried, but I could not sleep," replied Randalene, "just the thought of this demon attack keeps me awake."
"Well, just be careful later when the fight begins, lack of sleep could prove fatal on the battlefield," explained Silus.
"I know, anyway, why are you still up?" asked Randalene, "I thought you would want to get some sleep too, being that this is going to be a large battle, and you have been pretty busy lately."
"Dragons do not normally sleep every night like the other races, you should know that," explained Silus.
"True, anyway how is your armour coming along?" asked Randalene.
"Well I have to admit, when I walked in and Cirilla appeared, I was, a little concerned and confused, she seemed a bit clumsy," explained Silus, "but then I saw how passionately she talked about her work, and this new material she was working on."

"Yeah, she can be like that, you would see her and think, she is too young to be an expert smith, but the work she does, well it certainly can take your breath away," said Randalene, "is she working now?"
"No, she finished my armour pieces and has kind of fallen asleep in the corner," answered Silus.
"Poor thing, anyway let us see the armour," said Randalene.

Silus held the door open for Randalene, as she walked into the workshop, she saw Cirilla sitting in the corner, curled up with a blanket over her. Silus then held up one of the shoulder plates that Cirilla had forged. Randalene took the armour from Silus and began studying it closely. Randalene then turned to Silus with a rather confused expression on her face.

"I am not familiar with this metal," said Randalene.
"Well I did say she was working on a new material," explained Silus, "there is a large plate of this stuff on a manikin out there in the courtyard, I tried cutting into the metal but even with magic, I could not even scratch the thing."
"So you thought, it would be a good material to use for a massive battle?" asked Randalene, "not that I doubt Cirilla's work, but it just seems like a bad time to be experimenting with types of metal."
"I agree, but in this case, I am putting my faith in your recommendation and Cirilla's ability as a smith," answered Silus.
"Well, I do not think you have much to worry about, you do not exactly take damage in fights, you deal

most of it," sighed Randalene, "anyway, I will carry your armour upstairs, if you could carry Cirilla upstairs, I doubt that corner is very comfy."
"Alright," said Silus.

Silus walked over to the corner where Cirilla was sleeping, he wrapped the blanket around her, then lifted her up in his arms, resting her head on his left shoulder. As Silus turned around he saw Randalene examining each piece of black armour as she picked them up. Silus then noticed that Randalene had a large piece of darkened cloth over her arm.

"Come on, I will hold the door open so you can walk Cirilla through," said Randalene.
"Thank you," replied Silus.

Silus carried Cirilla across the room, taking care not to bump into any of the equipment as he walked. Randalene stood at the doorway to the shop, holding it open as Silus approached, Silus turned to walk sideways through the door, as he stepped into the front of the shop, Randalene pointed to a staircase to the left, Silus carried Cirilla up the stairs into a large room with a couch, a bed, a small fire place, a small table and a small water fountain on a balcony. Silus gently placed Cirilla on the bed, then adjusted the blanket to cover her body. Randalene then entered the room and quietly placed the armour pieces on the table, she then stood up to face Silus as he moved to stoke the fire.

"You know, I am slightly glad you are willing to try Cirilla's new armour," said Randalene softly.

"You were criticizing me for doing so in the workshop, what has changed?" asked Silus quietly.

"Well Cirilla had made that plate months ago, but no one was willing to test the armour," explained Randalene.

"That would explain her excitement when I asked her to make armour out of it," said Silus, "I just hope it does not get eaten by acid like my previous mithril set."

"Well, I suppose you can find out later," replied Randalene.

"Not like I have a choice about that," sighed Silus, "though at least Servana, the serpent demon is dead now."

"Keeping to your new armour, I think I have something that may go with the look," replied Randalene.

Randalene then unfolded the cloth over her arm and held it up to show Silus. Silus looked at the darkened cloth, it was almost completely black, and was styled like a jacket.

"This used to be a tabard worn by my great grandfather, who as you know fought the demons before, when they tried spreading from the south," explained Randalene, "he embedded the ashen remains of the demons into this cloth, and enchanted it so that, whoever wears the cloth can sense demons."

"Sounds like your great grandfather liked to experiment," said Silus.

"He did, however no other elf would do the same, even once my grandfather had proved its function," replied Randalene, "and it is not that I am ashamed to wear it, it is just the black look never really suited me."

"Well, that and you have an appearance to maintain as the Queen," chuckled Silus.

"Which is why, I want you to have it," insisted Randalene, "I have taken the liberty of having the cloth tailored into this jacket, and because I know you do not wear tabards or lots of armour for that matter."

"Randalene, I... I cannot possibly accept such a gift," said Silus, "this is part of your elven and personal heritage, it would be like stealing the eye of Galatia from the elven people."

"No, this is a gift for you Silus," replied Randalene, "please take this, as thanks for coming to help us and also as a token of our friendship."

Silus looked at Randalene, he then stood up and walked over to Randalene and examined the material closely. He then looked at Randalene again as she stared at Silus, her eyes almost shouted out to Silus, begging him to take it. Silus then took the jacket from Randalene and put it on. Randalene looked at Silus as he examined his appearance in a mirror and swung his arms around to check the fitting.

"Very well Randalene," said Silus, "I accept your gift."

"Thank you Silus," replied Randalene, "I am glad you accept it, because once I saw your new armour, I thought, this would be a perfect match for it."

"Well, that is a benefit," chuckled Silus, "though some might question why I suddenly wear black armour and a black jacket, but I suppose I can deal with that."

"I just hope this jacket and armour helps you end this war," replied Randalene.

"I have a feeling it might," said Silus, "anyway, suppose I best starting sorting my armour out."

"I will go and make some tea," responded Randalene.

Randalene took a kettle and collected water from the fountain on the balcony. Silus quickly disappeared from the room and returned with a handful of leather straps. Silus sat at the table, he began attaching the straps to the different armour pieces. Randalene chanted a small fire spell then started serving tea from the kettle into two small cups.

"So how are things looking out there?" asked Silus.

"Well, as I was heading here, I did see your squad return from their sabotage mission," explained Randalene, "they all looked to be fine, and as for the rest of the preparations, Gilnur reported that everything has been set up to your specifications."

"And what of the evacuation?" queried Silus.

"Everyone has successfully left the city, and are being escorted by the soldiers they should get to Selania sometime after sun rise," answered Randalene.

"That is good," said Silus.

Silus started fastening some of the metal plates to his legs, Randalene then watched as Silus started attaching the curved plates to the shoulders of the jacket.

"You know, the armour does suit that fabric really well," said Randalene.
"I know, but about this fabric," replied Silus, "you mentioned that your great grandfather said that the demonic ash embedded into the fabric allowed the wearer to sense demons, do you know if that is actually a fact, or is it possible that, this ability is just a myth?"
"Unfortunately, I cannot answer that Silus," sighed Randalene, "my great grandfather was the only person to have worn the tabard."
"Fair enough," replied Silus.
"You are not worried?" asked Randalene.
"Well, if the ability is a myth, it would not change anything for me, I would still fight the demons when they show themselves," answered Silus, "the only difference this material can make, is if the ability is not a myth."
"I guess," said Randalene.

Silus finished fastening the last armour piece to the jacket, Silus then stood up to try on the jacket again. Randalene watched as Silus then made slight adjustments to the shoulder plates to give himself more freedom to move his arms in the jacket.

"Even though no one would consider your look to be traditional, I would say that this look suits you Silus," said Randalene, "even though it is all black, I think that it still suits you, as it is a representation of your dragon form."

"Thank you Randalene," replied Silus, "now it is just a case of waiting for the fight to start."

Silus sat down again, Silus and Randalene continued talking, eventually the sun began to rise and the forest turned slightly amber in colour. Cirilla began to mumble as she moved around on the bed, as she picked herself up off the mattress, she looked around the room through lazy eyes. She could see Silus and Randalene sitting at the table.

"Morning Cirilla," said Randalene.

"Uh... Lady Randalene, what... I am so sorry, my Lady," stammered Cirilla.

"Do not worry," replied Randalene calmly, "I came to check on Silus, I did not really think you would work yourself to sleep."

"Well how could I sleep when Silus agreed to have armour made of my new compound," yawned Cirilla.

Cirilla stood up from the bed and walked over to the table and sat down on a chair that she conjured as she sat down. Randalene poured Cirilla a cup of tea. As Cirilla yawned, Silus took off the jacket and hung it over the back of his chair.

"Where did the jacket come from?" asked Cirilla.

"Lady Randalene gave it to me," answered Silus, "and thanks to her, I now have a new look and something to fasten your new armour to."

"The look does actually suit you," said Cirilla, "the mithril armour you were wearing yesterday kind of looked... awkward on you."

"I can accept that, the armour was light both in weight and colour," said Silus, "and speaking of armour, how much do I owe you for forging this new armour?"

"Well... you see... I...," stammered Cirilla.

"No need to be nervous, how much does this armour cost me?" asked Silus.

"I was not actually going to charge you for the armour," said Cirilla, "you see because no one would wear this compound as armour, I would not have been able to make and sell it as armour, and for that I do not think I can really charge you for the armour."

"Do not be silly Cirilla," said Silus, "you used resources and physical effort to make this armour, and I cannot in good conscience walk away without paying you for any of this."

Cirilla lowered her head and began twiddling her thumbs. Silus looked at Randalene who looked back at him, then Silus looked at Cirilla, who was clearly getting really nervous and agitated. Silus then stretched his left hand out and placed it on Cirilla's hands, Cirilla looked at Silus as he smiled at her, Cirilla smiled back.

"I tell you what Silus," said Cirilla, "you wear my armour today and prove its worth, if others wish to have me make more of it, then you can consider it a gift, to thank you for promoting my new compound, if not then I will charge you ten thousand gold for it, sound like a deal?"

"Sounds like a steep price, but fair enough, it is a deal," replied Silus, "but we cannot just keep calling it your new compound, this metal needs a proper name."

"I was thinking of calling it Black Steel," said Cirilla, "then I remember that is the armour Shiento has issued to his elite demons."

"If the metal is as impervious as Silus told me, then it should have a more individual name," responded Randalene.

"Ok then, why not call it impervious?" asked Cirilla.

"Well, the problem with that is we do not know if that is true," answered Silus.

"Why not call the metal, obsidian?" questioned Randalene.

"Obsidian?" said Silus with a confused look on his face.

"Yeah, if you were unable to scratch it with your dragon sabres, which let us be fair is made from magic and is a substance that never breaks," explained Randalene, "then this is a rather appropriate name for it I think."

"Well, I have no objections, do you Cirilla?" asked Silus.

"Sure, it is a cool name that matches the cool appearance," giggled Cirilla.

"Well then, that is settled," said Silus raising his cup, "to the future of the obsidian legacy."
"You sure you are not getting ahead of yourself Silus?" queried Cirilla.
"You should be more confident in your work," answered Silus, "you saw that my attacks bounced off of the original plate yesterday."
"Alright, to my new discovery," said Cirilla.

Cirilla, Randalene and Silus raised their cups and clinked them together over the table. They all drank from their cups, Silus and Cirilla smiled at each other. Randalene then stood up and walked to the balcony and looked to the south side of the city.

"Something wrong?" asked Cirilla.
"The demons must be getting near," answered Randalene.
"Yeah, we should be getting ready to start the fight," said Silus.
"I wish to join the fight," replied Cirilla.
"Do you even have any experience in a fight?" asked Randalene, "I am not being funny, but this is going to be a serious fight, and one that could very well last for hours."
"I know, but I was trained by my father to use a shield and spear, and I wish to put that training to use, and make my father proud," answered Cirilla.
"Your father was a soldier?" queried Silus.
"He was a solider until he suffered an injury that he lost his right eye and the full use of his left leg," answered Cirilla, "from that moment, he devoted

167

himself to making armour that would stop others from suffering the same injuries."

"All right then," said Silus.

"You cannot be serious Silus?" questioned Randalene.

"I can understand her reasons for wanting to fight," answered Silus.

"And you will just allow her to fight, without seeing how she handles herself or anything?" asked Randalene angrily.

"Cirilla's reason for fighting, is the same reason I fight," said Silus calmly, "and after seeing the passion and effort she put into making my armour, well that is all the demonstration I need to see, just promise me Cirilla, that you will not be drastic or careless out there."

"I swear on my honour, I will not let you down," replied Cirilla.

"All right then, I will head for the south of the city, make sure the Commanders are ready," said Silus, "Cirilla you best go get ready and meet me there when you can, Randalene, I assume you are fighting with us, so you best get ready too."

"How can you be so calm, when the demons are bearing down on us as we speak?" asked Randalene.

Silus stood up and grabbed the jacket off the chair, as he through the jacket over him and put his arms into the sleeves, he looked at Randalene and smiled.

"Because I have faith in the people I fight with, I know they will not quit, no matter how hard the battle is or how grim the situation looks, they will not surrender," explained Silus, "I am calm because I am fighting beside men and women who show more bravery then they think they have."

Randalene looked at Silus with a blank expression, Silus just smiled back then exited the room. Cirilla looked at Randalene then bowed to her before leaving the room. Randalene then looked out from the balcony again before walking across the room and down the stairs. As Randalene emerged into the front of Cirilla's shop, she could hear Cirilla moving around the workshop. Randalene walked out of Cirilla's shop to see Silus standing at the southern end of the street, he looked at her and lifted his right hand to show a thumbs up gesture to her, before running out of sight.

"I wish I could be as confident as you Silus," whispered Randalene.

Randalene walked up the street quietly, as she turned right and onto the main square, she looked at the war table that she and the others were standing around yesterday evening. Suddenly she felt more confident, as she clenched her hands into fists, she ran to the north of the plaza where a large oak tree palace stood.

~

To the south, Silus had arrived at the encampment where Commander Drake and the dragonkins were readying their weapons and arms, as Silus approached they all stood up and stood to attention as if on parade.

"Continue your preparations, do not let me disturb you," said Silus.

The dragonkins bowed to Silus before returning to their weapon and armour prepping. Commander Drake walked over to Silus and bowed to him briefly, Silus looked around as many elven troops glared at Silus briefly before continuing with their own preparations.

"I see you have found yourself some new armour my Lord," said Commander Drake.
"Yeah, and as I thought, it unnerves the elves," answered Silus, "it does not matter, we have a battle to win, is everything and everyone prepared?"
"Yes, my Lord," replied Commander Drake, "Corporal Scals completed his mission without incident, the demons should nearly be at the gauntlet of traps as we speak."
"Which means we should be able to see the explosions when they get within range," said Silus.
"Yes, my Lord," responded Commander Drake.
"Commander, stop calling me, 'my Lord', I may have led these soldiers here, but I fight as one of you today, today I am but an ordinary soldier, fighting a war that I was told to," explained Silus, "so just call me by my name, understood?"
"Yes my... I mean Silus," said Commander Drake.

"You are being a little harsh are you not, Silus?" asked Cirilla as she appeared from a street corner near the dragonkin encampment.

"I have never truly liked being call 'Lord', or even being referred to as 'my Lord," answered Silus, "I am no different to anyone else."

"That is not what I have heard about your deeds and exploits," said Cirilla.

"Forgive me, but who are you?" asked Commander Drake.

"Oh, my apologies, I am Cirilla," answered Cirilla.

"Cirilla is the armourer who made my armour," explained Silus, "Cirilla, this is Drake, Commander of Urendos' army."

"It is a pleasure to meet you Commander," said Cirilla.

"Just call me Drake," replied Commander Drake, "and it is a pleasure to meet you too, so you made this armour?"

"Well, I am still finding it hard to take full responsibility for this armour," said Cirilla bashfully.

"Why is that?" asked Commander Drake.

"Well... you see...," stammered Cirilla.

"It is ok Cirilla, you deserve full credit for this armour," said Silus, "and what she is nervous about is that this metal has not been properly tested in a battle."

"And you are going to wear it now?" questioned Commander Drake, "I know you are a capable fighter, but is it wise to wear unproven armour in a battle like the one we are about to face?"

"Well Cirilla..." said Silus.

"Ciri, just call me Ciri," interrupted Cirilla.
"As you wish, and I tested Ciri's armour at her workshop, I could not even scratch the metal," explained Silus, "besides it looks like it suits me more than mithril armour."
"Let us just hope it holds up better than your mithril armour," sighed Commander Drake, "anyway, we should start forming our defensive lines."
"Here we go," whispered Silus.

Silus looked south to see a large explosion of ice shards that erupted from the ground. The dragonkin and elven soldiers began grabbing their weapons and rushed to form a defensive line across a small ridge, the formation was four rows of soldiers, a mixture of elves and dragonkin in each row. Silus turned around to see Randalene walking towards him. Randalene was wearing a full set of plate armour, the armour was tinted blue, with a chainmail skirt over plate legs, Randalene carried two swords at her waist. His long blonde hair braided and tied back into a long ponytail.

"So, it begins," said Randalene.
"Guess I this answers my question if you are participating in the battle," replied Silus sarcastically.
"Normally I would dismiss your sarcasm to be a bit more comical, but now is not the time Silus," said Randalene.
"As you wish," replied Silus, "right to rally the troops then."

~

As the demons walked over the ridge to the south of the elven city, the four Commanders stopped to look at each other and discuss a battle plan.

"I say we just charge them and take them down quickly," scoffed the demon with a bastard sword. "Nonsense, let us outflank them and catch them off guard," snivelled the demon carrying swords and throwing knives.
"Both very good plans," said the scythe demon, "however your plans lack details, like how we will kill Silus."
"I will crush his skull with my battle-axe," grunted the demon with a bastard sword.
"Do not be so foolish," growled the multi-armed demon, "why do you think Lord Shiento sent four Commanders to slay the elves? To be prepared for Silus' involvement, and to work out a strategy to bring him down."
"We do not need a plan, we just have to cut his head off," snarled the demon with a bastard sword.
"No, separate Silus from his forces," said the scythe demon looking to the multi-armed demon, "if you could get Silus away from the troops, then the three of us will attack him together."
"Of course, and after I have separated Silus from his troops, I can enjoy a little vengeance for our fallen brethren," replied the multi-armed demon.

"So long as you can get Silus away from the troops first, you can fight the enemy until you have slain them all," chuckled the scythe demon.

"Then let us get to it," said the multi-armed demon.

~

Silus, Cirilla and Randalene quickly marched to the defensive line, as they approached two ranks of elven troops parted to create an alley for them to walk through. At the front of the line, Silus could see that the demons advance had been halted by the explosion of ice. Randalene then turned to face the four lines of soldiers.

"Warriors, the time has come to defend our home!" shouted Randalene, "the enemy is upon us, but to our aid are the dragonkin of Urendos and the Dragonborne, with them at our side, we shall vanquish this enemy and walk away as victors."

The elven soldiers began to cheer, Silus looked around to see the morale of the elven soldiers' rise dramatically.

"Silus, do you wish to say anything?" asked Randalene.

The soldiers fell silent and looked towards Silus, Silus conjured his dragon sabres and glanced across the faces of the elves.

"Warriors of the Dark Forest, I look around and see a mixture of anger and worry, to those who are angry, you should be, the demons have violated your homeland!" shouted Silus, "to those who worry, you should not be, for the demons are arrogant and weak, for it is in unity that we gain strength, the combined forces of the Dark Forest and Urendos will show these demons that it is not us who are afraid, but the demons who should fear us!"

The elven troops began to cheer again, the dragonkins roared with pride as Silus raised his left dragon sabre into the air. All the soldiers began to stamp their spears into the ground in unison, the sound of their armour clinking as they move. Silus started pacing slightly in front of the defensive line.

"Are we afraid of them?" shouted Silus.
"No!" echoed the soldiers.
"Who should be afraid?" shouted Silus.
"Them!" echoed the soldiers.
"Will you fight?" shouted Silus.
"Yes!" echoed the soldiers.
"Then let us show them, what hell is really like!" shouted Silus.

The soldiers continued cheering loudly, Silus turned to face the demon horde. The demons had begun charging towards the city, Silus could see four demons standing on top of the ridge in the distance. The demons rushing in cheering as they charged towards the defensive line.

"Archers, form up!" ordered Silus.

The front two lines dropped to their knees, the rear two drew their bows from their backs and loaded an arrow from their quivers. Silus raised his right dragon sabre above his head and watched as the demon charge drew closer. Randalene drew her two swords, Cirilla conjured a halberd and shield into her hands.

"Atula!" shouted Silus as he forcefully lowered his dragon sabre to his side.

The rear two ranks unleashed their arrows, Silus quickly raised his right hand dragon sabre again as the arrows flew over his head, the archers then loaded a second arrow into their bows and readied to fire. Silus watched as the first volley of arrows landed and slew the closest demons with ease. The remainder of the demons continued charging as if nothing had happened. Silus looked up to the four demon Commanders to see that the four-armed demon had begun to charge towards them.

"Atula!" shouted Silus as he dropped his right arm again.

The archers fired their arrows, Silus watched as the arrows sent another wave of demons tumbling to the ground, the four-armed demon had reached the line where the first demons were shot down. Silus stared at the four-armed demon as it charged toward him.

176

Silus then looked to his right as Commander Drake stepped forward.

"The four-armed demon is one of the Commanders," said Silus.
"Shall we leave him to you Silus?" asked Commander Drake.
"No... me, you, Randalene and Ciri will take him down," answered Silus, "while the rest of our forces, force them back."
"Sounds good to me," said Randalene.
"Chuntela!" shouted Silus as he began to run towards the oncoming demons.

As Silus charged towards the demons, the three demon Commanders on the ridge, looked at each other confused. As they looked behind Silus, they could see the rest of the defensive line charging forward. Silus started cutting his way through the nearest demons, heading straight for the multi-armed demon. Commander Drake, Cirilla and Randalene following close behind Silus. The elven and dragonkin troops crashed into the advancing line of demons. As the sound of swords clashing with one another, shields being bashed echoed in the early morning air.

~

In Qurendia, Amelia had woken up and got dressed to stand in the Keep's courtyard, Amelia was facing east, Fiona then exited the Keep to see Amelia standing outside. As Fiona walked over to Amelia, Amelia glanced over her shoulder then turned to looked forward again.

"The fight has begun," said Amelia.

"I am still staggered by how accurate your sensing ability is here," replied Fiona, "normally when people like us are in Qurendia, our ability to sense anything gets distorted by the amount of metal in the city."

"I would not say my ability is accurate," said Amelia, "I can just about sense Silus' magic from here, but I can tell that he is now charging into battle."

"I hope he is truly ready for this battle," replied Fiona, "what about the elves?"

"Well, I can sense Silus' magic resonating with others, but I cannot make out who is who," explained Amelia, "all I can say for certain is that Silus is focused on slaying a large four armed demon."

"Well, there is not much we can do about that," sighed Fiona.

"Good morning ladies," said Captain Frederick as he walked towards the Keep from one of the barrack doors, my, my, you two are up pretty early."

"Amelia has been sensing the battle going on in the Dark Forest," explained Fiona, "with Silus there, she will struggle to focus on anything else."

"That is not true Fiona," said Amelia.

"Well from what I know of Silus, he can single handily take down a large group of demons, and has been known to hunt larger prey alone," explained Captain Frederick, "so I do not think there is anything to worry about my ladies."

"It is not Silus we are worried about, Captain," answered Fiona, "it is Shiento."

A heavy gust of wind blew across the courtyard from the north-west as Fiona spoke the name, Amelia looked toward the wind and saw a black speck climbing a building. Amelia's eyes turned to a scarlet red as she looked through her phoenix eyes, she could see the black shape she was seeing had a bow across its back, and had two quivers of arrows, one on its back the other on his belt.

"There he is," said Amelia.
"Who?" asked Fiona.
"Look over there to that tall structure, can you not see the body climbing up the side?" queried Amelia.

Fiona looked to where Amelia was pointing, as her purple eyes changed to shine brighter and the pupils become slits, Fiona could make out the figure climbing the outside of the building.

"That is our demon," said Fiona, "Captain, gather your men, have them quarantine that area."

Fiona and Amelia turned to the Keep and started walking towards the front doors. Captain Frederick looked to the building in the distance, then turned to look at Fiona and Amelia.

"Wait that is it?" asked Captain Frederick, "you identify the demon then simply ask me to quarantine the area?"

"No disrespect Captain, but your men as not ready to face this demon," answered Fiona, "he is an archer and dabbles in poisons."

"And to make the situation more awkward, Silus told us that the demon can produce a poison that can be instantly fatal to a human," added Amelia, "so keep your men a safe distance from the building, me and Fiona will go in and take the demon out."

"But... but..." stammered Captain Frederick.

"That was not a suggestion Captain, if you value your men's lives, you will follow our orders," said Fiona.

"As you wish," replied Captain Frederick.

Amelia and Fiona walked into the Keep and disappeared from the Captain's sight. Captain Frederick then turned and ran towards the north side of the courtyard. As Captain Frederick reached the doorway to the barracks, he reached just inside the door to the left and pulled out a large horn. As the Captain blew heavily into the horn, a low bellowing sound echoed around the courtyard. As the horn sounded, the clinking of metal rubbing together began to grow louder as the courtyard filled with soldiers that immediately began to form a U-shaped formation of three ranks as if on parade. Captain Frederick waited until the soldiers had settled before stepping forward to speak.

"All right, listen up!" shouted Captain Frederick, "there is a demon assassin in the city, he intends to take the life of our Duke, he has been spotted in the vicinity of the church in the north west district, we are going to evacuate all those in a four block radius and quarantine the area, and then await further orders, do you understand?"

"Sir, yes sir," replied the soldiers in unison.

"All right, then move out!" ordered Captain Frederick.

The soldiers saluted Captain Frederick before turning to their rights and marching three paces before running to the north side of the courtyard, Captain Frederick turned to look north. As the sound of metal boots running on the ground faded, Captain Frederick kept watching the church staple, the sound of bells began to ring in the distance, Amelia and Fiona reappeared in the doorway to the Keep with their weapons and armour fitted.

"Everything ready Captain?" called out Fiona.

"My men have begun clearing the nearby area and the quarantine will be ready soon," replied Captain Frederick.

"Good, just remember that you and your men are not to approach or attack this demon," stated Amelia, "we will take care of the demon."

"I still feel hesitant to allow that, but as you wish," replied Captain Frederick.

"With all due respect Captain," said Fiona, "but do you or your men have any experience in fighting demons?"

"Well...I..." stammered Captain Frederick.

"Precisely our point," said Amelia, "we have dealt with demons a lot recently, so we have more experience and our magic will have a benefit in taking this demon down."

"All right, I concede the point my Lady," replied Captain Frederick, "just try and take it down fast and without too much damage to the city."

"We will do what we can," said Fiona.

Captain Frederick nodded his head then turned and led Amelia and Fiona towards the north end of the courtyard where a bridge leading into the city stretched over a line where the rock on which the city is built had been dug out to form a gulley between the main city and the military and Keep areas.

"Amelia, when we face the demon, we need to try and corner him," said Fiona.

"Agreed, but we also need to get close enough to kill him," replied Amelia, "a problem to taking this demon down is that he is an archer, and more than likely will be ready to fend off and keep attackers at bay."

"So, we stagger our attack," suggested Fiona, "you distract him, I move, then we switch tactics and keep going until we get within range."

"Or, we could just charge him together, use magic to deal with his attacks and then cut his blasted head off," scoffed Amelia.

"I can recognise that attitude, it is just peculiar to be coming from a woman," said Fiona.

"Can we just focus on taking this demon down before getting side-tracked?" asked Amelia.

"What is up with you?" queried Fiona, "before you were worrying about Silus and did not like being so far away from him, now you are almost trying to imitate him."

"I just want to be done with this assassin, and get out of here, the smell of oil and coal burning is rather horrific," answered Amelia.

"I know this city is unusual for those who are not accustomed to our ways," said Captain Frederick, "but you need to be a little bit more open-minded, Lady Phoenix."

"I guess you are right Captain," replied Amelia, "but if Shiento is only sending one assassin here, yet he intends not to make a further play on Qurendia, at least until we and Selania are dealt with."

"How can you be sure that Shiento will not attack us before Selania?" asked Captain Frederick.

"Because Silus will be in Selania, and Shiento wants him dead, so he will try to take him out first," explained Amelia, "with Silus dead, along with most of Urendos' dragonkin soldiers and elven forces, then the demon army will have minimal resistance in conquering the rest of Jarvlan."

"Minimal resistance?" said Captain Frederick in disbelief, "you do not think we can handle ourselves?"

183

"I mean no disrespect Captain," answered Amelia, "but your technological weaponry will only have effect against his lowest demons, the titans, Shiento himself, their power and resistances will allow them to rip Qurendia apart and sending it crashing to Earth."

As Captain Frederick, Amelia and Fiona walked down a wide street, a line of soldiers were standing across the street, they each held a shield and a spear, both held up and pointed towards the church at the end of the street. As they approached the line they stopped, the Captain turned to look at Amelia.

"I hope you two are ready to kill this freak?" asked Captain Frederick, "if you fail, then the Duke is as good as dead."
"Do not worry about us, just make sure that there are no civilians nearby," said Fiona as she drew her dragon sabres from her hips.
"Be ready to move your men in case he tries to make a run out of there," suggested Amelia as she drew her sword and shield.

The line of soldiers parted to allow Amelia and Fiona to pass through, as they began walking towards the church at the end of the street, the soldiers moved back to form a line. Captain Frederick looked from behind the line as the girls walked in silence. As Amelia and Fiona stood at the doors to the church, the air fell silent, the church doors opened slowly, Amelia and Fiona entered the church, as they did the doors closed behind them. The church was decorated with tapestries and symbols, the pews were forged out of metal, the faint sound of someone talking echoed through the air.

"This little pointy killed the butcher, this little pointy killed the maid," echoed the voice.

Amelia and Fiona had made it half way through the pews as the voice continued chanting to itself.

"And this little pointy slew the phoenix," hissed the voice.

Amelia and Fiona looked up as an arrow flew towards them, the two girls dived to separate sides and took cover between the pews. The voice then began chuckling to itself, the sound of an organ began to play as Amelia and Fiona try to look for the demon.

"Welcome to Groda's finest show!" shouted the voice, "here, you will face death!"

Amelia looked to the right side of the church to see the organ, but no one playing it, Fiona looked above the alter to see a shadowy figure crouched on one of the steel beams that ran across the ceiling.

"Amelia, he is on the beams," whispered Fiona, "you be ready to move, I will distract him."
"Right," answered Amelia quietly.

Fiona moved to the far end of the pew, before getting up and shooting a few fireballs up to the steel beam. As she did Amelia, darted out the end of her pew and ran for a small archway near the organ. The demon fired two arrows at Fiona before turning to fire one towards Amelia.

"Come on little mice, come out and play," said Groda. "Why do you not just come down and fight us face to face, instead of cowering like a scared child!" shouted Amelia.
"I do enjoy a good fight, however under the circumstances, I must be allowed to indulge in a game or two," chuckled Groda.
"Then we will have to force you down," said Fiona, "frustus!"

Fiona shot an ice cone towards Groda, Groda drew an arrow from his quiver on his waist and fired it at the ice cone, and the arrow split the cone down the middle. Fiona ran to take cover behind a steel alter on the side of the church as the two halves of the ice cone crashed into the ceiling behind Groda.

"Not bad ladies, but you will not best me with the way you are fighting," chuckled Groda.

Amelia took a deep breath before turning to run out of the archway, Groda turned and quickly fired an arrow at her. As the arrow flew towards Amelia, she just stared up at Groda.

"Not fast enough to outrun my arrows you whore," grinned Groda.

"Amelia, watch out!" shouted Fiona.

As the arrow was about to hit Amelia, her body became distorted and the arrow flew straight through her, the arrow crashed into the ground as Amelia's body began to evaporate.

"What the devil?" shouted Groda in disbelief.

Amelia appeared in a burst of fire that appeared on the steel beam next to Groda. Groda quickly raised his bow to block Amelia's sword as it was being thrusted towards his chest. Groda quickly pulled out a knife from a sheathe on his back, Groda then went to slash at Amelia's left shoulder. Amelia raised her shield to block Groda's attack.

"Hang on Amelia!" shouted Fiona.

Fiona used her magic and leapt up to the beam, as she landed, Groda quickly looked behind him. Amelia and Fiona had pinned Groda between them, Groda quickly dropped his knife and then pulled his bow apart to reveal they had to blades hidden in them.

"Let us end this," said Amelia.

"Gladly," replied Fiona.

The three began to cross blades as the sounds of Groda's knife hit the church floor, the sound of swords crashing echoed in the empty church. As Amelia and Fiona both tried to lunge at Groda, he jumped backwards and landed on the next beam. Amelia and Fiona's swords crashed together, Groda smiled.

"Not bad ladies, but I have a job to do, and I must get to work," said Groda as he put his bow back together and turned to face a stained-glass window behind him.
"Get back here you scum bag!" shouted Amelia.

As Groda jumped at the window, Amelia leapt across to the next beam, as Groda was mid-jump Amelia tried to slash at him, Groda twisted his body and all Amelia's sword did was cut away his second quiver on his hip.

"Curse you," grunted Amelia.
"Pythlon baz!" shouted Fiona.

As Fiona shouted the incantation, she raised her left dragon sabre to fire a large lightning bolt at Groda. Groda crossed his bow and his free arm across his chest, the lightning bolt hit Groda. As Fiona and Amelia jumped across to the broken window, they saw Groda crash onto the nearby roof, as he struggled to climb to his feet, Amelia and Fiona leapt from the church window to the rooftop.

~

Silus jumped backwards from the multi-armed demon as it tried swinging both his left swords at him. Silus looked around to see that the elven and dragonkin soldiers were holding their ground against the oncoming demon horde. Randalene, Cirilla and Commander Drake were standing around the demon, they were all breathing quickly.

"Silus, we need to cut him down to a manageable size," said Randalene.
"Agreed," replied Silus, "alright guys, be ready to strike."

Silus darted forward at the demon, as the demon went to thrust one of his right swords at Silus, Silus jumped and slammed his dragon sabres onto the demon's sword forcing it to crash into the ground. As the demon's sword crashed into the ground Silus leapt backwards.

"Frustus!" shouted Silus as he landed on the ground.

Silus watched as the demon's sword and arm became encrusted in ice, Silus watched as Cirilla and Commander Drake moved to the demons right and together charged and thrust their weapons at the demon's arm. The demon roared in outrage as it watched its arm smash into thousands of pieces.

"You wretched swine!" shouted the demon as it turned to swing its two left arms at Cirilla and Commander Drake.

"Not so fast, Syphdura!" shouted Silus.

Silus swung his dragon sabres toward the demon, as he did the blade transformed into an extending vine, the vine wrapped itself around the demons left hands. Silus then stretched his dragon tail out of his back and reached for a tree behind him to anchor himself in place, the demon tried to wriggle out of Silus's spell. Commander Drake then froze the demon's legs in place.

"Randalene, cut its arms off already!" grunted Silus as he struggled to restrain the demon.
"Right," said Randalene as she charged towards the demon.

As Randalene neared the demon, she leapt into the air and as she did a forward flip, she brought her twin swords in a downward motion over her head, they began to glow with a bright light.

"Intezra!" shouted Randalene.

As Randalene's swords hit the demon's arms, the bright light began to cut through the demon's first arm, the demon roared in pain. As the first arm was severed the demon began to struggle violently, first it backhanded Randalene and sent her tumbling backwards across the ground, then it broke free of Silus' last vine attack, as he did he grabbed Silus' vine and pulled on it heavily, Silus' tail lost grip on the tree and Silus went flying into the air, the demon lashed the vine round to the south before letting go, sending Silus flying through the air.

"Silus!" shouted Cirilla.

Silus hit a tree branch as he tried to right himself in the air, as Silus then crashed into the ground. Silus rolled to his feet and dug his dragon sabres into the ground to slow himself down. As Silus looked up from his fall, Cirilla and Commander Drake were dodging the demon's attacks as it raged around at the loss of its two arms.

"Well, cannot say that was unexpected," grunted Silus as he slowly tried to stand.
"Not so fast boy!" shouted a female voice.

Out the corner of his left eye, Silus could see a scythe blade flying towards him. As the blade was about to cut into Silus' neck, his body blurred.

"What?" shouted the scythe demon in disbelief.

Silus' body changed into a ball of lightning, as the demonic scythe passed through the lightning ball. the lightning ball then jumped away and landed in a forest clearing. As the lightning changed back into Silus, he looked up to see the female demon standing within the tree line. As Silus stood up he could see the demon wielding a battle-axe walking out of the tree line to his left, in the branches above to his right he could make out the knife wielding demon.

"Well, looks like you three are finally deciding to get your hands dirty," said Silus.

"Well, these two will just get in my way," grunted the demon with the battle-axe, "for I, Zoldrun, will be your demise!"

Zoldrun charged at Silus, his battle-axe held over his right shoulder, Zoldrun swung his axe at Silus, Silus stepped backwards to avoid it, as Zoldrun pulled his axe back across his body to take a second swing at Silus, Silus moved his left hand dragon sabre to block, then jabbed his right hand dragon sabre into the demon's right shoulder.

"Argh, curse you!" shouted Zoldrun.

"Looks like you are just over confident Zoldrun," chuckled the scythe demon, "why not let me and Folta help?"

"If you were any good in a fight Veronica, Silus would have died with your first blow," grunted Zoldrun.

Chapter 6: The Fire Burns

In the forest Randalene, Cirilla and Commander Drake were still fighting the now two armed demon, its raging flurry of swords slashes and grunts keeping them away. As Cirilla and Commander Drake leapt away from the demon, Randalene looked at them to see them breathing heavily. Randalene then turned her gaze to see the rest of the demons fighting the combined forces of the dragonkins and elves, the battle was fairly even.

"We need to restrain him again," said Cirilla.
"How would you recommend we do that?" asked Commander Drake, "his strength grows with his rage."
"Leave that to me," said Randalene calmly, "you two just be sure to take his head."
"As you wish," answered Commander Drake.

Commander Drake then charged at the demon and with his dragon sabres pointed at the ground. As the demon went to bring his left hand sword down at Commander Drake, the Commander raised his dragon sabres to block. As their swords clashed, a huge boulder appeared and smashed into the demon's chest causing the demon to fall backwards.

"Syphdura!" shouted Randalene.

As Randalene shouted the incantation, the forest floor became ripped as vines shot out the ground, and began to wrap themselves around the demon's neck, arms and torso. The demon roared in outrage as it tried to struggle out of Randalene's attack.

"It is now or never you two," grunted Randalene as she focused on maintaining the vines.
"Right," said Cirilla, "ready Commander?"
"Let us kill this mongrel," answered Commander Drake.

Cirilla dropped her shield and placed her free hand on the halberd shaft, Commander Drake let his dragon sabres disperse in a cloud of smoke, then he conjured a two handed long sword into his hands. The two stood on opposite sides of the demon, as they readied their weapons the Commander's sword began to glow with a fiery red tint and Cirilla's spear glowed with an icy white tint.

"Time to die demon," said Cirilla as she took a deep breath.

Commander Drake and Cirilla both leapt into the air, Commander Drake's sword began to waver as the blade became engulfed in flames, while Cirilla's halberd blade grew in size as its metallic blade became a giant ice shard. The demon looked up as he continued grunting and struggling in Randalene's entanglement of vines.

"Sazarach!" shouted Commander Drake as his sword became a raging torrent of fire.
"Frustus!" shouted Cirilla as her halberd blade disappeared in the blade of ice.

As the two fighters swung their weapons down at the demon's neck, the demon smiled briefly.

"It was a good fight," sighed the demon.

The demon closed his eyes as Commander and Cirilla's blades cut through the demon's neck. Randalene breathed a sigh of relief as the demon's body stopped wriggling, as Commander Drake and Cirilla stepped away from the demon's body it disintegrated to black ashes.

"We won, it is over," sighed Randalene.
"That could have gone worse," gasped Commander Drake.
"Wait, where did Silus get too?" asked Cirilla breathing heavily.
"He was thrown south, so he must have gone near the clearing after landing," answered Randalene.
"I am sure I saw the other Commanders' went after him, once this demon threw Silus away from our forces," sighed Cirilla.
"Then let us go help him," said Commander Drake as he let his two handed sword disperse, "he might need assistance."
"Agreed," replied Randalene.

~

In the clearing to the south, Silus was dodging and blocking the attacks from Zoldrun, Folta and Veronica. Silus dived to avoid a joint attack by Zoldrun and Veronica's weapon's but before he could stand up, Folta threw a trio of blades, two of the blades hit the ground in front of Silus, the third bounced off Silus' right shoulder plate.

"What the?" shouted Zoldrun in disbelief.
"It is not even scratched," gasped Veronica in shock, "what kind of armour could take a hit without even being scratched?"
"The kind forged by an elf with more heart and passion than any demon will ever know," sighed Silus.
"What would you know, it will not stop my scythe," grunted Veronica.

Before Silus could react, Veronica had darted towards him and begun swinging her scythe at him. Zoldrun and Folta watched in surprise as Silus failed to move to avoid Veronica's attack. As Veronica's scythe came down over Silus' shoulder.

~

On the edge of the clearing, Randalene, Cirilla and Commander Drake watched as Silus stood motionless as Veronica's attack continued uninterrupted. Silus watched out the corner of his eye as the scythe blade crashed into his shoulder plate.

"Silus!" shouted Cirilla.

Everyone watched in shock as Veronica's scythe blade broke once it hit Silus' shoulder plate, Veronica looked at her scythe in shock as Silus jumped backwards. As Silus stood up he saw the scythe blade flying through the air. Silus flicked his left hand dragon sabre up towards the scythe blade.

"Syphdura!" shouted Silus.

Cirilla watched as Silus's dragon sabre turned into a vine once more and stretched to catch the scythe blade fragment. Silus then spin to his right and flicked the blade piece towards the demons as Zoldrun attempted to charge Silus. Folta and Veronica watched as Silus pulled his dragon sabre backwards, causing his vine-like dragon sabre to hack the scythe blade into Zoldrun's left shoulder.

"Pythlon baz," said Silus.

A quick electrical charge travelled along the vine and into the scythe blade. Zoldrun roared in pain as the electrical charge jolted through his body. Silus' dragon sabre returned to normal as Zoldrun's body crumbled to dust.

"Well that is one of you dealt with," sighed Silus.

"But how?" asked Veronica in disbelief, "How could your armour possibly be strong enough to break my scythe and still not be scratched?"

Silus looked at his right shoulder plate and noticed that Veronica was right, there was not even the tiniest scratch or mark on his armour. Silus then looked back at Veronica.

"So, I guess you should surrender if you cannot cut me," said Silus sarcastically.
"I will sooner jump into a volcano," replied Veronica angrily.
"Well then... Let us see if I can accommodate that wish," chuckled Silus.

Veronica drew the two spears from her back, as Folta threw a flurry of knives at Silus. Silus dove and rolled into the tree line. As Silus stood up he saw a spear flying through the air, Silus ducked and spear embedded itself into a tree behind Silus.

"Curse you, you will die!" shrieked Veronica.

Folta watched from the branch he was sitting on, as Veronica's rage at Silus unfolded with her reclaiming her first spear followed by a frenzy of stabs and slashes from her spears. Silus blocked and parried Veronica's attacks, the two dancing around each other's movements and attacks. Folta sat back and watched Veronica struggle against Silus' strength.

"Guess you are not as strong as you thought, am I right, Veronica?" chuckled Folta to himself.

Veronica tried sweeping at Silus' feet, Silus flipped backwards into the air, and landed on a vine that had appeared from a nearby tree.

"You have put up quite a good fight, but I grow tired of this battle," said Silus as he caught his breath. "What are you talking about?" asked Veronica as she struggled for breath.
"Your plan was not half bad to begin with, send your multi-armed friend to separate me from the others, but since then you and your two friends have been fighting independently, which is the worst thing you could have done," explained Silus, "and because you were fighting amongst yourselves, you left yourself open to counterattacks."
"Go to hell!" screamed Veronica.

Veronica charged at Silus, Silus did not try to move away, he simply pointed his left dragon sabre at Veronica, and with a single breath, the blade changed to a vine and stretched from the sword hilt, the vine ripped through Veronica's chest. Veronica looked down to see her blood staining the vine, and with a heavy cough of blood, Veronica dropped to her knees.

"Now you die," said Silus calmly.

Silus pulled his dragon sabre away from Veronica, as the vine tore its way back out of Veronica's chest, as

Silus's dragon sabre returned to being blade. Veronica's body disintegrated, her spears dropped to the ground, Silus took a deep breath before turning his head to look up at Folta, who was still sitting against a tree trunk of a tree near the clearing.

"Not bad Dragonborne," said Folta as he stood up on the branch, "but you are wrong, working together would not have helped us, we all have different methods for killing our enemies, and my style was limited by their presence."

"So, you simply sat back and watched as your comrade as she died?" asked Silus.

"She was an arrogant cow, simply because she was the only female Commander sent to this forest she took it upon herself to order the rest of us about," scoffed Folta, "but I will prove myself a better opponent."

"You know, I really am getting tired of all you demons and your insufferable boasting," said Silus, "time for you to shut up."

"You will have a trouble getting to me Silus," chuckled Folta, "my daggers are conjured from my demonic magic and I have an infinite number of them."

"We shall see," said Silus, "tempas vaz!"

Folta threw two knives at Silus but watched in shock as Silus' body vanished from his sight, the daggers hit the ground where Silus was standing. Silus appeared on the branch near Folta, Silus then darted at Folta as he drew two short swords from his waist, the two began crossing blades quickly, as Cirilla, Randalene and Commander Drake watched from the ground.

"Should we not try helping him?" asked Cirilla.
"What good would that do?" queried Commander Drake, "Silus can handle this demon, and it is not like we would make much of a difference in the fight, Silus already took out two of the other Commander demons."
"Indeed, we should go help the troops," said Randalene.
"That is not necessary either," said Commander Drake as he turned to look over his left shoulder, as the troops began heading toward them, "the troops have finished dealing with the demons anyway."

Randalene turned to look behind her as the troops began running towards the clearing. Cirilla looked up as Silus jumped over Folta as he tried to jab his short swords at Silus. Silus then hacked his left dragon sabre at the branch, the branch cracked as Folta fell towards the ground.

"Frustus," said Silus calmly.
"No wait!" shouted Folta as he fell.

Silus watched as an icy patch on the ground appeared, with dozens of icy spikes pointing to the tree tops. Cirilla watched as the knife wielding demon fell, Randalene and Commander Drake turned back to see Folta's body be pierced with the spikes of ice. Silus then jumped down to the forest floor, the demon's body twitching as its blood trickled down the spikes.

"So, I lose," whispered Folta, "this fight is not over yet, one titan remains, and he has just the advantage needed to turn the tables on you scumbags."

Silus watched as Folta's body disintegrated to black ash on the icy patch. Silus then dropped to one knee and dug his dragon sabres into the ground. Cirilla ran over to Silus as he tried to catch his breath.

"Silus," said Cirilla softly.
"I am fine, only just realised how much that fight took out of me," gasped Silus.
"Well at least this new armour held up against the demon's attacks," said Commander Drake as he approached, "it is impressive to see that is it completely unscathed, I should see about getting myself some armour like that."
"Well here is your blacksmith Drake," chuckled Silus as he gestured at Cirilla.

Silus then raised his head to look west, the small smile on his face disappeared as the soldiers of elves and dragonkins reached them. Randalene looked around at the tired faces of the soldiers, and a smile crept onto her face.

"We are victorious!" shouted Randalene as she raised her left sword into the air.

The soldiers all raised their weapons and cheered, Silus did not move as he watched the skies to the west. Cirilla looked at the soldiers cheering before noticing Silus was not even smiling, Commander Drake also looked at Silus and noticed his expression was rather serious.

"What is the matter Silus?" asked Commander Drake.
"Amelia and Fiona are fighting the assassin sent to kill the Duke," answered Silus.
"How can you be so sure?" asked Cirilla, "I thought that a magical creature's ability to sense anything becomes clouded in or around Qurendia because it is made of mostly metal."
"I do not know how I can be so sure, I just am, they are struggling a little," answered Silus as he stood up and walked to the clearing, "not surprising when facing an opponent who will fight only from a distance."

Silus looked out to the horizon, in the distance he could make out some mountain tops, the sky was a bright blue, with not a single cloud in the sky. Silus closed his eyes as a gentle breeze blew across the clearing.

~

In Qurendia the guards were running through the streets trying to keep an eye on Amelia and Fiona as they jumped from rooftop to rooftop trying to get close enough to Groda while avoiding his arrows. As

Groda fired a smoking arrow, a large explosion forced
Amelia and Fiona to take cover behind chimney
stacks on two separate roofs.

"This is pointless!" called out Fiona, "he can just fire
an arrow and we try to avoid it, allowing him space to
move."
"Then we force him to move where we want him too,"
replied Amelia.
"You got an idea I suppose?" asked Fiona.
"Just get the Captain and his men to head back to the
Keep," said Amelia calmly.
"What are you... hey wait," called out Fiona as Amelia
began to charge at the demon.

Amelia started running across the rooftops towards
Grota, as Grota looked at Amelia, he smiled and
pulled back his bowstring. Fiona quickly jumped
down into the streets below, where a group of soldiers
were running towards the building where Grota was
standing.

"Soldiers, wait," said Fiona as she landed in front of
them.
"What now?" asked a guard, "we need to get this
demon under control."
"Amelia will direct the demon to the Keep courtyard,
gather all your men and prepare an ambush," ordered
Fiona.
"How will she direct the demon to the centre of the
city?" asked the guard.

"Never mind that, just get your troops organised," ordered Fiona as she jumped back onto the rooftops, a large gust of wind blowing upwards from beneath her feet.

The soldiers watched as Fiona flipped forward onto the rooftops and disappeared from sight, they turned around and ran back down the street. Fiona looked to her left to see Amelia shooting fireballs from her hands at the demon, forcing him to take cover behind a low chimney stack.

"Tempas vaz" said Fiona.

Amelia watched as a blur rushed past her towards the demon's hiding spot, as Fiona drew close to Grota, he looked up and saw her sword swinging towards his head, Grota raised his bow to block Fiona's attack, before kicking out her feet. As Grota stood up he fired an arrow straight at Amelia, only for his bow to break as the arrow fired.

"Curse you witches," cursed Grota.
"Oh dear, no bow, no defence," said Amelia sarcastically as she jumped across the street to reach the rooftop where Grota and Fiona stood.
"I would not be so cocky," scoffed Grota as he conjured a crossbow into his hands, "take this!"

Grota's crossbow had a circular barrel under the bridge, the crossbow had no string, but Amelia and Fiona could tell that the crossbow did not need it as

Grota had conjured the crossbow with magic. Amelia watched as the barrel turned clockwise loading a bolt into the nut of the bow, before Grota pulled the trigger to fire the bolt. Fiona dove towards Amelia, grabbing her and forcing her down onto the rooftop. Grota jumped to the next rooftop laughing manically as he did.

"Nice try ladies, but not good enough to end me," chuckled Grota.
"You bastard," scoffed Amelia as she stood up.
"Oh well, we know he does not have the skill to kill the Duke, seeing as he never leaves the keep," boasted Fiona.
"True, this demon just does not have the skill to make a killing shot," replied Amelia.
"To hell with you, how dare you mock me!" shouted Grota as his crossbow loaded the next bolt.

Amelia and Fiona took cover behind two tall chimney stacks near them as Grota fired multiple bolts consecutively, the barrel on his crossbow spinning rapidly as it loaded bolt after bolt. The air filled with the sound of bolts whistling through the air. Amelia glanced round the corner of the chimney stack to see Grota slowly stepping backwards as he fired.

"He is preparing to make a run for the Keep," said Amelia.
"Then we got him angry enough to rush for the Keep?" asked Fiona.
"Guess we will find out," answered Amelia.

Suddenly a bolt bounced off the side of the chimney stack that Amelia was standing behind. The whistling sound subsided, as Amelia glanced around the corner to see that Grota had stopped firing his crossbow and began jumping across rooftops towards the keep.

"Come on, we need to make sure he reaches the Keep," said Amelia.
"Right behind you," replied Fiona.

Amelia and Fiona ran from behind their chimney stacks and started chasing Grota again. As they ran, then fired magical projectiles near Grota to keep him running, Grota occasionally turned to fire his crossbow, forcing Amelia and Fiona to take cover behind chimney stacks or jumping down onto balconies hanging over the streets.

"Nearly there," said Amelia.

Amelia and Fiona watched as Grota fired a bolt with a cable attached to it at a tower on the guard barracks, Grota then grabbed the cable and turned to fire two more bolts at Amelia and Fiona as they chased after him. Fiona raised her right dragon sabre and stepped in front of Amelia, as Fiona spun her dragon sabre to deflect the bolts. Grota then jumped from the roof and swung to cross the gorge between the city and the Keep.

"Ready to end this?" asked Fiona.

"Need you ask?" queried Amelia.

"Alright, time to end this," said Fiona.

Grota landed with his feet on the wall of the barracks, as he began to climb the wall, pulling himself up on the cable, Amelia and Fiona unfolded their wings from their backs, as Grota reached the top of the barracks, he saw that the Duke was standing in the courtyard, Grota then took a few deep breaths as he raised his crossbow to aim at the Duke.

"And this little pointy, kills the Duke," chuckled Grota.

As Grota began to squeeze the crossbow trigger, he gasped for air as he felt his arms become heavy. Captain Frederick and Duke Horacio looked up to the barrack roof to see Amelia and Fiona standing next to the demon. Their swords shining red as Grota's blood trickled down the blades.

"No... how could... I fail?" coughed Grota.

Amelia and Fiona watched as Grota's body fell forwards off the roof, as he fell his, head separated from his shoulders and his torso separated from his waist. As Grota's body hit the courtyard floor it crumbled to dust.

"Well, that was fun," gasped Fiona taking a deep breath.

"He was more trouble than I thought he would be,"
sighed Amelia.
"At least he is dead, and we saved the Duke," said
Fiona, "two things we can be proud of."
"Yeah, we should go and check in with the Duke,"
replied Amelia.

Amelia and Fiona jumped forward off of the roof, and
stretched their wings to glide across the courtyard.
Duke Horacio and Captain Frederick watched as the
two slowed down and hovered before landing a few
paces away from them.

"Well, you two handled that well," said the Duke, "but
why order the guards away to set up an ambush, if the
ambush was not necessary?"
"The demon was not far off, so he would have heard
us, and we also mocked him, saying he had no chance
of killing you," explained Amelia.
"I see, demons do not take kindly to mockery," said
Duke Horacio, "I recall Silus telling me of how a
demon will pride themselves on any skill they have,
insulting their skills sends them into a frenzy."
"A frenzy which we played on," explained Fiona.
"Indeed," said Captain Frederick.
"Now that you have completed your mission will you
be departing the city?" asked Duke Horacio.
"Our orders were to await Silus and the dragonkins, I
imagine Silus wishes to speak with you too,"
answered Fiona.

"Very well," said Duke Horacio, "I am curious, the Captain was just telling me that you can sense Silus even from inside my city, is that true Lady Phoenix?"

"I can only sense the magic he is using," answered Amelia.

"How is the battle going in the Dark Forest?" asked Fiona.

"It would seem that most of it has been settled, I can sense Silus's relief at killing the Commanders," answered Amelia, "however, there is something off about Silus' magic now."

"What do you mean?" queried Duke Horacio.

"I do not know how to explain it," replied Amelia, "I can sense Silus' magic, but something feels different, his magic is resonating with something and through that I can sense a large demon not far south of where he is."

"How could you possibly be sensing a demon?" questioned Fiona, "no dragon or phoenix has ever had that ability."

"I know it sounds preposterous Fiona," answered Amelia, "but I am telling you, I can sense a powerful titan class demon, and I know Silus can sense it too, I just hope he and the others will be able to slay it."

"I am still hesitant to accept that you or Silus could sense a demon, but I will not question what you are sensing at the moment," said Fiona.

"Well, if we are going to wait for Silus, I guess we should get something to eat while we wait," replied Duke Horacio.

~

Randalene turned to look at Silus, the soldiers all became quiet as the sound of branches being snapped echoed into the forest. Silus turned to look south and saw a dark figure walking towards the clearing. Randalene, Cirilla and Commander Drake all entered the clearing.

"This is not over yet," sighed Silus calmly.
"It almost looks like a treant," said Randalene.
"A what?" asked Commander Drake.
"A treant is a creature made of a tree, which is possessed with a spirit of some kind," answered Silus, "but this is worse, that is the demon that Folta spoke of as he died."
"Men, ready for battle!" shouted Randalene.

The soldiers all held up their shields and spears ready to fight, as they did, the creature broke free of the trees and stomped into the clearing. Silus looked at the demon tree standing before him. The demon had a silvery-grey coloured bark, it stood on two stump like feet, its whole body a twist of tree bark, vines and demonic flesh, its eyes glowed yellow as it stared across the clearing at Silus. Randalene gasped in horror as the demon stood still.

"That is not possible," said Randalene quietly.
"That is a demon?" asked Cirilla.
"Worse, it is a titan demon that has possessed a very rare type of tree, one that is pretty much extinct,"

explained Silus, "its skin is now made of willo-steel, which means this is not going to be easy."

"Silus, that demon has possessed the last of the willo-steel trees," said Randalene.

"I know, but we have to destroy it otherwise it will wipe out this whole forest," replied Silus.

"Time of the demon has arrived, the time of the free must end, now you will face Ludron" grunted Ludron, "and you four shall be the first to feel the wrath I bear for you, for slaying my brethren."

"Oh great, another demon that can boast about itself," sighed Silus.

Ludron let out a deep roar, as it did the trees around the clearing began to sprout vines between them, the soldiers try to enter the clearing but got slammed by the vines and cannot get to the clearing before the vines formed a solid wall, a barrier between the clearing and the forest.

"My Queen, we cannot get through to help you!" shouted Gilnur.

"Do not worry about us," answered Silus, "you and the other soldiers tend to any wounded, if there are any who have fallen then prepare pyres for them, we will deal with this one."

"But..." stammered Gilnur.

"No, Silus is right Commander," said Randalene, "there is nothing we can do now, this demon is controlling the vines, so it is down to the four of us to defeat this monster now, just tend to the wounded and the deceased."

"Now let us end this," said Silus as he began to walk towards Ludron.

"Fool," grumbled Ludron.

Ludron stabbed his right arm into the ground, Cirilla and Commander Drake watched as a vine like spear shot out the ground, Silus moved slightly to the left and right to avoid each attack. As Silus neared Ludron his body blurred as he darted through the air, he hacked at Ludron with an air powered slash from his dragon sabres.

"That will not work Silus!" called out Randalene, "his bark like skin has the same properties as the willo-steel armour that we used to make, it is too durable to break."

"And what would you have me do Randalene?" shouted Silus angrily, "just give up and accept death, sazarach!"

Randalene watched as Silus conjured five fireballs and fired them quickly into Ludron's back. Cirilla and Commander Drake looked at each other and nodded, they then pointed their weapons at Ludron.

"Python baz!" shouted Cirilla and Commander Drake together.

Randalene watched as Cirilla and Commander Drake both fired bolts of black lightning at Ludron. Ludron groaned as it got hit by the combined attacks of Silus, Cirilla and Commander Drake, the clearing became filled with smoke. Ludron began laughing as they watched on.

"Not bad, but I cannot and will not be defeated so easily," cackled Ludron, "now it is my turn."

Randalene watched as a huge wooden spear flew out of the smoke towards her.

"Tempas vaz," said Silus.

Randalene blinked as the spear neared her, as she reopened her eyes, she could see Silus standing in front of her. Silus slashed at the spear, his dragon sabre splitting the spear, Randalene watched in shock as the two spear halves flew past her and imbedded themselves into the tree behind her.

"Silus," said Randalene quietly.
"Come on Randalene, do not stand here like a rag doll," ordered Silus angrily, "are you going to defend your realm or not?"
"But... how can we defeat him when he is like this?" Randalene thought to herself.
"Alright, let us focus on finding its weak points, its chest seems pretty tough so let us see about its limbs and head," said Silus as he, Cirilla and Commander Drake positioned themselves around Ludron.
"Defiant to the end," growled Ludron, "why not just accept your death Silus?"

"You have not won anything yet, mark my words, we will bring you down," said Silus as his dragon sabres began to glow an icy white.

Silus darted at Ludron and began hacking and slashing at Ludron's legs, Cirilla and Commander Drake used ice magic like Silus to attack its arms. Ludron grunted a little as he was attacked, eventually Ludron stomped his left foot down hard, Silus, Cirilla and Commander Drake were sent tumbling backwards as a shockwave forced them away from Ludron. Randalene looked on as Silus, Cirilla and Commander Drake climbed back to their feet.

"Randalene, could really use with some help here!" shouted Commander Drake.
"She is useless to you, she knows more of the wood that I have possessed and is too scared to even try and stand in my presence," chuckled Ludron, "it would be easier to let me kill her."

Ludron held up his right hand and pointed his fingers at Randalene, Randalene just stared blankly at the ground in front of her. Ludron laughed as his fingers extended and shot at Randalene like spears. Randalene closed her eyes then heard the sound of the willo-steel fingers grinding against metal. As she opened her eyes she could see Silus standing in front of her his dragon sabre crossed to his left, Ludron's spear like fingers either stopped by his shoulder plate or missed him and Randalene all together.

"Snap out of it Randalene!" shouted Silus, "we cannot allow this demon to succeed, you swore you would defend the honour of the elves."

"How futile," said Ludron as he retracted his fingers.

"If you give up now Randalene, then you will disgrace your people and your ancestors!" shouted Silus.

Randalene looked up at Silus, his black jacket waving in the breeze, she looked down at her swords, and clutched them tightly. Randalene looked up at Ludron with anger in her eyes, she then raised her right sword over Silus' shoulder and fired a bolt of lightning at Ludron's head. Ludron groaned as the bolt hit him in the face, as he stumbled backwards, Randalene stood beside Silus.

"Sorry about that," said Randalene, "now let us end this."

"Would not have it any other way," replied Silus, "ready you two?"

"Yeah," answered Cirilla.

"On your orders Silus," said Commander Drake.

As Cirilla and Commander Drake ran to stand alongside Silus and Randalene, Ludron looked up to see them all pointing their weapons at him, each crackling with electricity.

"Pythlon baz!" they shouted together.

Ludron watched as electricity from all their weapons formed a large ball of electricity in front of them, he then began to chuckle as he stood up straight. The ball of electricity then fired as a huge bolt of lightning, Ludron did not try to move or defend himself as the bolt hit him dead centre of his body, and Ludron disappeared from view in a cloud of smoke.

"Did that do anything?" asked Cirilla.
"Let us hope so," answered Commander Drake.

The four then watched on as the smoke cleared, Ludron stood still glaring at them, his body crackling with electricity as the residual force of their combined attacks ricocheted across the metallic bark.

"That is not possible," said Randalene, "our combined power should have done something."
"It did, look at his head," replied Silus calmly.

Randalene, Cirilla and Commander Drake looked at Ludron's head, to notice a small crack in Ludron wooden skin.

"We have cracked his armour, but we will now need a direct hit to end this, and that is just too narrow of an opening to do from a distance," said Silus.
"Then we get in closer," replied Randalene.
"Easier said than done," sighed Commander Drake.
"That was fun, but I have a feeling that you four will not last much longer," chuckled Ludron.
"He is about to use a massive area attack, be prepared to move," said Silus.

Ludron punched the ground with both fists, as he did the ground of the whole clearing became cracked as vines and wooden spikes ripped up through the grass, Silus and the others split up trying to avoid Ludron's attacks. Silus used his ice magic to stop various spike and vines from hitting him. Randalene conjured an earth barrier to block Grota's attack.

"Drake, Cirilla, look out!" shouted Silus as he jumped into the air and hovered using his dragon wings.

Commander Drake held up his left dragon sabre to block a thin looking vine as it lashed at him, the vine bent over the Commander's sword before slashing into his left shoulder. Commander Drake screamed in pain as he dropped his dragon sabre. Cirilla was diving and rolling to avoid Ludron's attacks, but Ludron then pointed his left index finger at Cirilla, as Ludron's finger fired like a spear, Cirilla was blocking more of Ludron's vines with her shield. Cirilla turned around to see Ludron's finger fly at her, but she could not act in time, the finger pierced through her armour and straight through her right shoulder, Cirilla screamed as Ludron's vines dispersed and Ludron lifted Cirilla up, Cirilla dropped her halberd and shield and held onto Ludron's finger to ease the weight on her shoulder. Silus then flew straight at Ludron, his dragon sabres down at his sides.

"Solva baz!" shouted Silus.

As Silus shouted the incantation, his body glowed with a misty blue aura, as Silus neared Ludron, he did not raise his dragon sabres to Ludron, instead Silus shoulder barged Ludron's chest, as he made contact the blue aura surrounding Silus created a huge shockwave that forced Ludron to instantly fall back to the ground. His finger pulled out of Cirilla's shoulder, as Silus turned to fly towards Cirilla.

"I got you," said Silus as he caught Cirilla.

Silus landed on the ground, Commander Drake managed to walk to Silus, and Randalene lowered her earth barrier and ran to Silus. Silus knelt down and lowered Cirilla to the ground. Randalene dropped to her knees as she approached Cirilla.

"I am sorry, I cannot continue this fight," grunted Cirilla as she clutched at her shoulder.
"I cannot go on either," hissed Commander Drake as he knelt on the ground beside Silus.
"Silus, if we do not treat Ciri's wound she may not make it," said Randalene, "and we will have to heal the Commander's shoulder too."
"Do not worry about me, I can heal myself, just focus on Cirilla's wound," grunted Commander Drake as he pulled a bandage from a pouch on his belt.
"Can you heal her Randalene?" asked Silus.
"I can but it will take time," answered Randalene.
"Take all the time you need," said Silus as he stood up and turned to face Ludron who was getting back on his feet.

"Silus, you cannot defeat him alone!" shouted Randalene.

"I do not have a choice," said Silus calmly, "this is who I am, and I promise I will not let him get to you three."

"Silus, be careful," grunted Cirilla.

"Do not worry about me," said Silus, "I got this, you just worry about getting that wound healed."

Ludron stood on its feet and stared at Silus, his yellow eyes meeting Silus' as they changed to his dragon blue eyes. Silus stood in front of Commander Drake, Cirilla and Randalene, his jacket blowing in the breeze as the two stood still, the air became still and Silus' jacket stopped waving.

"You managed to land an attack that penetrated my skin, how is that possible?" asked Ludron.

"Magic is magic, the only difference is that some spells can pass through certain resistances," explained Silus, "I just found one that you do not have much of a resistance too, not that it makes a difference really."

"Oh really, care to explain that?" questioned Ludron.

"Your so called impenetrable skin has more than a few cracks in it, now all I have to do is simply land a direct hit between the cracks and this battle is over," explained Silus, "so anything you want to say before I blow you all the way to hell?"

"You will not succeed in defeating me, I will rip you to shreds before you can get a chance to slay me," roared Ludron.

"Well, shall we dance then?" asked Silus sarcastically.

Silus' body blurred as he darted towards Ludron, Ludron tried to punch Silus with his right hand, but Silus had got behind Ludron before his fist could hit Silus. As Silus stood behind Ludron, he held his right hand dragon sabre across his body.

"Wo'dren" said Silus as he spun around and slashed his dragon sabre into a crack on Ludron's left leg.

Ludron roared in pain, as Silus cut off his left foot. Ludron stumbled as his severed foot turned to ash. Ludron then spun round and tried to sweep at Silus with his left arm, Silus leapt into the air and landed on Ludron's right shoulder.

"You will not be needing this where you are going," said Silus as he raised his left hand dragon sabre above his head, "sazarach!"

Silus' dragon sabre caught fire as he slashed at Ludron's right shoulder, the demon roaring in pain as Silus cut of his right arm. Silus jumped off Ludron's shoulder and landed between Ludron and the others.

"Hang on my Lord," grunted Commander Drake as he slowly stood up.
"Stand down Commander," said Silus, "no sense in you injuring yourself further, I can handle this freak now."
"But... Silus..." stammered Commander Drake.

"Stand down," said Randalene, "Silus is right, this beast is getting weak."

"How is Cirilla?" asked Silus.

"I have done all I can for her wound," answered Randalene, as she looked down at Cirilla who was asleep, "but she will need rest and time to recover properly."

"Right, well let me just finish with this freak first," said Silus.

"You will pay for destroying my foot and arm," roared Ludron as he stabbed his fingers into the ground.

Randalene, Silus and Commander Drake watched as several vines ripped out of the ground in front of them. In a flash of light, the vines all froze in place, as Randalene and Commander Drake looked around, the frozen vines were stopped just where Silus was standing, but they could not see Silus. Above them, the sky had turned dark as huge thunder clouds began circling over the clearing

"Where did Silus go?" asked Randalene.

"Guess your saviour was all talk," chuckled Ludron, "he ran away because he knew he could not beat me."

Ludron pulled his hands out the ground, as he did the frozen vines broke and crumbled onto the ground. Ludron began to walk towards Randalene, Cirilla and Commander Drake. Randalene looked up to see a small dark speck flying down from the thunder clouds above.

"Silus," whispered Randalene.

Ludron continued walking towards Randalene, completely oblivious to what was happening in the skies above. As Silus dove out of the sky, he held only his left hand dragon sabre, the clouds above rippling with thunder and lightning. Ludron stood over Cirilla and Randalene, as Randalene looked up to meet Ludron's eyes, she smiled.

"What are you smiling at?" asked Ludron.
"Oh, nothing important, just wanting a good view of your imminent demise," chuckled Randalene.
"What do you mean?" queried Ludron.

Randalene did not answer, she just looked up at the sky, as Ludron tilted his back to see Silus as he grabbed his dragon sabre with both hands and held the sword, so the blade was parallel with his eyes. The blade began to glow with a faint blue light.

"Pythlon baz!" shouted Silus as he thrust his dragon sabre into the crack on the Ludron's head.

As Silus jumped off the demon's head, a huge bolt of lightning erupted from the cloud and hit Silus' dragon sabre like a lightning rod, Ludron roared in pain as the lightning passed through the dragon sabre and into his body. Silus moved Commander Drake closer to Randalene and Cirilla before conjuring a stone wall that curved over them. Ludron's body began to crack as the lightning continued channelling into his body, a light blue glow shone through all the cracks in his wooden body. As Ludron's eyes went black his body exploded covering the forest clearing with pieces of burning bark and black ash, the thunder clouds in the sky dispersed and the sky opened up to allow the sunlight to shine down on the ground once more.

Chapter 7: When Plans Fall

In Selania, Celestia was sitting in a chair at the war table in the palace throne room, three of Selania's Commanders and a few dragonkin soldiers standing around the room.

"Right, so the elves should be within view soon," said Celestia, "that will mean more people will be in Selania, making Selania and even bigger target for Shiento."
"Why should we even allow the elves into Selania, they would not help us," scoffed one of the Selanian Commanders.
"You will help them because I command you too," said Celestia.
"You are not our ruler, and we do not have to take orders from you," replied the Commander.
"Wrong, she does possess the right to issue orders!" shouted a man who had just entered the throne room.

The man wore a bright crimson red garb, detailed with dark blue embroidery. The man was middle-aged, he had short brown hair and brown eyes. As the man approached the war table, the Commanders all stepped back from the table. The man looked around at the Commanders with an angry expression across his face.

"How disgraceful, that you would speak to royalty in such a way, I do not care if Lady Celestia is not

Selanian royalty, the soldiers of Urendos came to our aid, as did the elven forces from Birthaina or have you forgotten?" said the man angrily.

"But... Councillor Alistair," stammered the Commander.

"But nothing, you are soldiers, and should respect the chain of command," replied Alistair, "you are to show the proper respect to Lady Celestia as you would have to our late King Jacob."

"I... understood councillor," said the Commander.

"As it happens, I have news for you all, and especially for you Lady Celestia," explained Alistair.

"Proceed Councillor," said Celestia.

"Well, the Selanian council has actually come to a quick conclusion on how our hierarchy will continue," explained Alistair, "and the decision is to allow Silus the Dragonborne to become King of Selania..."

"What?" shouted the Commanders in outrage.

"Forgive me Councillor," said one of the Commanders as he stepped towards the war table, "but how can that be the council's decision, nominating one who once failed to fight alongside us as our King?"

"Without an heir, our late King Jacob's line cannot continue as the hierarch of Selania," explained Alistair, "however the council's decision to elect Silus as our King comes with a condition."

"And may I enquire as to this condition?" asked Celestia.

"The condition is as follows: that Silus can and will only be elected as the King of Selania, if and when he finally defeats Shiento," answered Alistair, "that is assuming he does not run away like he did when

Shiento attacked Selania the last time, have you any comment on that Lady Celestia?"

Suddenly a young soldier wearing minimal plate armour ran into the throne room, he carried a small round shield in his left hand and a small sword on his left hip.

"Lady Celestia," said the soldier breathing heavily.
"Yes, what do you have to report?" asked Celestia.
"The sentries report a large group of elves walking out of the woodland to the west, my Lady," answered the soldier.
"Very good, send word to prepare for their arrival," instructed Celestia calmly.
"Yes, my Lady, also another sentry reports a large contingent of dwarven troops moving siege weaponry are heading this way from the north-west mountain range, we cannot say if they are hostile or friendly though," added the solider.
"Dwarves?" queried Celestia.
"Yes, my Lady," answered the soldier.
"I guess Urthrad wishes to aid us as well," said Celestia, "very well, when they arrive let me know and I will speak with them."
"As you wish, my Lady," replied the soldier.

The young soldier took a step back and bowed to Lady Celestia, before turning to run out of the throne room. Celestia looked to the Commanders then at Alistair.

"You did not answer me, Lady Celestia," said Alistair.
"I can assure you, Silus will fight Shiento," replied
Celestia.
"Do you believe the boy can defeat this demon?"
asked the Commander.
"I have known Silus for my whole life, he may seem
brash and cocky in a fight, but in truth, he will not
engage in a battle that he knows he has no chance of
surviving, the fact is, Silus is cautious and will only
fight a battle he can win," explained Celestia, "and
seeing as Silus has set himself to trying to keep as
many of the races alive as Shiento tries to extinguish
all life on Jarvlan, I would think it is safe to say that
Silus will fight Shiento."
"But what about defeating him?" queried Alistair.
"Unfortunately, I cannot predict that sort of outcome,
whether or not Silus will be able to defeat Shiento,
that is down to Silus," answered Celestia.
"And what about if Silus fails?" asked Alistair, "what
if Silus dies in his conclusive battle against Shiento?"
"Then you best have your final prayers ready,"
answered Celestia, "Silus being Shiento's brother,
they have the same natural capacity for magic, but
Shiento has attained more raw magic power, while
Silus uses what power he has more conservatively."
"Do you truly believe that Silus is our only hope of
defeating Shiento?" asked Alistair.
"I do not believe that is the case councillor," answered
Celestia confidently, "I know that is the case, if Silus
falls, we all fall."

The room fell silent as Celestia finished talking, the Commanders looked around at each other before looking to Alistair and finally to Celestia. The Commanders then dispersed and left the throne room. Alistair looked at Lady Celestia and bowed before leaving the throne room as well, Lady Celestia stood alone at the war table, the dragonkin guards standing still as if on parade.

~

In the Dark Forest, the elves and dragonkin troops were tending to their wounded. Randalene and Commander Drake were walking around checking on their troops. Silus was sat just outside a tent in the dragonkin encampment on the south side of the city, next to him, Cirilla was lying down on an unrolled mat with a blanket over her. Silus was looking out of the tent as a group of dragonkin soldiers carry pieces of broken armour and weapons into the city. Eventually, Cirilla started to stir from her sleep, Silus looked around as she opened her eyes.

"Hey Ciri," said Silus, "how are you feeling?"
"Well my shoulder still hurts a bit," replied Cirilla as she opened her eyes and let her eyes focus on Silus.
"Do you feel you can move it?" asked Silus.
"I am not inclined to," answered Cirilla, "can you help me up?"
"Sure," said Silus.

Silus shuffled into the tent to crouch beside Cirilla. Silus placed his right arm behind Cirilla's shoulders and held Cirilla's left hand with his left hand. As Silus slowly lifted Cirilla's torso to get her to sit up, Cirilla winced with pain as her right arm draped down.

"You ok?" asked Silus.
"Randalene healed my wound right?" queried Cirilla.
"She did, but healing the wound does not necessarily take away the pain," answered Silus.
"Yeah, I noticed that," winced Cirilla.
"Here, I can put your arm in a sling," replied Silus.
"Ok," said Cirilla.

Silus pulled out a beige coloured cloth out of a bag in the tent, as Silus unfolded the cloth, Cirilla looked at his eyes, Silus' eyes were in their human state, but the colour was a match for Silus' bright blue dragon eyes. As Silus started tying the cloth around Cirilla's neck, she could feel the weight of her arm lightening as her arm is slightly lifted into the sling.

"There you go," said Silus as he finished tying the sling.
"Thank you Silus," replied Cirilla, "how did it go with that titan demon?"
"Well the fight was not easy, but the demon did die, and I collapsed once the demon was dead," answered Silus, "everyone is currently tending to wounded."
"Did we lose anyone?" asked Cirilla.
"I do not know just yet," answered Silus, "Randalene ordered me to rest and look after you, but I believe

Commander Drake and Randalene are coming over to inform us of just that."

Cirilla looked out of the tent to see Randalene and Commander Drake walking towards the tent from the left, Silus shuffled towards the front of the tent and sat in the entrance. As Commander Drake and Randalene reached the tent, they knelt down and sat on the ground outside the tent. Cirilla looked at her shoulder before looking up to Commander Drake and Randalene.

"How are you feeling Ciri?" asked Randalene.
"I have felt better, but I guess this cannot be helped," answered Cirilla, "how is your shoulder Commander?"
"Luckily the cut was not too deep," responded Commander Drake, "have you recovered your strength Silus?"
"Well I cannot say I am in my best state, but I have enough energy to move about, just as long as I do not have to carry heavy objects, I think I will manage," said Silus sarcastically, "how are things looking?"
"Well, the good news is we defeated the demons," answered Commander Drake, "now it is just a matter of how do we proceed from here."
"How many did we lose?" quizzed Silus as he played with a twig in his hands.
"Sixty-nine elves died with many more injured and we have lost twenty-two dragonkin soldiers with thirteen injured," answered Commander Drake.

"To hell with you Shiento," grunted Silus as he snapped the twig with his left hand.

"Though it is of little comfort," stated Randalene, "this fight could have very well ended the elven people of this continent, if it had not been for you and the dragonkins."

"I am assuming most troops are not in a condition for travelling?" queried Silus.

"There are healers going around ensuring all the wounds are healed and the troops should be ready to mobilise by tomorrow," responded Commander Drake, "what are your orders Lord Silus?"

"Nothing from me, not yet," said Silus quietly as he looked up to see Legolas rearing and kicking wildly, "Legolas, calm down!"

Legolas neighed and continued rearing and kicking, Silus stood up and noticed Legolas was facing towards the clearing in the south. Cirilla scooted herself to the front of the tent and looked out to see the Pegasus being restless.

"What has him so spooked?" asked Cirilla.

"I am not sure, but I have never seen him act like this," responded Silus as he began walking over to Legolas.

"It is clear that Lord Silus is unhappy that so many have fallen because of the demons," said Randalene.

"Well that is a complicated situation, Silus has gone around and helped nearly every city and race throughout his life, and it is because of that, that he feels akin to everyone, and as you have stated, he does not take news of fallen friends and allies lightly," explained Commander Drake, "never the less, he understands what it means to command and lead soldiers, for there is no Commander who truly believes that his or her command will ever mean that no one will ever be lost on the battlefield."

"What of those who fell?" queried Cirilla.

"Well those who are still able have begun building a mass pyre to commemorate the dead," answered Commander Drake.

Cirilla looked over to Silus and Legolas to see that Silus had calmed Legolas but both were staring off to the south. Silus then turned and walked back to the tent.

"Commander Drake, Randalene," said Silus.

"What is it Silus?" asked Randalene.

"I am going to need you two to ready the troops for a forced march to Selania as soon as you possibly can," responded Silus.

"That will take some time, my Lord," stated Commander Drake, "and I thought the plan was for the dragonkins to accompany you to Qurendia after we had defeated the demons here?"

"I know, but the sooner the better," replied Silus.

"Why the sudden orders?" asked Randalene, "a few moments ago you were saying that you had no orders for the Commander, now your issuing a marching order, so what has changed?"

"You are about to find out," said Silus as he started walking towards the clearing.

"But... Silus..." stammered Randalene.

As Silus walked towards the clearing, Cirilla looked to see Legolas following close behind him, as Commander Drake and Randalene stood up to watch Silus, they noticed a black cloud waving in the distance across the clearing.

"What is that?" asked Randalene.
"Whatever it is, it cannot be good," responded Commander Drake.
"Do you think it could be more demons?" queried Cirilla.
"I certainly hope not," answered Randalene, "most of our troops are injured and we cannot hope to stand a chance if another battle is upon us."
"Help me up, please," said Cirilla as she lifted her left hand to Commander Drake.

Commander Drake knelt down and placed his right hand under Cirilla's shoulder, holding her outstretched hand with his left hand. As the Commander lifted Cirilla to her feet, Cirilla looked to see Silus stepping into the clearing, with Legolas standing on the edge of the clearing. Commander Drake, Cirilla and Randalene all began walking towards the clearing.

"Figures you would show up now, brother!" called out Silus as he stood in the clearing.

Silus watched as Shiento emerged from the tree line opposite him. Randalene, Cirilla and Commander Drake rushed to Silus' side as the black wavering cloud dispersed around Shiento. Shiento looked at the clearing floor and smiled as he gazed over the ash covered ground.

"Well, well, you defeated my demons, but you struggled through it," smirked Shiento.
"Why are you here?" asked Silus as he conjured his dragon sabres into his hands.
"I came to observe the battle, guess I am a little late for that?" stated Shiento sarcastically.
"If you are looking for a fight, then look no further," said Silus as he moved his right foot back a bit readying to charge at Shiento.
"Now, now Silus, we both know in your current condition you would not survive," chuckled Shiento.
"I have always hated that cocky attitude," grunted Silus.
"But as it happens, I did not actually come here to fight," said Shiento, "I actually came to congratulate you for your victory, though I cannot deny, the temptation to kill you here and now, while you are weakened is rather invigorating."
"You think I will be an easy kill?" queried Silus, "then you are wrong."

Silus grunted as he collapsed to his right knee, Shiento chuckled at seeing Silus' weakness, Randalene and Commander Drake stepped in front of Silus as Cirilla knelt down beside Silus.

"Silus, you should not push yourself," whispered Cirilla.

"You should listen to your friends Silus," mocked Shiento, "you would not last long against me in your current condition."

"Then you are sorely mistaken," grunted Silus, "tempas vaz!"

Cirilla watched as Silus disappeared from right in front of her, Randalene and Commander Drake stumbled as a heavy gust of wind blew past them. Shiento drew his dragon sabres as Silus appeared directly in front of him with his left hand dragon sabre swinging across his chest from his right. As Shiento blocked Silus' attack, a huge shockwave rippled through the air, cracking the ground beneath their feet.

"Silus, stop!" shouted Randalene.

Shiento stared at Silus as his dragon eyes appeared, their light blue colour glowing with anger as Shiento's eyes turned to their menacing yellow colour. The two fighters began swinging their swords attacking and blocking each other's moves, the sound of clashing metal rang into the tree lines. Commander Drake looked over his right shoulder, to see several dragonkin and elven soldiers grabbing their weapons and rushing towards them.

"We need to help Silus," said Cirilla as she conjured her halberd.
"You are not in the condition to be helping him, neither is the Commander," replied Randalene.
"I am not going to argue with that," scoffed Commander Drake.
"So, we have to just sit here and do nothing?" queried Cirilla.
"Even weakened as he is, Silus is still the only person who can truly match Shiento in this fight," responded Commander Drake.
"What do you mean?" asked Cirilla.
"Look at the fight," answered Randalene calmly.

Cirilla looked up to see Silus and Shiento as they angrily crossed swords. Their swords reverberating with the symphony of a heated war.

"The fight would appear on the surface to be equal, but it is not an equal fight," stated Randalene.
"I do not understand, they appear to be equal fighters," replied Cirilla.
"That is where you are wrong," said Commander Drake, "you see, Shiento is using his strength to repel Silus' attacks, and for the most part, his strategy is working, however, Silus is clearly the better swordsman, he is using technique to try and get the upper hand against Shiento, however their strategies are keeping the fight equal."
"The only determining factor is that Shiento is not fatigued from the battle," explained Randalene, "if

Silus is not careful, Shiento could land a fatal blow against Silus."
"Then we should try separating them," said Cirilla. "Even if we used magic to do that Silus is fighting using his skills and senses," explained Commander Drake, "he would sense our attempts, and counter our attempts using his own magic and abilities."
"So unfortunately Cirilla, as much as we would interfere in this fight, our attempts would be for naught," stated Randalene.
"Commander!" shouted a dragonkin soldier as the able-bodied soldiers enter the clearing.
"Stand down and get back!" ordered Commander Drake, "This is Lord Silus' fight."

Cirilla watched as Shiento's and Silus' swords began to glow in different colours with each strike, their blades switching from black to blue, red to white, brown to yellow and more. Shiento then stepped towards Silus, as Silus stepped backwards with his left foot, his foot slipped on the ground. Silus looked up to see Shiento thrusting his left dragon sabre at his right shoulder.

"Silus!" screamed Cirilla.
"Time to taste defeat brother," said Shiento as he smiled.

Shiento's smile disappeared as his dragon sabre snapped as it hit Silus's obsidian shoulder plate. Silus then jumped backwards panting heavily. Shiento lifted his dragon sabre then threw it to the side and lifted his gazed to stare at Silus.

~

In Qurendia, Amelia, Fiona, Captain Frederick and Duke Horacio were sitting in the study, drinking tea and discussing the demon incursion in the Dark Forest.

"That is weird," said Amelia suddenly.
"Something wrong Lady Phoenix?" asked Horacio.
"Silus' magic has spiked again," answered Amelia, "I think he has engaged in battle again, but he is weak."
"What do you mean?" questioned Fiona, "can you tell who he is fighting?"
"He has not fully recovered his strength after facing the demon horde, and he is engaged in a high intensity fight against..." explained Amelia, "I cannot be sure, but whoever it is has a demonic presence but whose magic resonates almost in unison with Silus' magic."
"That must mean Shiento has made an appearance," said Fiona, "dragon magic resonates when used, but for it to resonate in unison it has to be against another dragon with similar magical abilities."
"And if Silus has not replenished his strength then he will not stand a chance against his brother," stated Horacio.
"Silus will not lose," said Amelia firmly, "I know he will survive."

"But, will he have the strength to carry on afterwards?" asked Captain Frederick, "if his strength is already diminished, then how much longer can he fight on before collapsing from exhaustion?"

"Knowing Silus, he will not stop fighting until his enemy is no longer present," explained Horacio, "my men once brought Silus to me after a huge fight in a nearby valley, not too far north from the city, he was unconscious for two days before he awoke."

"You are all wrong, Silus will be fine," said Amelia, "you will see, Silus will fend off Shiento and be here soon."

"I admire your confidence my dear, but Silus has not changed much over the years, he will reach his limit soon if he does not stop engaging in battle after battle," urged Horacio, "as far as we have discussed, Silus has lead an attack on Shiento's fortress in the south, reducing it to rubble as you described, then the next day facing the assassin sent to kill King Jacob."

"Which as far as you could sense, Silus was angered at that demon, so we are assuming that that demon succeeded in slaying the King," interrupted Fiona.

"Quite, and that was yesterday, now on this one day, he has fought off the demon incursion in the Dark Forest, which I am assuming he fought against the tougher demons and is now facing another extremely powerful foe, one who is to all measurements, the most powerful foe Silus has ever or will ever face," continued Horacio.

"I do not care what any of you say, Silus will be fine, you will see," said Amelia as she stood up rapidly.

Amelia turned and stormed out of the study. Captain Frederick went to stop Amelia, but stopped when he saw Duke Horacio raise his left hand signalling for the Captain to remain still. Fiona watched Amelia walk out the doorway before sighing.

"I am sorry your grace," apologised Fiona.
"No need to apologise, I understand completely," said Horacio calmly, "she is a very passionate woman, probably the most passionate woman I have ever met, her words and her actions are true of herself, I cannot hold her against that fact."
"Should I not assign a guard to watch her?" asked Captain Frederick.
"No, she is not in any immediate danger here," answered Horacio, "so there is no need to treat her like a delicate flower."
"As you wish, my Lord," responded Captain Frederick.

Amelia rushed down the balcony staircase and out into the Keep courtyard. Amelia turned to face east, as she watched the skyline, she saw a bright light flash in the distance. As Amelia took a deep breath she noticed a figure standing on the church roof where Grota once stood. The figure was covered in a crimson cloak, the figure then jumped from the rooftop and disappeared from view, Amelia then looked back to the east, as she stood there silently she raised her right hand to the centre of her chest and clenched her hand into a fist.

"Silus, I believe in you, please come back to me soon," said Amelia quietly.

~

"That is not possible," scoffed Shiento, "how could your armour be strong enough to break my dragon sabre?"

"It has nothing to do with my armour," answered Silus as he shrugged his shoulders and examined his shoulder plate.

"Then how!" roared Shiento in outrage, "our dragon sabres are an invincible object, no force should ever cause them to break!"

"That is where you are deluding yourself, brother," grunted Silus, "our dragon sabres are our souls given solid form, so long as our soul's remain strong, no force could hope to break them, but you surrendered part of your soul when you became the demon dragon, you weakened your own swords."

"That, that cannot be right!" shouted Shiento, "how can they be so weak, when I am strong?"

"Your magic is strong, your form is strong," explained Silus, "but neither of those things make up for your weakened soul."

"Curse you," grunted Shiento, "I will rip out your heart and crush it in my hands with you still watching for this outrage!"

Shiento's remaining dragon sabre became enshrouded in black fire, Silus watched as the fire expanded both width ways and length ways. Shiento raised his right hand and then quickly swung his arm to his side, as he did the black flames died out to reveal a large bastard sword. The blade was pitch black, the front side of the blade was straight and sharp while the back side of the blade was serrated like a saw. The hilt was a white dragon head with its mouth opening over the blade.

"Even in my condition, I can hold my ground against you Shiento," smirked Silus as he readied to start the fight again.
"So it would seem," replied Shiento with a heavy sigh, "you are clearly a better swordsman than I, however my magic is far superior to yours."
"So, let us end this," said Silus.
"It will not end on this day," chuckled Shiento, "not for me."

Shiento raised his bastard sword above his head and gripped the handle with both hands. Silus held his dragon sabres at his sides, the blades pointing at Shiento.

"Well, you are not beating me without a significant fight," said Silus.

The two fighters stood poised ready to strike at one another. Cirilla, Randalene, Commander Drake and the soldiers watched eagerly, waiting to see who would move first, suddenly Silus slipped his right foot back and crossed his dragon sabres across his waist. Shiento and Silus then both lunged at each other.

"Draconom vaz!" they shouted together.

Silus' dragon sabres generated a fiery red plasma that covered the blade, Shiento's bastard sword generated a pitch black plasma. Everyone watched as Silus raised his dragon sabre's across his chest crossing them to meet Shiento's sword as it swung down towards his head. As the three blades crashed into one another, a huge shockwave splashed into the air, everyone watching could not help but to cover their eyes as the clashing of the fighter's blades began to generate a bright white light. Shiento and Silus roared at each other.

"Silus!" shouted Cirilla.

As the white light appeared to consume Shiento and Silus, a loud explosion erupted from the light, Silus was sent tumbling backwards across the clearing floor. Silus crashed onto his shoulders, his grip on his dragon sabres loosened and the blades slapped onto the ground in front of Silus as he stopped rolling, Silus lay flat on the ground in front of Cirilla, Randalene and Commander Drake.

"Gods no, Silus!" gasped Cirilla as she rushed to Silus' side.

Randalene and Commander Drake looked up to see Shiento, who had crashed into an oak tree on the far side of the clearing, his bastard sword embedded in a maple tree behind him to his left. The two fighter's body's crackled with electricity as they struggled to climb to a kneeling position.

"Not bad brother," wheezed Shiento, "I would even go as far to say that I underestimated you."
"This is not over," grunted Silus as he tried to stand but collapsed to his knee again.
"That is enough Silus, you are not in a condition to continue fighting," said Randalene, "and neither is Shiento."
"Unfortunately, the elven Queen is right," grunted Shiento, "our final confrontation will have to be postponed for now."
"Why wait, I will end your traitorous life now!" shouted Silus.

Suddenly the air filled with the sound of hooves trampling upon the ground, Silus looked around to see Legolas running towards him. As Legolas stopped in front of Silus acting like a wall between Silus and Shiento. Silus then looked up to see Legolas looking at him.

"Enough is enough Silus," growled Legolas in a deep voice.
"He can speak?" asked Commander Drake in shock.

Legolas' body began to turn black as the Pegasus reared up onto its hind legs, and its neigh turned into a roar. Everyone watched on in shock except for Silus who merely smiled.

"Guess you have grown tired of the charade?" said Silus sarcastically, "welcome back to your normal life, Dragonnoth."

Everyone watched as the Pegasus' body grew larger and larger, it skin changing from horse hairs to black scales, the head warping and growing horns and the tail changing from hair into a long scale covered tail. As the transformation ended, Shiento looked on in disbelief as a black dragon now stood between him and Silus.

"What just happened?" asked Randalene.
"So, that is where you have been hiding my brother," chuckled Shiento, "hiding in plain sight, in the form of another, it is good to see you again, Dragonnoth."
"Silus enough is enough, you cannot continue this fight," growled Dragonnoth.
"Yeah, kind of realising that, but I do not want to simply let Shiento get away with what he has done." Explained Silus.

Shiento chuckled as he climbed to his feet, but fell back against the tree behind him. Dragonnoth used his tail to help Silus stand up and support him, Silus looked at Shiento his dragon eyes shining with anger.

"Shiento must be made to pay," growled Silus.
"As much as I wish to end it right here, right now," chuckled Shiento, "I must adhere to my plan for conquering the whole world."

"So, you are turning tail to run?" asked Silus, "that is just like you, a dragon who could not bear the weight of his responsibility, now cannot admit defeat when death is presented to him."

"I would love to debate this with you brother, however you might want to conserve your energy for saving your little birdie," grunted Shiento as he managed to climb to his feet.

"What?" shouted Silus in outrage, "what have you done to her?"

"Me? Nothing," chuckled Shiento, "Lady Drask wished to prove her tactical value to me, and so she set herself to capturing the phoenix, and use her as bait to force you to surrender."

"You bastard," grunted Silus.

"Now, now, I warned her that if she chose to go through with her plan that no demon would aid her," explained Shiento, "so here is your chance to save the phoenix and potentially end your former friend's life."

"And why would you warn me of this?" asked Silus as he tried to stand without Dragonnoth's aid, "what could you possibly gain from warning me?"

"You may find this hard to believe, but I have a very specific image of my conquest of this continent, and it specifically details me being the one to defeat you in a final, all or nothing battle," explained Shiento, "I will not be satisfied with my conquest if Lady Drask's plan were to come to fruition, that was my purpose for coming here, to warn you, not to fight."

"You were right, I find that hard to believe," hissed Silus, "and what of yourself?"

"Well, I will return to our family home, I expect to see you there in three days, I wish only to talk at that point, to detail how my next move will play out," explained Shiento, "I have created the circumstances for my grand victory over you, I just need you to understand your role in my plan."

"Go to hell," grunted Silus.

"Three days' brother, you will meet with me, and the final preparations for our final battle will be ready," explained Shiento.

Shiento turned and walked to his bastard sword, Silus stood panting as he watched Shiento. As Shiento removed his bastard sword from the tree, Silus lifted his hands toward his dragon sabres, with a slight gust of wind, the blade flew straight into Silus' hands. Shiento turned around to look at Silus, Silus' dragon eyes faded to reveal his human eyes as Shiento unfolded his dragon wings out of his back. Shiento smiled before taking off and flying north over their heads.

"I am not so sure we should have allowed him to go," said Cirilla nervously.

"If Shiento did not intend on ending Silus today, then the fight would have continued," explained Commander Drake, "so it is safe to assume there was some truth in his words."

"We should be glad that the fight did not meet a real conclusion," stated Randalene.

"Randalene is right about that," said Dragonnoth, "if the fight continued Silus would have fallen."

"I would have managed," hissed Silus as his body swayed.

"All these years and you have not changed Silus," growled Dragonnoth, "you should be more than aware of your limits by now."

Silus collapsed to his knees, his grip on his dragon sabres loosened. As the dragon sabres slipped out of Silus' hands, they disappeared in a burst of fire. Cirilla knelt down beside Silus and wrapped her left arm around Silus, and rested her head on Silus' left shoulder.

"Are you alright Silus?" asked Randalene.

"Just fatigue, I will live," answered Silus.

"You are lucky to be alive, you were already dead on your feet before Shiento arrived," stated Randalene, "what in the hell were you thinking?"

"That I had enough in me to end him quickly," responded Silus.

"Do you believe he was telling the truth about Amelia?" queried Commander Drake.

"I do not intend to take it lightly," answered Silus, "Commander ready everyone for their march to Selania as soon as you can, and I will join you in Selania as soon as I can, with Lady Fiona and Amelia."

"You should not be rushing off in your condition," said Cirilla as she lifted her head.

"I do not have a choice, I have to go," replied Silus as he stood up again.

"Well, it is not like we could stop you, just take care Silus," urged Randalene, "we will mobilize as soon as we can."

"Very good, I will see you all in Selania as soon as I can," said Silus.

"I shall accompany you my Lord," stated Commander Drake.

"No, stay with your troops, return to Selania and inform Lady Celestia of what transpired here Commander," replied Silus, "you have your orders, Commander."

"As you wish my Lord," responded Commander Drake.

"Dragonnoth I know you are only looking out for me, but can you go with them?" asked Silus, "you will be of more help in moving the wounded and the weapons then travelling with me."

"Knowing that you are headed for Qurendia and I lack the ability to fully transform into human form, I agree with you," answered Dragonnoth, "just take care brother, you have rejuvenated some magic now that I have broken the enchantment you placed upon me, but you are still in a weakened state."

"I know, but I will be fine," replied Silus.

"Silus, I want to question how your Pegasus changed into a dragon, but now is not the time," said Randalene, "so for now, you get to Qurendia, and we will go to Selania as you have ordered, just be careful will you?"

"Of course, I will see you in Selania soon," responded Silus.

Commander Drake raised his right hand to his chest and bowed to Silus before turning to face the soldiers. As the Commander began issuing orders, Randalene placed her right hand on Silus' left shoulder before nodding and following Commander Drake back into the forest. Silus looked at Cirilla and smiled.

"I guess this is goodbye for now?" asked Cirilla.
"For now, but I will see you in Selania soon," responded Silus, "thank you for all your help Cirilla, I cannot repay you enough for what you have done for me."
"Oh, I have not done that much," blushed Cirilla.
"You made me an amazing set of armour that prevented me from being hacked and skewered throughout this day, and you fought alongside me, against some of the toughest demons I have ever faced," explained Silus, "I would hardly say that you have done little for me."
"Well, you took a great risk in using my new armour, even though it had not been tested properly," said Cirilla.
"With the way you talked about it so passionately, how could I doubt you?" queried Silus.
"Because it had never been tested properly," answered Cirilla.
"That does not matter Ciri, if a blacksmith is passionate about their work then it is clear that what they forge is worth putting your trust in," explained Silus.
"Thank you Silus," said Cirilla, "do not worry about paying me for the armour, regardless of our deal, I

cannot thank you enough for giving me the boost I
needed in forging that armour, and for saving me
earlier."
"You know I cannot..." replied Silus.
"Just let it go Silus," interrupted Cirilla, "we are even
now, agreed?"
"As you wish," said Silus, "well I best get going, take
care of yourself Ciri."

Silus hugged Cirilla lightly, Cirilla hugged Silus back.
As the two stepped apart, Cirilla watched Silus' wings
unfold from his back, Silus then smiled and turned to
face west. Silus took three steps forward before taking
off into the sky and soaring straight up into the sky.
Cirilla and Dragonnoth watched as Silus became a
speck in the sky before disappearing from view,
Cirilla and Dragonnoth then walked into the forest
heading back to the city.

~

The sky had turned a bright orange, the air was still,
only a few thin clouds filled the sky, the sun had
disappeared beyond the skyline of the city. Amelia
was still standing in the courtyard facing east, Fiona
emerged from the Keep and saw Amelia standing to
the right of the doors, Fiona looked left to see that the
phoenix guards had set up a small encampment in
the Keep courtyard. Fiona approached Amelia slowly,
as she got close Amelia turned to see Fiona.

"Amelia, I just wanted to say that I am sorry for a little while ago," said Fiona.

"That is ok Fiona, I hope the Duke was not offended for my outburst," replied Amelia.

"No, he understands completely," responded Fiona, "how does it look?"

"Well, Silus' magic has calmed down again, I believe that the fight between Silus and Shiento ended in a draw," explained Amelia, "but I cannot sense much else at this moment, unless his magic is resonating I cannot sense anything outside the city."

"Well, can you tell if Silus has collapsed or if he is still on the move?" asked Fiona.

"I could tell that he felt his fatigue during the fight, but I do not think he has collapsed from exhaustion," answered Amelia.

"You should go get some rest Amelia, you look tired," said Fiona.

"I am fine Fiona, I do not need to rest just yet," replied Amelia.

"You sound just like Silus," chuckled Fiona.

"What is that?" asked Amelia pointing to a small speck that appeared in the sky.

Fiona looked up to see what Amelia was pointing at, as the speck grew larger, Amelia and Fiona could make out that whatever it was had wings, as the speck got closer they could make out that it was a human body attached to two large wings. Amelia then smiled and placed her right hand on Fiona's left shoulder and shook her a little.

"It is Silus," chuckled Amelia.

"He made it here after all," replied Fiona, "sorry I doubted you Amelia."

"It does not matter, what matters is Silus is here," responded Amelia.

"But, if that is Silus, then where are the dragonkins?" asked Fiona, "was it not the plan for Silus and the dragonkins to arrive here together?"

"I guess things in the Dark Forest did not go as well as planned?" pondered Amelia.

As Silus flew over the edge of the city, several Qurendian soldiers looked up and saw Silus swoop over the city. Amelia and Fiona watched as Silus hovered over the Keep courtyard, a large group of soldiers rushed out of the barracks and surrounded Amelia, Fiona and Silus as he landed.

"Halt intruder!" shouted one of the guards.

"Stand down everyone, it is only Silus," replied Fiona calmly.

"Lady Fiona is right!" called out Captain Frederick as the Keep doors open, "everyone, stand down."

As Silus stood in front of Fiona and Amelia, his wings disappeared into his back, Silus looked up at Amelia. Amelia ran at Silus and launched herself onto him, wrapping her arms around him. As Amelia rested her head onto Silus's right shoulder, Silus wrapped his arms around her waist.

"I knew you would be alright," whispered Amelia.

"Of course I am, I was not going to stay away from you that long," replied Silus as he smiled.
"That is a rather interesting look Silus," said Fiona as she approached the two.

Silus and Amelia separated, Fiona then quickly gave Silus a hug, Captain Frederick approached them as the guards began heading back towards the barracks. Fiona and Amelia examined Silus' clothing and armour.

"Where did you get this stuff?" asked Fiona.
"Well the armour is a long story," answered Silus.
"I am sure we would all like to hear it Silus, however I believe you wished to speak with the Duke," said Captain Frederick, "so please, come this way."
"Right you are Captain," replied Silus, "lead on."

Captain Frederick turned and led Silus, Amelia and Fiona into the Keep. Silus looked around and took in the décor of the Keep. Amelia kept examining Silus' jacket and armour as they walked.

"So Captain, how is your wife?" asked Silus.
"Not too bad, thank you Silus," answered Captain Frederick, "I have a daughter now too."
"Really, what is her name? How old is she?" queried Silus.
"Her name is Abigail, she is four years old now," answered Captain Frederick.
"Wow, time flies by without us knowing, right?" asked Silus.

"Indeed it does," responded Captain Frederick. "Although, this place has not changed much, except for the fortifications outside," stated Silus.
"Well, I am sure the Duke will be happy to see you again," explained Captain Frederick.
"Again?" asked Silus, "the Duchy of Qurendia has not changed?"
"See for yourself," answered Captain Frederick.

Captain Frederick opened the door to the study and beckoned Silus to enter first. As Silus stepped into the study he looked over to the window and saw Duke Horacio standing there, the Duke turned to face Silus.

"Horacio?" said Silus in shock, "you are still functioning?"
"It is good to see you too Silus," chuckled Horacio.

Silus and Horacio met in the centre of the room, as they shook hands, Amelia, Fiona and Captain Frederick entered the room and the door closed behind them. Horacio gestured for everyone to sit down. Silus remained standing but walked over to a counter and began pouring everyone cups of water, and gradually handing out the cups to everyone.

"So, if you are still alive, I am assuming that your mechanics managed to create the replacements limbs and body parts that were damaged in that raid?" asked Silus.

"It is as you say, my boy," responded Horacio, "though, even with those replacements, my time grows short."

"What do you mean replacements?" asked Fiona.

"In the last bandit raid, where the rest of my family was killed, I was also badly wounded, and in my people's last attempt to save me," explained Horacio, "they replaced my damaged limbs and heart with mechanical parts, so I am not necessarily human, not anymore."

"Not true Horacio, your body may be half human, half machine, but you are the true architect of your actions and therefore your freewill is your own," described Silus, "therefore, to all possible explanations or possibilities, you are still human."

"I still find it amusing how you look like a normal human, but possess power and wisdom far beyond that of any human alive," replied Horacio.

"Same can be said for Amelia or Fiona though," responded Silus.

"Very true my boy," replied Horacio, "however your new attire can be considered rather disconcerting."

"Well it is a slightly long story, but I can shorten it if you like?" joked Silus.

"Go on then," chuckled Horacio.

"Well after getting to the elven city, Birthaina, I quickly discussed battle plans with Randalene and her Commanders, after which I asked if Randalene could recommend an armourer for me," explained Silus, "so I get introduced to Cirilla, who showed me an experimental metal she had created, but not tested or sold, so I tested it then asked her to make me some armour."

"Just like that?" asked Amelia, "a small test and you were satisfied with a new untried metal?"

"Well considering I have had demons hitting the plates on this jacket and they have not left a scratch, shows my trust in Cirilla was well placed," answered Silus, "anyway, after Cirilla made the armour plates, Randalene came by the shop and brought a cloth that was made by her ancestor, the cloth was nothing special until her ancestor imbued demonic ash into the fabric, I accepted Randalene's gift and applied Cirilla's armour plating to it, and here is the finished product."

"Why would an elf imbue demonic ash into anything?" questioned Fiona.

"That is because, Randalene's ancestor was trying to gain an advantage over the demons," explained Silus, "this fabric allows whoever wears it to partially sense a demonic presence, which I have noticed does work, if the demon's presence is strong enough."

"Fair enough, well regardless of my previous comments, this look does suit you," said Horacio, "you wearing chainmail or even plate armour just looked absurd."

Silus laughed as he poured himself a second glass of water, Silus then turned and sat down in a chair opposite Horacio and to Amelia's left. Silus left out a heavy, exhausted sigh as his weight was fully supported by the chair.

"By the way Lady Phoenix, have you received a second message yet?" asked Horacio.

"No, but now that you mentioned it, I read the message but it was signed C.C. and I have no idea who that could possibly be," explained Amelia.

"C.C, you mean the Crimson Crusader?" queried Silus.

"What was that Silus?" asked Fiona.

"You said this message was signed C.C." answered Silus, "C.C. stands for Crimson Crusader..."

"How..." stammered Amelia.

"So, the vigilante is still in Qurendia... how interesting," pondered Silus as he looked up to see a board with several stabbing marks on it, "I am assuming that the vigilante has been in contact with you Horacio?"

"That is correct," responded Horacio.

"Amelia, can I see this message, or at least know what it concerned?" asked Silus.

"Sure thing Silus," answered Amelia as she pulled out the rolled up message from a pouch on her belt.

"Thank you my dear," responded Silus as he took the rolled parchment from Amelia and unrolled it.

"So, what do you think Silus?" questioned Horacio.

"What do I think about what?" queried Silus.

"The vigilante, what do you think about this person?" asked Horacio.

"I do remember this vigilante living here the last time I was here," answered Silus, "I never had a run in with this vigilante, and as far as I know, the vigilante had not made a large impact back then, so I am guessing this person had not been in Qurendia for long at that time."

"And what about this person's identity?" asked Captain Frederick, "there are tens of thousands of people in this city that are worried who is this person, and whether or not to feel safe or insecure knowing such a person should be allowed to live amongst us."

"I understand your concerns and the concerns of your citizens Captain," answered Silus, "however, from what I have heard of this vigilante, this person clearly means no harm to any civilian, they are only a threat to the bandits and criminals who see Qurendia as their hunting ground."

"I thought you would say that Silus," said Horacio calmly, "however I would like to ask a favour if you have time to indulge me."

"Well, I do not have a great deal of time here," responded Silus, "after all, I find myself at the centre of this war between demons and the races of this world."

"Of course, I was only going to ask that you look into this vigilante, determine who this person is, and if possible establish a real mutual trust, rather than this hope filled trust that we have had to deal with since the vigilante's first appearance."

"Well that is the issue that I find in front of me right now," explained Silus.

"What do you mean Silus?" asked Fiona, "does this have anything to with the last part of your fight in the Dark Forest, where Shiento showed up?"

Silus looked at Fiona in surprise, Fiona stared at Silus with a look of curiosity. Silus then turned his gaze to Amelia before taking a deep breath.

"How do you know Shiento showed up?" asked Silus. "Amelia was able to sense your magic every time you used it," answered Fiona, "and she described your last magic resonation as 'resonating in unison' with your enemy."

"Fiona explained that your magic would not resonate like that if you were fighting a demon, so she ruled it out to being a dragon or other beast who would be able to use the elemental magic," added Amelia.

"And based on that, you assumed it was Shiento, correct?" asked Silus.

"Yes," answered Fiona, "she also mentioned that when Shiento showed up you were badly fatigued."

"Well, she was right about that, and yes Shiento did actually show up, but he claimed that he did not actually show up in the Dark Forest to slay me," explained Silus, "I was actually the one to strike first, even given my weakened state."

"So, what actually happened?" asked Fiona, "I thought the plan was you and the dragonkin soldiers were supposed to come here after the battle?"

"It was, unfortunately things did not go as I thought, the demons were stronger than I originally thought, and even with myself and the dragonkins aiding the elves, we lost quite a few troops, both elf and draconic," explained Silus, "that does not include those injured though, given the state the soldiers were in, I ordered Randalene and Commander Drake

261

to march their soldiers to Selania when able to do so, as for the elven citizens, they were evacuated yesterday evening, shortly after my arrival to Birthaina."

"Well, at least you saved any innocent lives," said Horacio.

"Indeed, but what was Shiento's goal for appearing there?" asked Amelia, "you mentioned he claimed to not be there to kill you or anyone else, so what was his goal?"

"Well, for starters he warned me that Lady Drask, his second in command, had made her own plans for my demise," answered Silus.

"Why would he do that?" queried Fiona, "that just does not make sense for him to warn you."

"According to Shiento, he has a very specific plan for how he wants to conquer Jarvlan, and it includes me being in a final massive battle with him," explained Silus, "and it seems he did not fully approve of her plan, which she intends on using Amelia as a hostage to force me to surrender."

"That will not happen," said Amelia standing up quickly.

"Calm down Amelia, no one is saying that you would not be able to stand against her, or that you are inadequate as a fighter," replied Silus.

Amelia looked at Silus who was looking at her as she stood up, Silus gestured to Amelia's seat. Amelia calmly sat back down, Silus then sat forward in his chair.

"Shiento also had another reason for appearing like that," said Silus calmly.

"And what could that have been?" asked Amelia.

"Apparently he wishes for me to meet him in three days, Shiento wants to give me a sporting chance to organise a defence against him for the final battle," answered Silus, "it would seem Shiento is rather mocking me, by showing a small sense of the notion of fair play."

"Do you intend to meet with him?" queried Horacio.

"I think it is a case of, 'do I have a choice?'" pondered Silus, "regardless, I will meet with him, in the meantime, I can have a small look into your vigilante while trying to dispel Lady Drask's plan to kidnap Amelia."

"Thank you Silus," replied Horacio.

"Have you or Captain Frederick got any hints of where I should begin looking?" asked Silus, "I understand the vigilante operates across the city, but I cannot just wander the streets in the hope the vigilante shows up."

"How about the north west side of the city?" asked Amelia.

"Why would you recommend that?" queried Silus.

"Well, once me and Fiona were escorted to the Keep I noticed someone standing on a rooftop to the west in a crimson coloured cloak and hood," explained Amelia, "and after the assassin was dealt with I noticed someone who was dressed in a similar fashion atop the church spire where the demon had tried hiding."

"Fair enough," said Silus, "well, I could do with a stroll through the city, so I will have a brief look this evening, but ultimately I should not be doing much as I should be resting."

"If you should be resting then just start your investigation tomorrow morning," urged Fiona.

"I could, but there are some things that you just do not see in the morning light," replied Silus.

"If you insist on going for a walk this evening, then I shall accompany you," added Amelia.

"I was not actually going to give you a choice on that point, this message was addressed specifically to you, so maybe our combined presence would pull this vigilante out into the open."

"Take care you two, even though this vigilante has reduced the criminal activity of bandits within the city, there are still a large number of bandits who live here," explained Horacio, "this goes especially for you my boy, you have admitted to being fatigued from your series of fights, and without you, Shiento will sweep across the land without any resistance."

"But earlier..." said Fiona.

"Let it go Fiona, Horacio can be quite partial to certain people," explained Silus as he stood up, "coming Amelia?"

"With you... of course," answered Amelia standing up too.

Silus held out his right elbow for Amelia to hold. Fiona, Horacio and Captain Frederick all watched as the two quietly left the study, Fiona shook her head in disbelief as Silus and Amelia disappeared from view.

Horacio looked at Fiona, then waved for Captain Frederick to leave.

"Something troubling you, my dear?" asked Horacio. "I was just thinking that Silus has never taken anything serious, and even given his current physical and mental state, he is not changing much," explained Fiona, "one of these days, Silus will get himself into a situation and I fear he will not take it seriously enough before he gets hurt."
"Sounds just like what Silus would end up doing," replied Horacio, "but I would not worry too much about him Lady Wythernspine, Silus is far stronger than he appears, and I know for a fact he has not ever used more than twenty percent of his full power."
"How could you quantify that?" asked Fiona.
"When you get the chance, ask Silus about his Omega Wheel," smiled Horacio.
"Omega Wheel, what could you know of such a thing?" queried Fiona.
"I will not explain it, I believe Silus should be the one to do that," answered Horacio, "for now, I think I shall go to see the engineer, so feel free to grab something to eat, or go for a stroll, for the evening is still young, as are you."

Horacio stood up and bowed briefly to Fiona, before walking towards the study door. Fiona stood up and walked to the window, as she gazed out over the city, she noticed that the sky had turned to a royal blue colour. As Fiona stood alone in the study, a light breeze flicked at Fiona's long hair. As Fiona gazed out into the growing darkness, she began to gaze through her dragon eyes, she noticed a small figure jumping from rooftop to rooftop, and Fiona knew that it would be Lady Drask. Fiona then ran out of the study and back to her room to grab her armour.

Chapter 8: Separated, Now Reunited

As Silus and Amelia walked across the north bridge out of the Keep courtyard and into the city, Silus gazed up to the sky, and noticed the sky had become freckled with stars. Amelia and Silus walked through the city streets, Silus asking Amelia about how she and Fiona dealt with the assassin sent to kill the Duke, occasionally Silus would laugh at the details of how Amelia and Fiona struggled so much.

"So that is how it happened," said Amelia, "he was a pain in the arse to deal with, but we eventually got him."
"Playing on his ego was a lovely touch," replied Silus as he smiled at Amelia, "I am glad that you and Fiona are safe though."
"Well, it is not like we would have just waited for you to come and save the day," mocked Amelia, "one less job for our saviour."

Silus stopped chuckling, Amelia noticed as the smile on Silus' face disappeared quickly, Amelia held Silus' arm tighter and rested her head on his shoulder.

"Sorry, that was uncalled for," apologised Amelia.
"Do not worry, it is fine," said Silus, "you know, I used to hate that."
"Hate what?" asked Amelia.
"Being called a saviour," answered Silus, "when the King of Selania adopted me, all I ever heard was, 'one

day the world will herald you as a saviour', or, 'one day you will be called upon to save the people of this world', I hated hearing that every day."

"So, you do not hate that anymore?" asked Amelia, "being called a saviour?"

"I learnt a while ago that, if you are destined for something, then it will happen, no matter how hard you try to stop it," explained Silus, "but regardless, Shiento has been allowed to go on for too long, regardless of what the world chooses to do, I must fulfil my duty and end that traitorous bastard."

"I see, so you still believe you have no choice in what you do?" queried Amelia.

"I can choose what to do, but there are something's that just have to be done," explained Silus, "and can you honestly choose to ignore Shiento, especially now after he has destroyed Flammehelm."

"I guess you are right," replied Amelia.

Silus and Amelia continued walking, after a while Silus and Amelia came to a terrace area, with a huge balcony area where you could look out over the mountains, if it were light enough. Silus and Amelia continued walking heading towards the western end of Qurendia. As they walked under a bridge they noticed the houses were slightly bigger and the streets were wider. Silus slightly turned his head to the left and glanced out the corner of his eye over his shoulder.

"Something wrong?" asked Amelia.

"Feels like we are being watched," answered Silus quietly, "keep going, we can take a right up there, it is a dead end, but that will not be a problem."
"Alright, if that is how you want to play it," replied Amelia.

Amelia held Silus' arm even tighter, as they rounded the corner into a dead end street, Silus conjured his dragon sabre into his left hand. Silus and Amelia walked halfway down the street before stopping. They turned around waiting to see who comes round the corner.

"Do you think it is the vigilante or just a bandit?" asked Amelia quietly.
"I am thinking, not a bandit, I can sense that something is different about this person," answered Silus.

Silus and Amelia watched as someone stepped out from round the corner, the person's whole body was covered in a cloak with a hood up, Silus could not make out if the cloak was crimson coloured or not, as the person stood in the middle of the street facing Silus and Amelia, the cloaked figure then took a few steps forward to stand in the light shining down from a nearby street lamp.

"It is nice to see you both here," came a female voice, "kind of a shock to see you here Silus, I knew Amelia was here, and I sent that letter, but it is good to see you again."

"How do you know me?" asked Amelia as she moved slightly behind Silus.
"Oh, come on Amy, surely you remember me?" queried the woman.

Amelia looked at the cloaked stranger, her face riddled with confusion, Amelia looked at Silus who closed his eyes, and let out a heavy sigh and then smiled.

"I recognise your voice, and I must say, I am rather surprised that you would have ended up here of all places... Samantha," said Silus.
"Samantha?" said Amelia in disbelief, "as in my sister, Samantha Phoenix?"
"Right you are," replied the woman as she removed her hood.

As Samantha lowered her hood, Silus and Amelia saw a young beautiful face, Samantha has long brunette hair, plaited into a three braid ponytail. Her eyes were a bright red colour that almost shone in the dark street. Amelia looked at Samantha, her body paralysed with shock, Silus looked at Amelia before wrapping his left arm around her shoulders.

"Amelia, hey Amelia," said Silus.
"Wha... what?" stammered Amelia.
"No need to act so shocked, just relax, it is your sister," replied Silus.

"I know, but I have not seen her in years and we all thought she was dead," explained Amelia, "why did you not send a letter or anything?"

"I wanted to, believe me sis, I wanted to," replied Samantha, "it was just, well... it is difficult to explain."

"What could be so difficult to explain that you could not send a letter to me, mum and I were so worried about you and we had no idea where you had gone," said Amelia as tears came into her eyes.

"Amelia calm down," said Silus calmly as he tightly hugged Amelia, "Samantha, seeing as you have lived here a number of years now, I am guessing you got a house or something?"

"Yes, it is not that far from here either, I live here in the noble quarters," answered Samantha, "come, it is this way."

"Lead on Samantha," replied Silus.

Silus wrapped his left arm around Amelia's shoulder, Samantha put her hood back over her head and began walking down the main street into the western district. Silus and Amelia followed Samantha in silence, the streets were void of anyone, except for Silus, Amelia and Samantha.

"Silus," whispered Amelia.

"Yeah?" asked Silus quietly.

"Do you not find it weird that Samantha would appear here, when we all thought she had been killed?" queried Amelia.

"Just because you did not hear from her, does not mean she was dead," explained Silus quietly, "besides it was a surprise for me to find her here as well."

Samantha turned and climbed up a staircase between two shops, as Silus and Amelia reach the bottom of the staircase, they could see Samantha walking towards a large mansion. As Silus and Amelia reached the top of the staircase, they looked around to see they were in a square shaped garden area in front of the mansion. The garden had two large maple trees standing on either side of the main pathway leading from the staircase to the mansion doors, there was a circular pathway that lead around the maple trees. The outside of the circle was filled with a vast array of flowers and bushes.

"Welcome to my home," said Samantha.
"This is where you live?" asked Amelia.
"Not too shabby, Sammy," replied Silus.
"Do not call my Sammy, you know I hate that Silus," said Samantha angrily.
"I know I was just kidding with you," chuckled Silus, "but I am wondering how you got a place like this, being a vigilante is not exactly a well-paid vocation."
"Agreed, but before I actually started the Crimson Crusader myth, I actually did a fair few bounty hunts here in Qurendia," explained Samantha, "so I earned quite a bit from those and then I also got a steady stream of income because I bought out a few shops and get shares from their profits."
"Impressive," said Silus.

"Come on, let us get inside," replied Samantha as she walked towards the front door.

Silus and Amelia followed Samantha into the mansion, inside Silus looked around to see the walls decorated with pictures of Flammehelm and portraits of the Phoenix family. The floor had a long red carpet that lead straight down towards the kitchen area, to the left of the door was a living room, to the right a small study area and a staircase leading upstairs. Amelia looked around and saw a portrait above the living room fire place, the portrait was of Silus standing with two young girls with brunette hair standing at his side. The living room had two large couches positioned either side of a low table, the floor was covered in a red carpet.

"Brings back memories does it not sister?" asked Samantha.
"I had forgotten that we had met Silus before," answered Amelia, "mother sent me to find him and I did not even know who I was looking for, nor did I truly recognise him when I found him, and when I brought him to mother, even she did not recognise him."
"That is partially my fault, I was playing with potions before and one of my bottles exploded, the smoke produced from that erased parts of your memories," explained Samantha, "I am sorry Amelia, it must have been hard dealing with my disappearance."

Silus walked into the living room after having a quick look around the mansion. He looked at Amelia and Samantha as they hugged, Samantha then looked at Silus and smiled.

"I wondered where that portrait went," said Silus, "I did not see it in Flammehelm."
"From what I have heard, there is not anything left to see of Flammehelm," replied Samantha as she sat on a couch.
"Unfortunately," sighed Silus.
"I know of Flammehelm's destruction, I also know that you were there Silus, you held the demons back while the city evacuated," detailed Samantha, "but what I do not know, is how you end up getting from the far east, to the far west, especially when you have a war on your hands."
"It is the war that has caused me to make such a trip," replied Silus, "but on the grounds of what you do or do not know... what have you heard of Cynthia?"
"My mother?" asked Samantha, "I know she evacuated with the rest of Flammehelm, I assumed you got Flammehelm to evacuate to Urendos and that is the last I have heard of her."

Silus took a seat on the couch opposite Samantha and rested his elbows on his knees and placed his head in his hands. Amelia sat next to Samantha, Amelia held Samantha's left hand with her right hand.

"What... what is wrong?" asked Samantha.

"Samantha... mother, she..." stammered Amelia as tears covered her eyes.

"I am sorry Samantha, but your mother is dead," said Silus.

"That... that cannot... it cannot be true," stammered Samantha as Amelia hugged her tightly.

Samantha and Amelia hugged each other, their sadness showing in their tears. Silus stood up and walked around the low table to sit next to Samantha on the opposite side to Amelia, Silus then hugged Samantha and Amelia as the two cried over the loss of their mother.

~

In the Dark Forest, Commander Drake and Randalene were beginning their march to Selania. Several soldiers were placed on carts being pulled by horses. Dragonnoth was pulling four glaive throwers in a line behind the main group, Cirilla was walking beside Dragonnoth.

"So, you are Dragonnoth?" asked Cirilla.

"Indeed I am, I am one of Silus' other siblings, me, him and Shiento are all that is left of our family," answered Dragonnoth.

"But you were Silus' Pegasus earlier?" queried Cirilla.

"When the former King of Selania adopted Silus, our parents only allowed it if I was to be taken with Silus," explained Dragonnoth, "however, the King did not want a dragon wandering in or around the city, so

I was a distant guard for Silus, and when Shiento attacked Selania before, I helped Silus escape." "Could you not have faced Shiento and forced him away from Selania?" questioned Cirilla. "Things are never quite as simple as they appear," answered Dragonnoth, "you see, without being trained in the magic that Silus or I possessed, I would not have been able to stand against Shiento any better than Silus would have." "I see, still, how is it that you came to be a Pegasus?" asked Cirilla, "even shape shifting into a Pegasus would have left your magical aura exposed." "You are right about that my dear, but Silus and I had learnt as much about our magic as we could, following the attack on Selania," explained Dragonnoth, "then to help stop Shiento from sensing us, Silus used an enchantment spell to convert my form into Legolas, which altered my aura and Silus' so Shiento could not track us, it was also our disappearance that lead to Shiento leaving Selania, without us there, Shiento had no reason to completely wipe out all life there." "Is that because he was only there to kill you two, because you were the greatest threat to his plans?" queried Cirilla. "That is correct," answered Dragonnoth. "I see, so that is how all this fighting began," replied Cirilla. "Well, it all started because of the prophecy of the 'Dragonborne King', Shiento then hated Silus and sought to end the prophecy before it could come to fruition," explained Dragonnoth, "after the attack on

Selania, Shiento then tried boosting his power by killing other dragons and then the worst of it all, becoming the demon dragon to reach his full power."

Cirilla looked up at Dragonnoth in shock, Dragonnoth continued looking forward as they walked. The long convoy of soldiers and weapons marched quietly through the forest heading east along the same path that Silus and the dragonkins used the day before.

"It seems like your lives have been filled with nothing but fighting and death," said Cirilla.
"I cannot deny that, but I can say that there have been good points, we have met some people who are truly amazing, like yourself making that armour," explained Dragonnoth, "and there are people like Lady Fiona, Commander Drake, Lady Amelia who all stood up to make a difference in this war."
"Does not mean that you had to choose this life," replied Cirilla.
"If there is one thing that me and Silus has learned in our lifetime, it is that you do not often get to choose the life you lead, but you get to choose where this life leads you," responded Dragonnoth, "it is true, that we have seen many deaths and fights, but it is also true that the friends and alliances we have forged will never break, and that is what keeps us going, knowing that we can face the enemy, with people who have the courage to stand up with us."
"So, you do not regret anything?" asked Cirilla," there is nothing you would change about your life?"

"Even if we could turn back time to change something, we are content to let things stay as they are, because if we changed something, would we still have met all these people? would we have made these alliances?" explained Dragonnoth, "regardless of how you view this situation, we are where we are supposed to be, and it is in that knowledge and wisdom, that Silus and I have pushed through the hard times and have gotten to the point where we can nearly see the end of our struggle, and we can start hoping for a much brighter future."

The convoy continued marching through the forest, Cirilla grew tired, but climbed onto Dragonnoth's back and lay there asleep. Dragonnoth forged a path out of stone to cross the gorge where Silus and the dragonkins landed the day before. The night was still, only a gentle breeze accompanied the convoy of elves and dragonkins to Selania.

~

In Selania, Celestia was sitting in a bedroom in the palace, she was wearing a pale blue dress, with a white dressing gown over the top. Celestia sat at a dresser, brushing her long blonde hair with a dark brown brush. Suddenly there was a loud knock on the bedroom door, Celestia put the hairbrush down before turning in her stool to face the door.

"Come in," said Celestia.

As the door opened, Celestia could see that is was the Guard-Captain of Selania entering through the door.

"Forgive me Lady Celestia, I hope I am not keeping you up?" said the Guard-Captain humbly.
"Not to worry Captain, what seems to be the problem?" asked Celestia.
"A very large contingent of dwarves has arrived outside the city, they have also brought with them siege weapons, such as cannons and trebuchets," answered the Guard-Captain, "they have stopped outside the city and one dwarf has come forward as King Urthrad and insists on speaking with whoever is in charge of Selania."
"So, they know that the King is dead?" queried Celestia.
"Only after I explained the situation to them," responded the Guard-Captain, "once I mentioned that you are our acting ruler for the time being, he then insisted on being let in alone to see you."
"So where is King Urthrad now?" asked Celestia.
"I asked him to wait in the throne room, given that he arrived with an army, I have had two soldiers stand with him," explained the Guard-Captain.
"Very well, I shall speak with him," replied Celestia, "please inform King Urthrad that I will be down shortly."
"As you wish milady," responded the Guard-Captain.

Celestia stood up and walked into the bedroom wardrobe to get changed, the Guard-Captain left the room and made his way down the corridor towards a large spiral staircase on the east side of the palace. Celestia got changed into a dark purple dress, which only stretched down to her shins, she also wore black boots. As Celestia made her way out of the room and towards the staircase on the east side of the palace, she glanced out of the windows to see the city being lit up by street lanterns. Celestia stopped as she reached the staircase, she turned to look out of the window.

"I wonder how they are all doing?" pondered Celestia, "I just hope they are all alright."

Celestia then turned and descended down the stairs. As she reached the bottom of the staircase, she could hear the Guard-Captain and Urthrad voices echoing from beyond a door at the end of the corridor. Celestia walked slowly towards the door, as she approached the door it opened. As Celestia stepped through the doorway into the palace throne room, she looked to her left to see the Guard-Captain talking with Urthrad. Celestia walked towards them slowly, around the throne room, were several dragonkin and Selanian guards standing to attention.

"King Urthrad, it is good to see you again," said Celestia.
"Not as good as it is to see you well, my Lady," replied Urthrad humbly, "from what I have heard, things for yourself and Silus have been rather hectic?"

"Indeed, first an assassin sent to Selania, then an attack on Birthaina and another assassin sent to Qurendia," explained Celestia.

"Aye, Worbarg lies in ruins too," sighed Urthrad.

"The demons attacked your city too?" asked Celestia, "but Silus did not..."

"Slow down lass," urged Urthrad, "as for the demons, nay, they did not attack Worbarg, however I fear that the huge demonic presence in our world has started affecting the beasts of our land."

"I see," replied Celestia

"We were already mobilizing our forces to bring our artillery and troops to Selania to help with those blasted demons," responded Urthrad, "however what we could not have predicted, was that the critters known as podra, a subterranean mole like creature, just in case you are unaware of these beasts."

"So, these podra have destroyed Worbarg?" asked Celestia, "what about your people? You have not marched both civilian and soldiers here have you?"

"Of course not, and now that you mention my people, I am afraid I must apologise," said Urthrad.

"Apologise?" queried Celestia, "what for?"

"In my haste to evacuate my people when the podra appeared, my soldiers were already marching but my civilians could not get to the same path as the soldiers and I had to send them on the direct tunnel to Urendos, where I hope they will be safe," explained Urthrad.

"So, your citizens are either en route to Urendos or are currently in Urendos?" asked Celestia.

"That is correct my Lady, I am sorry to be burdening your people in this troubling time," answered Urthrad.

"Actually, I would agree that you made the right decision," replied Celestia, "we cannot keep filling Selania with refugees from the various races, and our troops are a heavy presence here already.

"Lady Celestia, what should we do, the elven people are already filling the arena and we have very little room left in Selania to house anymore people," asked the Guard-Captain.

"Do not stress yourself about me and my men Captain," said Urthrad calmly, "me and my men will remain outside the city walls, we have already started setting up camp and will remain outside readying our weapons for the oncoming battle."

"You do not even know if Shiento will launch another attack on Selania yet, for all we know he could attack Qurendia, and all we could do at this moment is let that attack happen because we cannot mobilise fast enough," argued the Guard-Captain angrily.

Celestia and Urthrad looked at each other and smiled, the Guard-Captain's angry glare moved from Urthrad to Celestia and back to Urthrad. Celestia smile faded before looking at the Guard-Captain.

"Silus believes, no, he knows Shiento will focus on Selania first, for it seems that nearly the entire continent is now housed here within Selania," explained Celestia, "Shiento would not waste time on a small scale battle with Qurendia before he has destroyed the elves, dwarves and humans who now take shelter here, as for the forces of Urendos, Shiento knows that we will react and go wherever he may attack, thus we are here, and it is here that a massive battle between the demon army of Shiento, and the combined force of all races on Jarvlan will take place."

"You assume much my Lady, but have very little to back up your assumptions," replied the Guard-Captain angrily.

"Perhaps you should have more faith in Silus and what he is trying to do," responded Celestia.

The Guard-Captain looked around at Celestia then to the dragonkin soldiers before looking at Urthrad. Lady Celestia then looked at Urthrad, the Guard-Captain then sighed and bowed to Celestia and Urthrad, before turning and walking out of the throne room heading towards the palace doors.

"Well I give the lad credit for passionately thinking of his people, it is soldiers like that make armies as strong as they are," sighed Urthrad, "any final words my Lady?"

"I just want to thank you for bringing troops here, the end of this war is fast approaching, and I am glad that you and Randalene have helped us as much as you can," replied Celestia, "this war can only be won if all the races band together to stand against Shiento."

"Well, even if the different races stood apart in these times, we would only ensure a swift end to our own races," explained Urthrad, "and given that Silus spent a number of years trying to help out all of the races on Jarvlan in turn, how can any of us turn down his call for help at the pinnacle of this blasted war."

"Thank you, my friend," replied Celestia.

"Do not fret about the small details my dear, now I should let you get some sleep, and I should return to my troops," responded Urthrad, "one last question, when does Silus intend on making an appearance here?"

"He was here a few days ago when we were trying to deal with the assassin, since that was settled, he went to the Dark Forest to help Randalene with the horde sent to eradicate the elves," explained Celestia, "if all goes according to plan, he should have reached Qurendia by now and the assassin sent to kill the Duke will be dealt with, so it should not be long for him to return."

"Very good, well when he gets back, hopefully we can get to planning an effective defence," sighed Urthrad.

"And until then, we should do what we can," replied Celestia.

"Indeed, but for now I will bid you goodnight your Ladyship," said Urthrad humbly, "hope you have a pleasant sleep."

"And to you as well King Urthrad," replied Celestia, "I shall see you tomorrow."

Urthrad and Celestia bowed to each other, before Urthrad turned to head out of the throne room and down to the palace door. Celestia turned and headed back through the door that leads to the spiral staircase. The night in Selania grew still, as the soldiers and citizens fell asleep, the sky was clear of clouds and shining bright with millions of stars, the moon was half full, only the gentlest breeze disrupted the stillness of the evening.

~

In Samantha's mansion, Silus, Samantha and Amelia were all sitting on the same couch. Silus and Amelia were explaining how they met and got to Flammehelm, as well as how the evacuation went. Samantha occasionally stopped them to ask a question or two. A butler walked in and brought each of them a cup of tea before leaving the room again in silence.

"So, what happened after you got to Urendos?" asked Samantha as she tried not to cry.
"Well Silus collapsed, we did not know why until he awoke again the next day," explained Amelia, "when he woke, we found out that Shiento had cast a spell trying to remove Silus as a defender, so Shiento's demon Generals who were sent to eradicate all life in Urendos."
"How would demons even get into Urendos, I thought the gates were enchanted to prevent such a thing?" asked Samantha.
"You are correct, the gates are enchanted, but the crevice in the roof of Urendos, that on the other hand is not enchanted," answered Silus, "I also found a traitor in Urendos, the same one who sent an assassin to kill both of you and Cynthia."

"And it was after the assassin was dealt with, that you then left Flammehelm right?" queried Samantha. "Yes and no, I stayed in Flammehelm for a year after that assassin's death, but I was trying to unthread myself from both of your lives," responded Silus, "after the traitor was dealt with I had to rush straight into helping everyone else fight off the demon Commanders, who all wore the Black Steel armour, which is a sign that they were top ranking warriors in Shiento's army."

"The demon who was sent to Selania and Qurendia did not wear such armour," stated Amelia.

"No they did not, and that is because Shiento sent all of his top Commanders to Urendos, he has no other left, well apart from his newly selected ones which are now all dead," explained Silus, "and sadly it was near the end of the demon attack where I was weak and nearly unconscious, that the last of the demon Commanders tried to kill Amelia, but Cynthia pushed her aside and took the blow, it killed her instantly."

"I see, I cannot say I am glad to have been informed of this, this is the gravest news I have ever heard," replied Samantha, "but at least mother had a noble death."

"She did, and honoured along with the soldiers that we lost that day too," stated Silus.

Silus stood up and drank the last of his tea, Amelia and Samantha remained seated and sipped from their cups. Silus gazed at the portrait of him standing next to the younger Amelia and Samantha and smiled.

"All of these things have been occurring, attacks on my home, my family... and, where was I?" sobbed Samantha.

"Do not blame yourself for what has happened Samantha," said Silus, "even if you were there, what could you have possibly changed?"

"I could have... I could have..." stammered Samantha.

"Samantha, there was nothing you could have done," interrupted Amelia.

"Samantha, none of this is your fault, do not hold yourself accountable for what has happened in your absence," added Silus, "what is in the past, should remain in the past, what matters most now, is how you proceed to the future."

Silus yawned and raised his arms to stretch, Amelia held Samantha's left hand with her right. As Samantha looked up to Silus, she placed her cup of tea on the saucer on the table in front of her.

"I am sorry, I have kept you up talking about this when you have had a trying day," said Samantha.

"Oh, do not worry about me," replied Silus, "a good night's rest and I will be ready to go another round with Shiento."

"Let us hope not," whispered Amelia, "I would rather you stayed out of fights for a few days."

"I know, I know, and I will try my best," responded Silus, "that may be hard with Lady Drask trying to capture you or to kill me."

"Regardless of that, you can sleep in one of my guest bedrooms," said Samantha.

"I appreciate the offer my dear, but I cannot sleep very well in a bed," replied Silus, "with that said, if a situation or even a question should bother you, I will be in the garden, good evening miladies."

Silus bowed to Amelia and Samantha before removing his jacket, hanging it on a coat stand inside the door. Samantha watched in amazement as Silus walked out the door and closed it behind him. In the garden, Silus looked around to notice the high walls preventing any of the neighbours from looking in. Silus then walked over to the maple tree to his left, Silus looked up to the branches quickly before lying down against the trunk. Silus rested his head on the trunk, he rested his hands on his stomach. As Silus lay at the base of the tree, he slowly began to close his eyes and a gentle breeze crept across the garden. In the mansion, Amelia sat on the couch looking at the portrait of Silus and younger versions of her and Samantha, Samantha looked at Amelia and smiled.

"So, you do not remember Silus being our friend and protector when we were young?" asked Samantha.
"I told you that I do not," answered Amelia, "and it is not fair for you to use that against me."
"I know, but what do you think of him now?" queried Samantha, "I watched the two of you walk from the Keep, you two seem to be pretty close."
"Well I met him in Selania nearly three weeks ago, and since then we have been nearly inseparable," explained Amelia.
"So, you love him?" asked Samantha.

"Why does that matter?" queried Amelia.

"Hey, I do not mean to upset you sister, I just want to understand how the two of you feel," answered Samantha, "I would be asking him the same questions if he were still in here."

"Well, leave Silus alone, he has been through a lot these last few days, and he has more pressing matters to deal with than your questioning," replied Amelia.

"Woah, you are making it sound like I am doing something wrong, what has gotten into you?" asked Samantha.

Amelia did not answer Samantha, instead she stood up and walked over to the window. Samantha watched as Amelia gazed out of the window, she looked to the left to spot Silus lying under the maple tree. Samantha sat back on the couch.

"What is the matter, Amelia?" asked Samantha, "why are you getting so defensive over this?"

"Because it does not matter how I feel," answered Amelia, "I know how Silus feels and I know I cannot be with him, not now, and not for a while."

"I am not sure I understand," replied Samantha.

Amelia took a deep breath before turning to face Samantha. Samantha looked at Amelia and saw that her eyes were filled with sadness.

"Why can you not love him?" asked Samantha, "are you afraid that he does not love you?"

"It is not that," answered Amelia, "he told me that he does care for me, but he cannot put his feelings first, he has to end this war first."

"Then why do you sound sad about that?" queried Samantha, "to me that sounds like he is promising you that he will stay by your side until the end."

"That is not what is bothering me," said Amelia quietly.

"Then what is bothering you?" asked Samantha.

"The King of Selania is dead, and the question is who would succeed as King," answered Amelia, "although the history of Selania would paint Silus as a villain, they may reconsider knowing that Silus has been the architect of their survival since the moment he came to them."

"What are you talking about?" questioned Samantha.

"Think about it, Selania hated Silus for abandoning them when Shiento first attacked Selania, but Shiento did not kill everyone in Selania," explained Amelia, "Shiento was looking for Silus, and when he realized Silus had left the city, he left as well."

"So Silus knew why Shiento was there, and drew him away," pondered Samantha.

Samantha sat forward and placed her elbows on her knees, she placed her head on her hands. Amelia glanced out the window to Silus once more, before taking a seat on the couch opposite Samantha.

"Silus though once hated by Selania, has always been their protector, and he is making a return to defeat Shiento once and for all," explained Amelia, "and with the way things are going, I would not think it impossible for the Selanian council to make Silus their King."

"So, you believe that if that happens your time with Silus will come to an end?" asked Samantha.

"If Silus becomes King of Selania, then I will not be able to stay with him, the hierarch of Selania rules alone, as it has always been," answered Amelia.

"Silus might not have to face that decision, he may just refuse such a thing and choose to remain a vagabond," explained Samantha, "you need to bear in mind sister, that Silus never puts himself first, he will always do what is best for others before himself."

"In which case he would put the citizens of Selania before himself," said Amelia quietly.

"If he loves you as you love him," replied Samantha, "then he will always put you first."

"Do you really think so?" questioned Amelia.

"What does your heart tell you?" queried Samantha.

Amelia looked down at the floor and stared blankly, Samantha smiled before getting up to walk over to the window. Samantha gazed out into the darkened garden, she could just about see Silus lying under the maple tree.

"What would you do in my place Samantha?" asked Amelia.

"What would I choose?" queried Samantha, "I do not think that would be a hard question to answer."

"What do you mean?" questioned Amelia.

"From what we have discussed, your question is basically a choice between staying with the one I love or deny how I feel and let that love die," explained Samantha, "and to me, that is a simple decision sister, I would choose to stay with the one I love."
"Even if you would not be able to actually be with Silus if he is made King?" asked Amelia.
"You are worrying that Silus will be made King, you do not even know if that will happen," answered Samantha, "so stop worrying sister, you do not need to be worrying about something that may never happen."

Amelia stood up and walked over to Samantha. As they both looked over to where Silus was sleeping they smiled.

"Come on, you got the most amazing dragon in the world choosing to stay around you and protect you," explained Samantha, "what more could you want?"
"You make it sound like a dream," replied Amelia.
"But it does not have to be a dream, dear sister," responded Samantha, "perhaps you should talk to Silus about what he intends to do in regards to how he feels for you, and if he would jeopardise that to simply to become a King."
"I do not think that is something easy to bring into a conversation," sighed Amelia.
"Just think it over," replied Samantha, "in the meantime, I think we should get some rest, it is nearly midnight, come on."

Amelia turned to follow Samantha, as she headed for the staircase in the study across from the living room. The two climbed the stairs simultaneously, the upper floor of the mansion had four rooms, on both the left and right hand side of the house, there was two bedrooms in the front and back corners and between the two bedrooms was their own separate bathrooms.

"That room on the back corner is my room, you can sleep in any of the other rooms, they all have their own bathrooms and if you should need anything, there is my butler and my maid who will get you food or a drink," explained Samantha.
"Thank you, Samantha, but I think a good night sleep will be all I need," replied Amelia, "good night Samantha."
"Good night Amelia, you know, I am really glad we got to meet again," responded Samantha.

Samantha walked into her room at the back left corner of the mansion, Amelia walked to the room on the front left hand side of the mansion. The room had a large King size bed against the opposite wall, the room was decorated with crimson carpets, curtains and bed sheets.

"Any hint who the Crimson Crusader is?" whispered Amelia sarcastically.

Amelia walked over to the window and looked down into the darkened garden, Amelia could just about see two legs sticking out from under the leafy canopy.

293

Amelia smiled as she turned to face the bed, Amelia walked over to the bed and sat on the left side of the bed. As Amelia started to take off her boots, Amelia could hear Samantha running a bath in her bathroom.

"It is easy for you to talk about love," said Amelia quietly, "it is not you who has found love with someone, who could potentially be snatched from you by the laws of man."

Amelia got changed into some silk pyjamas that was left in the bed side cabinet, Amelia used a small wind spell to extinguish the candles and lanterns around the room. Amelia lay down in the bed as the last of the flames died out, in the darkness Amelia breathed slowly and closed her eyes. Samantha had her bath and got changed into her pyjamas, Samantha quietly walked out of her room with a small candle burning in a candle holder, she walked down to the door of Amelia's room. Samantha opened the door to Amelia's room slowly, as Samantha looked into Amelia's room, she could see that Amelia had fallen asleep.

"I guess I will speak to you tomorrow sister," whispered Samantha, "sweet dreams Amelia."

Samantha quietly returned to her room, as she went around the room and extinguished the various lanterns and candles around the room, before getting to her bed and sitting on the edge of the bed.

Samantha placed the candle holder on her bedside cabinet, then she lifted up the bed sheets and covered herself as she lay in the bed, Samantha blow out the candle on the bedside cabinet and then turned to lie on her left side. As Samantha lay still in the bed, the mansion fell quiet, Samantha slowly drifted off as she lay in the bed. In the garden, Silus was turning in his sleep, as he rolled onto his right side. His dragon tail stretched out from his lower spine, the tail reached up to the lower tree branches, as Silus slept peacefully his tail coiled around a tree branch, the tail lifted Silus so he was hanging upside down, his arms crossed over his torso, his legs crossed like he was sitting on the floor.

Chapter 9: Friendships Stand Strong

Morning dawned over Qurendia, the sky painted a light pink as the sun shone over the horizon, the sound of blacksmiths and engineers started to work, as the sound of metal clanging against metal echoed across the city. Amelia awoke to the sound of a blacksmith's hammer, repeatedly banging a few streets over, as her sleepy eyes opened to gaze around the room, she saw that her clothes had been picked up off the floor and replaced with a clean set left on the dressing cabinet to her left. As Amelia sat up in the bed, she could also make out the sound of someone grunting and swinging a sword outside.

"What is he up to now?" asked Amelia.

As Amelia climbed out of bed, she covered herself with a red dressing gown hanging on a hook next to the bed. As she walked over to the window to see Silus standing on the central path in the garden swinging his dragon sabres, practising his technique.

"Do you ever stop to relax?" Amelia asked herself.

Amelia then turned and walked to the dressing cabinet and pulled her clothes off the hangers, Amelia then looked up into the mirror to notice her hair was slightly fuzzy, Amelia then put her clothes back onto the hooks and then entered the bathroom. As Amelia began to run a bath, there was a knock at the bedroom door. As Amelia walked to the door to answer it, a maid let herself in.

"Oh, forgive me, my Lady," said the maid as she saw Amelia tying up her dressing gown.
"No, it is quite alright," replied Amelia, "is something wrong?"
"No, not at all, my Lady, I have your original clothes, they have been washed and ironed," responded the maid bashfully
"Thank you," said Amelia as she took the folded clothes from the maid, "so how long have you worked for my sister?"
"About ten years now, my Lady," replied the maid.
"You do not have to keep calling me 'my Lady', just call me Amelia," chuckled Amelia.
"As you wish," said the maid, "so you are Amelia, Lady Samantha's younger sister?"
"I am, have you met Silus yet?" asked Amelia.
"The gentleman with the twin swords in the garden?" queried the maid, "yes, he is rather charming in his own way, he does seem a bit strange to me."
"How so?" queried Amelia.
"Well, it is not uncommon for people to wake early to start working the forge or building a mechanical device, but there are not many who start the day by sitting cross legged with balls of magical energy floating around them, or swinging swords around like they are envisioning a battle," explained the maid.
"Well Silus is a rather unusual dragon I guess," laughed Amelia.

"Indeed, but I hope I am not out of line for saying such things?" asked the maid.

"Do not worry, even if you had said those things straight to Silus, he would not be offended in the slightest," explained Amelia.

"From what I have heard of Silus, he is a bit of an isolationist, so I was wondering why he is here, and staying in plain view of everyone?" questioned the maid.

"Well I suppose the first thing to say is that he is trying to end this war between the races of this world and the demon army," explained Amelia, "but as for why he is here, as in outside this mansion, that is because he was with me when my sister appeared."

"I believe my Lady mentioned that you two are lovers, is that true or is that simply my Lady spreading gossip and rumours?" queried the maid.

Amelia looked around the room quickly, then turned and entered the bathroom to stop the running water filling the bath. The maid then walked and stood in the bathroom doorway and looked at Amelia.

"I am sorry, I should not have been so nosey," apologised the maid.

"No, it is fine, just…" stammered Amelia, "it is just I am unsure of what will happen across the next few days, and how my relationship with Silus will be affected by the events that will soon happen."

"Oh, I see, but with the way you make it sound, it is almost like a forbidden love novel, and those are just so romantic, perhaps you will get your happily ever after," replied the maid.

"I may not be so fortunate, only time will tell," sighed Amelia.

"Keep your chin up Amelia, where there is hope, there is always potential," said the maid, "anyway, I shall let you have your bath, I should get to making breakfast, any idea on what you would like?"

"Some jam and toast would be lovely, and maybe some tea would be nice," replied Amelia.

"Any particular tea?" asked the maid, "some dragonroot tea or maybe a tea with a fruity flavour?"

"If you have any foltesta tea, that would be amazing," responded Amelia.

"Ah, you and your sister like the same tea then, a refreshing flavour made for those who live in mountain regions, not to worry I shall make a second pot of foltesta for you my dear," answered the maid.

"Thank you, if you bring it to the garden after I have had my bath, I will be there with Silus," replied Amelia.

"As you wish," responded the maid.

The maid closed the bathroom door as she left, Amelia could hear her closing the bedroom door too. Amelia then slowly got undressed and slid into the bath, as the warm bubbly water covered her body, she closed her eyes and relaxed with a deep breath. In the garden, Silus had stopped practising his technique with his swords and had returned to sitting under one of the maple trees, as he sat down he looked up at the sky.

"Where is Lady Drask?" Silus asked himself, "I doubt Shiento would have told me about Lady Drask's plan as a joke to hurry me to Selania, especially since his army is stationary in the south and he headed north to the draconian ruins."

Silus crossed his legs and then held his left hand out in front of him with his palms facing upwards. A small glowing light appeared above his hand as his dragon sabres appeared before revealing them to be the Crystalline Sabres. As Silus looked over the surface of these swords, the light blue tint of the metal speckled with the shining of star light in the metal.

"Well, I cannot leave this city until Lady Drask is dealt with, but can I defeat Shiento with the power I have?" Silus questioned himself quietly, "I suppose I will just have to find that out when I have to stand toe-to-toe with him."

Silus watched as the Crystalline Sabre returned to looking like Silus' dragon sabres. Silus then let the dragon sabre disperse in a quick burst of fire, Silus then let his hands rest on his knees. Silus closed his eyes and began to breathe rhythmically. Eventually, Amelia quietly emerged from the mansion front door, she slowly closed the door behind her. Silus did not move or open his eyes as Amelia slowly approached him.

"Good morning Amelia," said Silus suddenly.

Amelia gasped as if someone had snuck up behind her and tried scaring her. Amelia then sat down in front of Silus as he opened his eyes.

"Did you sleep alright?" asked Silus.
"I did thank you," answered Amelia, "what about you? Do you feel any better?"
"Much better now, thank you, I hope you and Samantha did not stay up too late?" queried Silus.
"Not really, we spoke for about an hour after you came out here, but then we both decided to hit the sack," answered Amelia.
"Fair enough, you two talk about anything interesting?" questioned Silus.
"I would rather not remember that conversation," said Amelia as she looked away.
"May I inquire as to why you say that?" asked Silus.
"Please, just drop it," answered Amelia.
"Amelia, if we are going to stay together and take things forward, you are going to have to trust me enough to talk to me about anything and everything that bothers you," explained Silus, "so I shall ask again, what did you and Samantha talk about?"
"We cannot take things between us further," sobbed Amelia as tears began to flood her eyes.
"Why can we not become a real couple?" questioned Silus.
"Do not pretend you have no grasp of what is happening," replied Amelia as tears began to run down her face.

"What are you getting upset about?" queried Silus, "what have I done to bring this up, or is this got something to do with anything that Samantha said last night?"

"It is because you will have to become the King of Selania, then there is no chance for us to be together," cried Amelia as she lifted her knees and wrapped her arms around them and lowered her head to her knees.

"Ah, now I understand," said Silus.

Silus lifted himself into a crouched position and moved towards Amelia, as he sat next to her he wrapped his arms around her, his right leg sat bent on the ground forming like the back of a chair. As Silus pulled Amelia closer to him, she raised her head to rest on his right shoulder.

"You should not be worried about something that may not happen," said Silus calmly, "I have no intention of becoming the King if it means I am separated from you."

"What?" sobbed Amelia.

"If the Selanian council ask me to become King, then I will turn them down, unless they agree to allow you to rule at my side as Queen," explained Silus, "I helped raise and train you after your father died, but at no point, did I ever consider myself to be in a position where I would replace him, and in the last few weeks that we have been together, I think I have found someone that I would happily devote my life to,

I would never abandon you for anything, I would sooner die then have to force you away."

"Si... Silus," stammered Amelia as she wiped away her tears, "you really mean that?"

"Would I lie to you Amelia?" asked Silus, "the short time we have spent together has been the happiest time in my life, and I would never put myself through a situation that would potentially make you sad."

"What about your duties as a dragon?" queried Amelia.

"My duties have nothing to do with ruling a city, and there is nothing the draconian law, that could force me to become a King against my will," answered Silus, "besides I have always hated this prophecy that predicts that I would be the King of both human and dragon races, I have always thought that destiny was unavoidable, but I have learnt that a destiny can be changed with the right circumstances."

Amelia wiped away the last of her tears, before wrapping her arms around Silus. The two sat quietly for a few moments, they embraced each other more tightly as Amelia moved her head closer to Silus' neck, Silus then rested his head on Amelia's and began rubbing Amelia's right shoulder with his left hand.

"You would really turn down the appointment of being Selania's King, just to be with me?" asked Amelia.

"No matter what anyone else says Amelia, I want you to remember my next words, remember them and never let anyone else change what you have heard me say," answered Silus.

"Ok," said Amelia.

"I will always be with you, in this life and every life we lead beyond this one, time will not keep me from you, I vow to always stand by your side and to never let you face the world alone," stated Silus, "I love you, Amelia."

"I love you too," replied Amelia.

Silus and Amelia lifted their heads and looked at each other for a moment, Silus then lifted his left hand and cupped it to Amelia's right cheek. As the two moved their heads together, Samantha looked out of her living room window to see the two as they kissed. Amelia tightened her arms around Silus' body, as Samantha saw the two, she went to the front door and opened it slowly to step outside.

"Try not to disturb the neighbours you two," said Samantha.

Silus and Amelia stopped kissing and smiled at each other, as Samantha stepped down off the porch and onto the pathway. Silus and Amelia looked up at Samantha to see she was wearing a crimson dress that draped down over her legs to cover her feet, there was a slit in the left side of the dress that stretched from the bottom of the dress to Samantha's knee, her hair was tied back into a long ponytail.

"Good morning to you too Samantha," chuckled Silus, "one question though, do you have anything that is not coloured a bright crimson red?"

"You do not like the colour?" queried Samantha.

"It is not that I do not like the colour, it is just that is the only colour I have seen here at your home, as well as seen you wear since seeing you last night," explained Silus, "do you not get bored of the same colour?"

"It is not a question of growing bored of the colour, it is simply a preference of how I define who I am," explained Samantha.

"A cutthroat vigilante?" joked Silus.

"How dare you, I will have you know..." shouted Samantha in disbelief.

"Relax, I was just kidding around with you," chuckled Silus as he and Amelia began laughing.

"I forgot how irritating you can be sometimes," sighed Samantha.

"But I am not a bad person, I just have a different view of the world," replied Silus.

"And you are the most valuable person in this war," said Samantha.

"The war should not take much longer to finish, Shiento will make his final move soon and then we can end this," responded Silus, "it is simply a matter of when he chooses to play his hand."

"Well I have been thinking about that," stated Samantha.

"About what?" asked Amelia.

"How this war ends," answered Samantha.

"Why would you need to think about that?" queried Amelia, "it will be the same as any other war." "True, but I mean how the final battle will go, and I have come to the decision that I should help," explained Samantha.

"There is no need to force yourself to fight Samantha," said Silus, "this war has seen enough bloodshed, and it will see more than enough blood added to the ground before the final swing of the sword."

"I understand that, but now that the war has reached a point where Shiento could swoop down on us at any moment, it is vital to ensure that any who are able to fight, should be fighting the final battle," explained Samantha, "and I have not forgotten the lessons which you taught me Silus, I request, no, I beg you to let me fight alongside you."

Silus looked at Samantha as her determined eyes met his eyes, Silus looked to Amelia who looked from Silus to Samantha and back. Silus then looked up at Samantha once again before letting out a heavy sigh.

"You do realise, I could not stop you from fighting even if I wanted to," explained Silus, "if you to fight, then the combined forces of all the races will be glad to have you on our side."

"Thank you Silus," replied Samantha, "but what about Qurendia?"

"What about Qurendia are you concerned about?" asked Silus.

"Has the Duke offered any of his troops?" queried Samantha.

"Not yet, I have not actually asked him, I was going to do that today anyway, but he did ask if I would look into who the 'Crimson Crusader' was," answered Silus, "since that is done, I can reply and tell him that the Crimson Crusader is someone he can trust, but I will not reveal you, that would make you a target for bandits."

"No, I think it is time I spoke with the Duke face-to-face," replied Samantha.

Silus sighed as he stood up, before helping Amelia to help feet. Silus then looked around to notice someone flying to the north and south of the mansion, Silus then looked to Samantha then Amelia.

"Looks like this morning is going to be eventful," sighed Silus.

"What are you talking about?" asked Samantha.

"Silus!" came Fiona's voice as she landed on the north side of the garden, "Lady Drask is on the move, I have been trying to chase her all evening."

"We knew she was here already Fiona," replied Silus calmly, "though she has taken her sweet time about making a move."

"Silus get back from her!" called out Fiona's voice as another Fiona landed on the south side of the garden.

"What? Two Fiona Wythernspine's?" questioned Amelia in disbelief.

"Well played Isabel, well played," sighed Silus as he clapped his hands sarcastically.

"Isabel?" asked Samantha, "but there are two Fiona's here?"

"Only in appearance," explained Silus, "one is the real Fiona Wythernspine, the other is Lady Drask otherwise known to me as Isabel Redding."

"But how can we tell who is the real one?" queried Amelia.

"Silus, please that is Lady Drask, you have to believe me," urged the Fiona standing on the south side of the garden.

"Do not listen to her Silus, she is trying to trick you," urged the other Fiona.

"This is going to give me a headache if these two keep doing that," said Silus as he looked at Amelia and Samantha.

"How should we decide who is who?" asked Samantha, "get them to conjure their swords?"

"Would not work, shape shifting magic allows someone to accurately reproduce such things with enchantments," answered Silus.

"What about an item on their body, like that amulet that you and Fiona had?" asked Amelia.

"Same problem as the swords, with enough magic and perception, a spell can replicate that sort of thing too, even if it is an item in a pouch, a shape shifter could manage that," sighed Silus, "I know, a shape shifter cannot replicate memories."

"Memories?" said Samantha, "like a specific memory that you and Fiona share?"

"So long as I know of a memory in Fiona's life, that is evidence enough," replied Silus.

"It is worth a shot, I guess," whispered Amelia.

Silus beckoned the two Fiona's to stand under a maple tree each, as Silus stepped forward he looked from one Fiona to the other.

"Ok here is how it will work, I will specify a date and a point of that day, all you two have to do, is correctly relay the events that actually occurred at that particular time gap," explained Silus, "do you both understand?"

"Yes," replied both Fiona's' in unison.

"Alright then, on the eve of Fiona's thirty-seventh year on earth, so in dragon years, that would make it the day before her second birthday, in case anyone is unsure of the time scale," explained Silus, "what exactly happened between myself and Fiona on that evening?"

The Fionas' looked at each other before nodding at Silus, as Silus took a step backwards, he then pointed to the Fiona under the maple tree to his right.

"First, you can tell us of what happened," said Silus. "That night you waited outside in the courtyard under my window, after I snuck out we went to Selania and sat on the harbour wall, talking, laughing and eating until sunrise which we watched together," explained the north Fiona.

"Alright and now it is your turn my dear," said Silus as he smiled at the other Fiona.

"That evening, we went to the Qurendian mountain region to do some training and hunting, but just before dawn, a large subterranean beast called a podra attacked, the beast was strong and you took a stone spike to your left leg, what we did not know was that Celestia followed us, just after you got hit, she conjured a huge bolt of lightning and slew the beast, we then had to cauterize your wound with a lump of iron heated up with a fire spell," detailed the south side Fiona.

"Perfect, well done Fiona," said Silus turning to face the other Fiona, "as for Lady Drask, your little charade has failed."

"Curse you both," cursed Lady Drask as she reverted to her normal appearance.

Fiona and Samantha watched in shock as the second Fiona's visage faded to reveal Lady Drask, her black leather corset and leggings wrapped around her as the magic faded. Her height slightly increased as her black boots formed around her feet in a cloud of smoke, finally her face blurred as the brunette hair changed to a light blonde and her face changed slightly.

"Now she could do with a makeover," joked Samantha.

"Insolent whore," scoffed Lady Drask as she raised her left hand, "you will pay for that."

"You first bitch," grunted Amelia.

"Amelia wait..." said Silus.

Before Silus could turn around and stop Amelia, her body blurred as she used magic to charge at Lady

Drask. As Amelia got close she conjured a sword into her left hand, Lady Drask had just enough time to conjure her own sword before Amelia could hack at her torso. Silus looked up at Amelia as she and Lady Drask began crossing blades repeatedly, Silus sighed and looked from Fiona in front of him to Samantha just over his shoulder.

"Silus we need to stop her, she is not fighting properly," urged Samantha, "she could be killed."
"She will not fall to Lady Drask," said Silus calmly, "though I do agree with you, her anger has gotten the better of her."
"So, you are just going to stand here?" asked Fiona.
"This is a battle that Amelia has wanted ever since we attacked the Black Fortress, but at that time I engaged Lady Drask," explained Silus, "since then, Amelia has learnt why I was trying to end her quickly, and it is because Lady Drask has a fragment of Shiento's soul bound to her own, but it was done with her permission, so I cannot do anything for her, except to end her existence."
"But…" stammered Samantha.
"Silus is right Samantha," interrupted Fiona, "this is not our fight, Silus will only intervene if Amelia looks like she will lose."
"So that is what you meant by Amelia would not fall to her," replied Samantha, "but that does not mean I cannot."
"Stay out of this Samantha," grunted Amelia loudly.

Samantha stood in shook, she watched as Amelia and Lady Drask start channelling magic in their sword strikes. Silus stood still and crossed his arms over his chest, as the battle between Amelia and Lady Drask heated up, Silus noticed that Amelia's aggression subsided a bit as Lady Drask leapt backwards to stand at the top of the staircase leading down into street below. Amelia went to charge at Lady Drask but found she could not move, as she glanced over her shoulder she noticed Silus had raised his right hand, and that his hand was glowing with a faint white light.

"Silus I thought you were not going to interfere?" asked Amelia angrily.
"Hang on a second Amelia," answered Silus, "Lady Drask has not moved backwards to manoeuvre, but to catch her breath."
"I did not think you would give it a second thought, Silus," gasped Lady Drask.
"I just find it amusing you did not question me when I said earlier that we knew of your plan here in Qurendia," explained Silus.
"Well I did have to maintain my disguise," stated Lady Drask, "but while we are on the topic, how did you know that I intended to force you to surrender by using your pet bird as a hostage."
"You whore, I will end you!" shouted Amelia angrily as she tried to wriggle free of Silus' spell.
"Amelia enough, stand down or I will have to use a knockout spell to put you in an unconscious state," said Silus calmly.

"Fine," sighed Amelia as she let her sword disperse as water onto the ground.

Silus lowered his hand, as he did the white glow disappeared, Amelia's body regained its ability to move. Amelia then walked to stand beside Silus, as she turned to face Lady Drask, her eyes glared at Lady Drask like an arrow flying straight at a target.

"I knew of your plan simply because your Master told me," explained Silus.
"You lie!" screamed Lady Drask, "why would Lord Shiento help you in any situation?"
"As he explained it to me, he has a very specific vision of how his conquest of this continent should happen, and your plan would interfere with that vision," explained Silus, "and so, as the battle in the Dark Forest ended and we started to lick our wounds, he appeared, and in a similar fashion to what you and Amelia just did, we fought before both of us were stricken with a temporary paralysis, after a joining of our draconic might, at which point he detailed why he was there, and how he wanted to proceed from that point."
"That cannot be possible, why would he snitch out my plan to you, he despises you and wishes only for your death, yet he would simply tell you of how I had a solution that would strip you from this world," ranted Lady Drask, "none of what you are saying makes any sense!"

"If you have an issue with what has transpired, then I suggest you take it up with Shiento, at least he will not kill you for questioning him," said Silus angrily. "What are you talking about?" asked Lady Drask, furious with Silus' almost entirely calm demeanour. "Do not tell me that you have not figured it out yet?" queried Silus.

"If you have something to say you filthy punk, then just spit it out!" screamed Lady Drask.

"Shiento did not part with a fragment of his soul simply to give you powers, he did it as it was a new way for him to give himself a chance for resurrection," explained Silus, "if I had slain Shiento in the Dark Forest for example, he could be reborn through you, you are his key to returning to this world, even more powerful than before if you escaped from the final battle, he will take your life and resurrect himself to pray upon the world once more."

Lady Drask looked at her hands, she gritted her teeth as she clenched hands into fists. Her breathing became quick and heavy, as she roared with outrage, she darted towards Silus, Amelia, Samantha and Fiona. Before Amelia could conjure her sword again, she looked up to see Silus conjure his left hand dragon sabre, as Silus' sword crashed into Lady Drask's, a shower of sparks flew off their blades. Lady Drask grunts as she gazes into Silus' eyes.

"You are nothing more than meat to Shiento's feast, just like the rest of us," grunted Silus as he forced

Lady Drask away with a small wind spell, "you are as expendable as the rest of us."

"You lie!" roared Lady Drask angrily.

"Go and ask him then, ask him what would happen if he perished before you, ask him what he truly intends for you," replied Silus loudly, "he will be at the draconian ruins if you are wondering."

"And how would you possibly know that?" asked Lady Drask angrily.

"Simply because he has demanded that I speak with him there in two days' time, which is strange, but it was so I would know what my 'role' in his little conquest scheme is," answered Silus.

"I... I can..." stammered Lady Drask, "I cannot accept that this is true."

"I can end your life here if it would help you," said Silus as he pointed his dragon sabre at Lady Drask.

"I... I do not... How could..." stammered Lady Drask, "How could he use me like this?"

Silus lowered his dragon sabre and nodded to the others to go into the mansion, Amelia did not move a muscle. Samantha and Fiona quietly walked into the mansion, before they stood at the living room window, as they peered out of the window to watch what would happen.

"I... I must... I must mean more to him than that," whispered Lady Drask.

"She is all yours to finish," said Silus.

"If that is how she is going to be, then it is not worth the effort," replied Amelia as she looked at Silus, "it is not considered honourable to strike a defenceless enemy, and to me, it does not matter if they are part demon or not, I will not stain my honour."

"Fair enough," responded Silus, "Isabel!"

"What?" asked Lady Drask as she looked up at Silus.

Silus could see that Lady Drask's eyes were looking at him, but it was as if her body was just an empty shell. There was nothing behind the eyes, no emotion, no life. It was as if Silus' words had torn out Lady Drask's soul.

"Look, whether you take my word seriously or not, but you currently have three options," explained Silus, "you can either surrender now and be given a quick and painless death, you can fight and die with some honour, or leave to confront Shiento about this, whatever you choose, it does not bother me in the slightest, but if you continue to stand there like a lifeless husk, I will just execute you on the spot."

"I... I will not," stammered Lady Drask, "I will not be bullied by you!"

Lady Drask conjured a second sword into her hand, her body began to glow with a dark red energy that waved over her body like a flame. Silus watched as she lunged at him once again, Silus conjured his other dragon sabre into his right hand. As Lady Drask neared Silus, she lifted both her swords to stab Silus, Silus raised his left dragon sabre to block and parry Lady Drask's attack, Silus then tried to slash at Lady Drask's chest. Lady Drask's body blurred as a gust of wind blew across the garden, Silus watched as his dragon sabre passed through Lady Drask's body as if it were air. Silus then conjured a large stone in front of him, which hit Lady Drask in the chest forcing her back.

"You are in no condition to be putting up a real fight, all this aggression is making you sloppy," said Silus. "Stop spouting your blasted teachings!" screamed Lady Drask as her left sword sparked with electricity, "take this, pythlon baz!"

Silus watched as Lady Drask fired a lightning bolt from her left sword at Silus and Amelia, Silus held up his right dragon sabre as the bolt neared him. Amelia watched as Silus' dragon sabre absorbed the attack.

"What the hell!" shouted Lady Drask in disbelief. "This is getting boring Isabel, either fight me properly or get out of here, I grow tired of this pathetic display of swordsmanship," said Silus calmly.
"To hell with you!" roared Lady Drask in outrage.

Silus sighed as Lady Drask lunged at Silus once more, Silus closed his eyes and took a deep breath before raising his right hand dragon sabre lazily. Amelia watched as Silus parried Lady Drask's attack with his eyes still closed, as Lady Drask managed to regain control of her sword, she tried to spin and swing both swords in unison at Silus' torso. Silus turned and moved his right dragon sabre to block Lady Drask's attack. As the two fighter's swords met, more sparks went flying off their blades.

"Fine, have it your way," said Silus, his voice full of disappointment, "sazarach!"

Silus stabbed his left dragon sabre into Lady Drask's lower torso, Lady Drask flinched in pain as Silus' sword easily pierced through her whole body, the blade tip stuck out of her back. Lady Drask coughed up a small patch of blood, which slapped onto the floor at her feet as Silus' sword burst into flames in her stomach. Silus then threw Lady Drask back, she crashed to the floor like a corpse.

"Are you ready to face death with honour now?" asked Silus, his voice growing darker with aggravation, "I automatically cauterized your wound that time, simply because I pity the state you are in, do not think I will be doing that again."
"I will not..." grunted Lady Drask before dropping her swords to grasp her wound with both hands.

Silus watched as Lady Drask curled over in pain, Amelia watched in silence watching as Silus flicked his left dragon sabre cleaning it of blood. Silus then glanced around to Amelia.

"As I said she is not worth the effort," said Amelia. "To be perfectly honest, I agree with you, but it is a case of do I fulfil what my duty would demand of me in this situation?" pondered Silus, "or do I follow

what honour would have me do, which is to show mercy?"
"Let her go, she will either fight us properly another time, die trying to confront Shiento, or she can end her own life," replied Amelia, "there is no need to taint our honour over this waste of flesh."
"Agreed, I will open a portal to send her straight to Shiento," said Silus, "you use a nature spell to throw her through it."
"Very well," replied Amelia.

Silus began chanting quietly, as he did a portal opened just in front of him, as Amelia looked into the portal she could see a set of ruins on a plateau on a mountain side. Amelia then conjured a vine into her hands, as she slung the vine at Lady Drask, Lady Drask dropped to her knees. The vine coiled itself around Lady Drask, Amelia then yanked on the vine tightening the vines. As Silus finished chanting Amelia flicked the vine sending Lady Drask flying through the air and into the portal, Silus then waved his hand and the portal disappeared. Silus let out a heavy sigh as he turned to face Amelia.

"Well that is finally done," said Amelia.
"I think we let that go on too long," replied Silus.
"True but neither of us would allow our honour to be compromised simply because she has part of Shiento's soul bound to her own," stated Amelia.
"I imagine we are going to have hell to pay with those two, and anyone else who hears of this," sighed Silus.

"So long as you are by my side, I do not care," smiled Amelia.
"And by your side I will stay until the end of time, gods willing," said Silus.

Silus and Amelia smiled at each other, before standing next to one another and holding hands before walking into the mansion. Inside Samantha and Fiona were standing by the window, as Silus and Amelia walked into the mansion, Fiona and Samantha turned to stare at them, their faces depicting anger.

"What the hell was that?" shouted Samantha in disbelief.
"You said so yourself Silus, Lady Drask has a fragment of Shiento's soul bound to her own, so why not end her and bring us closer to ridding this world of Shiento once and for all?" added Fiona.
"I knew you two were going to be like this," sighed Silus as he sat on the couch further from the window.

Amelia sat down next to Silus, she rested back and crossed her right leg over her left. Samantha turned and stood against the windowsill staring angrily at Silus, Fiona sat on the couch opposite Silus, as she sat down she placed her elbows on her knees and rested her head into her hands.

"Why did you two let her go?" asked Fiona.
"With the sorry state she was in, neither of us could bring ourselves to end her, she was barely able to

defend herself, and it is disgraceful to strike an unarmed or defenceless person," explained Amelia, "why should we end her if it tarnishes our honour?"

"So, you instead send her through a portal?" queried Samantha.

"She was devastated that I revealed that she is a tool for Shiento to use for resurrecting himself," answered Silus, "so instead of trying to get her to fight properly, I opened a portal to where Shiento is, so they can have a little chat."

"What would Celestia say to all this?" pondered Fiona, "you two will have a lot of explaining to do."

"Maybe we do, then again maybe we do not," said Silus, "in any case, we should get going soon, we still need to speak with the Duke before leaving, we should think about heading back up to the Keep soon."

"Lady Phoenix," said the maid as she appeared out of the doorway to the kitchen.

"Yes," answered Samantha.

"Should I bring through everyone's breakfast now?" asked the maid.

"Yes please, wait, have you asked for anything Silus and Fiona?" questioned Samantha.

"I am not hungry, so do not worry about me, thank you for offering," answered Silus.

"I could possibly have some toast, jam and some water," said Fiona.

"Then just bring through food for us three, please," said Samantha.

"As you wish my Lady," replied the maid.

As the maid disappeared back into the kitchen, Silus looked at Amelia and she looked at him and they both smiled. Samantha sat down on the couch next to Fiona, as the maid brought through a large tray with two tea pots, and two plates of toast and one bowl of porridge, Silus stood up and walked over to the window.

"Are you sure you do not wish to eat anything Silus?" asked Amelia.

"I am sure, Samantha would you mind if I had a quick shower before we head off?" questioned Silus.

"No of course not Silus, the bathrooms are all upstairs in adjacent rooms to each bedroom," answered Samantha.

"Right, thank you, I shall let you three enjoy your breakfast," replied Silus as he turned to leave the room.

Amelia and Fiona tucked into their jam on toast, while Samantha slowly consumed her porridge. Amelia could hear water running coming from upstairs, Samantha and Fiona smiled at each other as they watched Amelia looking towards the upstairs balcony.

"Amelia," said Samantha.

"Yes?" replied Amelia.

"I was wondering, what I said last night, I hope I did not upset you?" asked Samantha.

"About Silus being King, and that meaning I could not be with him, you mean?" queried Amelia.

322

"Yes, that," replied Samantha.

"Not to worry, I spoke with Silus about that this morning," explained Amelia, "so now I am alright."

"Must have been an unpleasant talk you two had?" asked Fiona.

"No, me and Silus..." answered Amelia.

"No, not you and Silus, I meant you and Samantha," interrupted Fiona, "if Samantha is worried she upset you, and you had to speak with Silus about it, it does not sound like an entirely pleasant conversation."

"Well I was simply asking what would happen if Amelia wanted to be with Silus, and Silus wanted to stay with Amelia, but I was concerned with what would happen if Silus was made King of Selania," stated Samantha.

"Silus would not be made a King," replied Amelia.

"Amelia, I do not mean it..." said Samantha apologetically.

"No Samantha, Amelia is not blaming you, Silus obviously told you that no dragon can be forced to become a King or Queen," interrupted Fiona, "and he is right, regardless of what Selania decides to do to replace Jacob, the one thing they cannot demand is that Silus unconditionally becomes the King, prophecy or not."

"So Silus would not become King if it would separate him from you?" asked Samantha.

"He vowed on that point," answered Amelia.

As the three girls continued talking, the sun had begun its ascent into the sky. The sky turning from blood orange to a vibrant blue, the skies surrounding

Qurendia were partially cloudy, the city now in full motion, the trains running around on their steel highways. The merchants and craftsmen plying their trade, children playing in the streets.

~

In Selania, the people of Selania awoke to find their city playing home to the dwarven race, as well as the elven race. Celestia was speaking with Urthrad outside the city wall in the dwarven camp, Urthrad looked to his left to notice movement coming from the forest to the west.

"We have company," said Urthrad as he pointed out the elves leaving the shade of the forest.
"It is Randalene and her troops," replied Celestia happily, "they made it."
"Well it is good to see that so many survived," chuckled Urthrad, "wait, I thought you told me the dragonkin soldiers would be with Silus in Qurendia?"
"That was the plan, but I can see a large majority that went with Silus, are actually with the elves," answered Celestia.

Celestia and Urthrad began giving orders to soldiers to start helping the approaching elves, Celestia then looked to the forest to see a tall black dragon emerge, the dragon dragged four glaive throwers in a row behind him, the dragon also had an elf sitting on his back.

"Is that, Dragonnoth?" Celestia asked herself quietly.

Celestia began walking straight towards the dragon, but as she reached the edge of the dwarven encampment, Randalene stopped her to talk.

"Celestia, before you question anything that has happened, please bear in mind that things in the Dark Forest did not go as well as you or Silus could have hoped," urged Randalene, "we lost a lot of troops both elf and dragonkin."
"Where is Silus?" asked Celestia.
"He is where his heart is," answered Commander Drake, as he helped a wounded elf lie down in front of a field medic's tent just behind Celestia.
"So, he did go to Qurendia alone?" queried Celestia, "cannot say I am entirely surprised with that."
"It has been a long time, has it not Lady Celestia," came the deep voice of Dragonnoth as Lady Celestia turned to look up at the dragon.
"Dragonnoth, I thought that was you," replied Celestia as the dragon lowered his head to meet Celestia's head height.
"For the first time in a very long while, I am back to being Dragonnoth," responded Dragonnoth.
"So, it was you, you were Legolas, Silus' Pegasus?" questioned Celestia.
"Indeed, but circumstances have lead me to break the enchantment that hid me from Shiento, and now I must stand ready to help in the upcoming battle against Shiento," answered Dragonnoth, "although the circumstances of this war, it seems things have

grown to be more complex than what I believe anyone originally conceived."

"How so?" asked Celestia.

"Well after the battle in the forest, Shiento made a sudden appearance," explained Commander Drake, "Silus, who was practically dead on his feet when Shiento showed up, engaged Shiento quite fiercely, but..."

"But what?" queried Celestia.

"But it seems Shiento had a different motive for showing up like that," answered Randalene.

"What are you talking about?" questioned Celestia.

"After Silus and Shiento stopped trying to kill each other, Shiento said he had come to the Dark Forest to warn Silus that Lady Drask would try to capture Amelia, to force Silus to surrender and in addition to that, kill Silus," answered Randalene.

"So that is why the dragonkin soldiers did not accompany Silus to Qurendia?" quizzed Celestia.

"With all due respect my Queen, you instructed me to follow Silus' orders like he was a higher rank than myself, and I have done just that," answered Commander Drake, "besides even if I chose to disobey his orders, I could not have gone with him, nor could any of my troops for that matter, we lost a small portion of our fighting force, the rest received injuries that would impair their flight."

"So, Silus was only weakened from using his strength and magic, he was not wounded?" asked Celestia.

"Indeed, but after hearing what Shiento said, I personally told Silus to get to Qurendia, and we all agreed that we would tend to our wounded before heading here," answered Randalene.

Celestia looked around as the elven and dwarven soldiers began to mix together in the encampment, some of the more able soldiers began pitching more tents, while medics looked after the dragonkin and elves who suffered more severe injuries. Cirilla climbed off of Dragonnoth's back and stood next to Dragonnoth, Celestia turned and looked at her.

"And I do not believe we have met, might I ask you, your name?" asked Celestia.
"I am Cirilla, a blacksmith by trade," answered Cirilla, "it is a pleasure to meet you, Lady Celestia."
"A blacksmith? May I enquire as to why you remained with the soldiers instead of travelling with the rest of your people?" questioned Celestia.
"Well I would have, except that Silus, who was brought to my shop by Queen Randalene to get some new armour made, so I ended up working on the armour when the evacuation was happening," answered Cirilla, "the morning of the battle, I was so happy that the armour I made for Silus was to his liking, that I then asked to fight alongside him, Randalene and Commander Drake."
"That was very brave of you my dear, might I now ask if you could possibly get ready for more weapon and armour maintenance?" queried Celestia.
"More than happy to lend a helping hand," responded Cirilla, "is there a normal forge I can set up with or

possibly an area where I could get a hand using a mana forge?"

"I am sure we can arrange something," replied Celestia, "in the meantime, Dragonnoth I might need to ask you to help move and build some fortifications for the battle, Commander Drake, I am trusting you to work with the Commanders not just of Selania but with the dwarves and elves as well, let us try and get a foundation to a battle plan ready, then we can build and change it if need be, Randalene and Urthrad if you can, can you manage a balance between tending to your troops needs and counselling with the battle plans."

Everyone nodded in agreement, Commander Drake walked off to gather some Commanders of both the elven and dwarven races, while Randalene and Urthrad began giving orders to their troops. Dragonnoth found an area for Cirilla to set up a mana forge, and with the aid of an elven mage they managed to get a mana forge going, Cirilla set to work forging weapons and armour on a large anvil that Dragonnoth had scavenged off a dwarven blacksmith, who had an extra anvil. Dragonnoth then went with a Selanian resource team who were trying to find materials to make weapons, armour, and fortifications. Selania was bustling with people, all trying to make a difference with Selania's preparations for the battle.

~

In Qurendia, Silus was climbing down the staircase, Amelia, Fiona and Samantha were talking in the living room. As Silus stood in the open area between the entrance hall and the living room, the three girls look up to see that Silus had changed his look. Instead of his shirt and trousers, he wore a black pair of trousers with black boots on that covered the bottom of his trousers, he had a black short sleeve shirt on, with a dark grey leather strap that wrapped over his right shoulder and across his left side just below the ribs, a second strap was attached to the main strap at the centre of the chest and back and ran over Silus' left shoulder. Silus had his original belt on with several pouches placed on his sides, with two larger pouches on his back.

"Going for a whole new look now Silus?" asked Fiona. "Well seeing as my new jacket and armour are both black, I thought it would be best to at least adhere to some sort of fashion statement, rather than wearing whatever I can," answered Silus.
"Ignore Fiona, this look suits you Silus," replied Amelia, "the Dragonborne, who is a black dragon, showing his true colours."
"Seriously Amelia?" questioned Samantha in disbelief, "you are only saying that because you are head over heels for Silus."
"That is not fair Samantha and you know it," said Fiona, "besides I actually agree with Amelia on this one, if you consider that when we talk about good and evil, the typical belief is that good is the shining white knights, while evil is the darkness, and yet Silus and

Shiento flip that around, because Silus is a black dragon but Shiento is a white dragon."

"I agree with that comparison, but I am not too sure that this appearance change will sit well with many others," replied Samantha.

"I am not bothered with what people think of me, if they do not like my appearance, then once this war ends, I can disappear away from those people," stated Silus, "as far as I am concerned, Samantha, after Shiento's head rolls, I am happy to simply get up and walk into amnesty."

"What?" shouted Samantha in disbelief, "you would simply walk away from everyone? What if you became King of Selania?"

"If it would separate me from Amelia, then I do not intend on taking on any such title," replied Silus, "the people of Selania managed to move on from the death of my adopted father, they can do so again without me."

"But Silus..." replied Fiona.

"I am not going to discuss this any further, I do not have to justify myself on this matter," said Silus as he turned and grabbed his jacket off the coat stand.

Amelia stood up and walked over to Silus as he put the jacket on. Samantha and Fiona looked at each other before standing up at the same time, as Fiona turned to walk towards Silus.

"Silus I did not..." said Fiona apologetically.

"Let us get back to the Keep, the Duke is probably wondering where we have all got to," interrupted

Silus, "Samantha are you coming with us, or are you going to head there on your own terms?"
"I think I will head up with you," answered Samantha.
"Alright I will wait for you in the street, I want to quickly grab something from a shop near here," replied Silus, "so I do not know if you want to get your cloak or anything, but if you meet me at the bottom of the garden stairs I should not be too long."
"Alright Silus," responded Samantha, "see you in a bit."

Silus turned and opened the front door and stepped outside into the daylight, as he went to pull the door shut Amelia slipped through the door behind Silus. Silus looked at Amelia standing beside him, as the door shut behind them.

"I guess you want to come with me?" asked Silus sarcastically as he started walking through the garden with Amelia holding onto his right arm.
"I would rather be with you, than have to listen to either of them, and the inevitable questions they would ask," answered Amelia.
"Are you feeling alright Amelia?" queried Silus.
"Of course, why would I not be?" responded Amelia.
"Well, it is just, you seem to be acting differently than before," stated Silus, "I am worried that you are letting what others say affect you not just mentally but emotionally."
"I am fine Silus, I promise," replied Amelia.

"Alright, well, we will not have to go far, the shop is just to the left as we reach the bottom of the staircase," explained Silus.

"What are you getting?" asked Amelia, "If you do not mind me asking?"

"I am going to pick up an order I placed a long time ago, back when Lady Drask was still Isabel," answered Silus, "The shop owner had specific orders to add certain bits and pieces to it, should I not collect it for a certain time."

"And you believe that this person will still have your order waiting?" queried Amelia.

"He should do, there are not many elves that choose to reside within Qurendia," responded Silus, "but he is the best engineer I have ever met, he actually was the one responsible for the Duke's replacement body parts."

"An elf, you say?" pondered Amelia out loud.

Silus and Amelia climbed down the stairs into the streets below, Silus steered Amelia to the left and walked past three shops, before coming to a shop that had a gear as the shop sign. Amelia looked up to read the shop sign, 'Godfray's engineering, the best firearms in the world'.

"Come on Amelia," said Silus as he opened the shop door.

"Alright," replied Amelia.

Silus and Amelia stood in a fairly small room, there were four chairs organised in a line in front of the shop window. In front of them, was a counter that stood to waist height. On the desk was a small note pad and a small bell to the left of the desk, Silus stepped forward and rang the bell twice.

"One moment please," called out a male voice. "What kind of order did you have placed Silus?" asked Amelia.
"Did I hear that right?" came the voice as a man peered round a doorway to Silus' right behind the counter, "it is, Silus Drago, so you have returned."
"Godfray, it is good to see you my friend," replied Silus as the two shook hands over the counter.
"And you too, Master dragon," chuckled Godfray happily, "and you travelled here with a Lady friend, and quite a lovely one at that, sorry my dear, where are my manners? I am Godfray, Master engineer and the only engineer in Qurendia to use a mana forge for my weapons."
"I am Amelia phoenix, it is a pleasure to meet you Godfray," replied Amelia.
"Phoenix, you are the daughter of Lady Cynthia are you not?" queried Godfray.
"I am, unfortunately my mother is no longer in this world," sighed Amelia.
"I am sorry to hear that my Lady, you have my condolences," said Godfray humbly, "anyway Silus, you are obviously not here to reminisce of the past, you are here for your order."
"I am curious what alterations you would have made to it, especially given the time between placing the

order and now," replied Silus, "so why not show us what you have created?"

"With pleasure," chuckled Godfray happily.

Godfray quickly disappeared back through the doorway, the sound of wooden draws sliding in and out of a shelf echoed back into the front of the shop. After a few moments, Godfray reappeared carrying a small black box. Godfray placed the box on the counter in front of Silus, Silus looked at the box for a moment, before lifting the lid of the box away to reveal a small piece of forged metal. Amelia looked at the metal in the box, then she looked up to Godfray and then to Silus, her eyes screaming with confusion.

"The alterations made to your original order are quite significant I am afraid," explained Godfray, "I had to start from scratch at one point, Qurendia devised the technology to create a firearm that could load ammunition from a box called a 'magazine' or 'clip' as the guards call it, rather than the rotating barrel design which you originally ordered."

"It is truly a masterpiece," said Silus as he picked up the firearm with his left hand, "but if I may say so, it seems to be rather light for even a small firearm."

"A h, that is something I think you will actually enjoy," chuckled Godfray as Silus handed him the firearm, "you see the traditional steel that we originally would use for any type of firearm, was deemed too unruly when you consider the rifles that the guards use, however our miners discovered a huge vein of naturally occurring mithril in the mountain quarries and mines, and so I managed to get quite the large shipment of the stuff, first thing I did was to recreate your revolver firearm into this clip loading firearm."

"Well that does explain the weight," replied Silus.

"But how did you get it to be such a dark colour?" asked Amelia, "I thought that all mithril metalwork's have either a bright white or a slightly pale blue complexion to it."

"Very true my dear, however this mithril is naturally occurring which was completely unheard of, and when applied to the forge from this natural state, the most amazing thing occurred," explained Godfray, "the metal not only darkens but grows in size and durability, this firearm will be stronger than most swords made by the rest of my kind."

"What about the unique request I made of you when placing the order?" asked Silus.

"The enchantable ammunition you mean?" queried Godfray, "that I think you will find has worked out wonderfully, this clip has glass bullets, but the way the clip and the weapon itself have been designed like your original designs, you channel your magic into the weapon, the bullets will never leave the clip and you can continue firing and firing until you cannot pull the trigger because you grow tired, which for you my boy, the rest of us will crumble to dust by the time that happens."

"It seems like you have done an exceptional job, my friend, so given all expenses to you now, how much do I owe you? queried Silus.

"Well I will not charge you for all the pieces I had to change, simply because I got more for your original weapon than I would have made, charging you for making it, so let us just settle on the original price of five thousand zon," answered Godfray.

"Are you sure?" questioned Silus in shock.

"Of course I am my friend, you may not have picked up your weapon when you were supposed to, but I will not rip you off given that your delayed collection has benefited me to some degree," responded Godfray.

"Very well, as agreed here is your payment," smiled Silus as he produced a large coin bag from a large pouch on his belt.

"Thank you very much," replied Godfray as he accepted the coin bag and began counting the contents which contained five hundred gold coloured coins, "well everything is in order, so I shall let you go on your way, I am sure you are eager to try out your new weapon?"

"First I have to tend to some matters which are far more important," responded Silus, "take care Godfray."

"And to you both, farewell," said Godfray humbly.

Silus shook hands with Godfray before turning and holding the door open for Amelia. Amelia walked through the doorway followed closely by Silus, as the door shut behind them, Amelia looked back down the street and saw Fiona and Samantha waiting at the bottom of the staircase. Silus loaded the clip into his firearm and then placed the weapon into a new pouch which Silus conjured onto the side of the strap on his torso. Silus and Amelia then walked towards Samantha and Fiona.

"Are you ready?" asked Fiona.
"Indeed I am, although I do have a question Samantha," answered Silus.
"Which is?" queried Samantha.
"Are you sure you are ready to reveal your identity to Duke Horacio?" questioned Silus.
"A trust can only be established between friends, you cannot truly expect a stranger to trust you, if they know nothing about you," answered Samantha.
"Fair enough, then shall we get going?" asked Silus.

As they began heading up the street towards the bridge on the north side of Qurendia. The sun had almost reached the peak of its climb into the sky, the sky was completely clear, the sun glared down upon the whole city. Amelia and Silus walked side by side, behind them Fiona and Samantha stood slightly apart as they strolled gently through the streets.

Chapter 10: Brothers Stand Apart

In the north of Jarvlan, Shiento was knelt down on the ground in the centre of the draconic ruin plateau. He sat still and with his eyes closed, the chilly mountain air did not seem to bother him at all. After a while his face began to show agitation, as he opened his eyes and gazed around him, he noticed Lady Drask crawling on the ground near the path which was leading up to the plateau from a mountain trade route far below.

"So, you come crawling back to me," said Shiento quietly as Lady Drask nudged closer to him, "I am surprised you made it out alive."
"My Lord... is it true?" asked Lady Drask clutching at her wound, "Have you... truly been... using me? All this time?"
"Silus has obviously told you what could potentially happen should I fall, did he not?" queried Shiento.
"So, it is true?" questioned Lady Drask.
"Know this, the part of my soul which is attached to your own, is more than just a way of channelling my magic into you, it can also allow me to be resurrected through you," answered Shiento, "however, that can only happen if you choose to surrender your life to resurrect me, and it is not something which I intend to do by choice for myself."
"What?" asked Lady Drask.
"Silus may believe that I can resurrect myself by using the fragment of my soul which is bound to you,"

explained Shiento, "however I cannot force myself to be resurrected through you, if I fall, you can choose to kill yourself which would resurrect me, but if I fall, I want you to carry on my work, build a new army and reignite this war anew."

"You would ask that of me, even after what I learnt?" grunted Lady Drask as she tried to stand in front of Shiento.

"Relax Lady Drask, you have been wounded, let me see that wound," urged Shiento calmly.

Shiento stood up and walked to Lady Drask, Lady Drask fell backwards against a broken stone column to her right. As Shiento knelt down next to Lady Drask, he held her right hand with his left hand, Shiento then examined the wound lightly lifting the clothing around Lady Drask's wound. Shiento then placed his right hand over the wound and began chanting, as he chanted a pale green light shone from under his hand.

"My Lord," said Lady Drask quietly.

Shiento lifted his hand as the green light faded, Lady Drask looked down to see that Shiento had fully healed the wound, the skin looked like it had never been cut.

"I can understand how Silus would confuse you, but he himself would not know how this type of magic works," explained Shiento, "for he has never had to use this type of magic, and now to the matter at hand."

"What do you mean my Lord?" asked Lady Drask. "Tomorrow Silus will come here, simply because I told him too, he will learn his final purpose for this world," answered Shiento, "and when that is done, he will have a few days to prepare for the final battle, once Selania has been levelled, then Qurendia will be easy to destroy."

"What are my orders, my Lord?" queried Lady Drask. "You will stay with me for now, when Silus gets here, I think it is important that you bear witness to what is said," responded Shiento, "after that, we shall return to our forces and ready them for a long march."

"Should I not go ahead and ready them for you?" questioned Lady Drask.

"Why rush? The longer we leave it, the more time we give the various races to make their pathetic preparations and more importantly, the more of our enemies' flock to Selania," chuckled Shiento.

Lady Drask and Shiento stood in the centre of the plateau, as they began to laugh manically together, their laughter echoed across the mountain range.

~

In Qurendia, Silus, Amelia, Fiona and Samantha had reached the Keep courtyard, as they walked across the courtyard from the north bridge, the doors of the Keep opened to reveal Captain Frederick and Duke Horacio standing there. As Silus looked around he could see a lot of the soldiers in the courtyard staring at him.

"Ah Silus, there you are," said Horacio.

"Sorry, I had myself a nice little nap," replied Silus.

"So, I must ask, have you made any head way on that request I made of you?" asked Horacio.

"You wanted to know who your vigilante is, I now present to you that vigilante," answered Silus waving hand to his left, "Duke Horacio meet Lady Samantha Phoenix, Samantha, this is Duke Horacio, the Archduchy of Qurendia."

"It is a pleasure to meet you, your Excellency," said Samantha as she bowed to the Duke.

"You are the Crimson Crusader?" questioned Horacio.

"I am, and I am also Amelia's sister," responded Samantha.

"Interesting, I would not have guessed that a member of the Flammehelm royal family has been living in my city for so long," chuckled Horacio, "I consider this meeting an honour your majesty, it is good I get to find out who has been protecting my city, while avoiding trouble with the guards, your talents are nothing short of astounding."

"You humble me, your Excellency," replied Samantha.

"Well, it is nice to have a face to put to the name of this city's hero vigilante," chuckled Captain Frederick, "but I do have one question, if I may?"

"Sure Captain, what is it?" asked Samantha.

"I know you and your sister have a history with Silus, but my question concerns whether or not you will remain here, or go with him?"

"For the moment, I will go with Silus," answered Samantha, "I need to avenge my mother and Flammehelm, and so my place is on the battlefield, wherever the demons decide to show themselves."

"That is entirely understandable your ladyship," replied Captain Frederick.

"However once this war is over, I do intend on returning to Qurendia and resume my role as the Crimson Crusader, if that is alright with you, your Excellency?" asked Samantha.

"That would be fine my dear, Qurendia will be honoured to have you return," answered Horacio, "but we must press on to graver matters, is that right Silus?"

"Indeed, old friend," replied Silus.

"Very well, you have come seeking aid for you battle against Shiento, and I have considered this matter very carefully," explained Horacio, "however, I am afraid I cannot simply send my men to defend another city and leave my own vulnerable to attack."

"I understand," replied Silus.

"On the other hand, I will make you a promise," responded Horacio, "my scouts will monitor the demon's movements, and if no threat is posed against us, I will send the full might of Qurendia's armada to aid you."

"Thank you, my friend," said Silus as he bowed slightly to the Duke.

"Now I shall not keep you, I know you should be getting back to Selania to make your own battle preparations," replied Horacio, "So for now, farewell to you all, I hope that fate is kind enough to bring us together again, and good luck to you all."

Silus, Amelia, Fiona and Samantha all bowed to the Duke, the Duke then stepped forward to shake Silus' hand. As Silus and Horacio stepped apart, the Duke and Captain Frederick turned and headed towards the eastern barracks. Silus and the others watched for a moment as they crossed the courtyard slowly. Fiona and Samantha turned around to face Silus.

"So, what now Silus?" asked Fiona.
"Now it is a case of I need to go see my brother, here what his 'vision' for the final battle is, then I will return to Selania to devise a plan to ruin it," answered Silus.
"You cannot seriously be considering going and seeing Shiento?" queried Samantha, "How can you even be sure that he will actually be there, or that he will not just try and kill you the second you get there?"
"I am not looking for permission Samantha," responded Silus, "I am going and there is not a single thing you can do about it."
"I am going with you Silus," stated Amelia.
"No, no, absolutely not, you are out of your mind, if you think I am going to..." roared Samantha.
"Well you decided to disappear and not even keep in contact with me or with mother!" shouted Amelia, "so

you do not get to tell me what I can or cannot do, do not think that just because you are now looking out for me, that this makes up for all those years that you were not there."

"Amelia calm down," said Silus calmly, "as for how we all proceed from here, Samantha and Fiona return to Selania and inform Celestia of everything that has happened here, in the meantime, me and Amelia will head to the draconic ruins where I was born to meet with Shiento, and then we will head to Selania from there to prepare for the battle."

"But Silus..." replied Fiona.

"I am not going to argue over this," interrupted Silus, "this is how we will proceed, and I am really not going to listen to any arguments against this plan."

"Alright," agreed Samantha, "you do what you have to do, but you must understand that there will undoubtedly be repercussions to the risks you are taking?"

"When that happens, I will deal with it, I am not going to stress over things that could or could not potentially happen," replied Silus.

"You should be careful Silus," urged Fiona, "you may very well be marking yourself as a renegade."

"As I said, I am not worried about that," responded Silus, "now go."

Fiona and Samantha looked at each other and sighed, the two then turned around as their dragon and phoenix wings unfolded from their respective backs. Silus and Amelia watched as the two took off and flew over the city. Amelia then turned to Commander

Hawke, who was standing quietly over her and Silus's left shoulder.

"Commander, you and the rest of your troops will return to Selania as well," ordered Amelia.
"I cannot in good conscience..." replied Commander Hawke.
"Just go, I will not listen to any objections, just follow your orders," interrupted Amelia.
"I... as you wish my queen," responded Commander Hawke.

Amelia watched as Commander Hawke approached his troops, the Commander ordered them to quickly pack up and move out. Silus looked to the north east and noticed a small black cloud, stirring over a distant mountain top. Commander Hawke and the phoenix troops took to the sky and followed closely behind Fiona and Samantha as they flew over the city limits, Amelia then looked at Silus.

"I guess we are both setting a bad image at the moment?" asked Amelia.
"Does it matter?" questioned Silus, "if we had a say in anything, we would both be gone once Shiento is dead."
"True, whatever happens, we will face it together, right?" queried Amelia.
"Of course, I will go anywhere, so long as I am with you," answered Silus.

Silus and Amelia hugged each other tightly, as they did, their wings unfolded from their backs. The two then leapt into the air and with light flapping of their wings they hovered over the courtyard, before leaning forward and with a heavy flap of their wings, they began soaring north over the city. Once they reach the city edge, Amelia followed Silus as he began a steep dive down into the mountain range below. As the two rocketed down towards a ravine between two mountains, the ravine snaked away to the north. Amelia and Silus pulled up from their dive and began gliding at speed up the ravine.

~

In Selania, Celestia was standing in the market plaza, in front of her was the war table that had previously been in the throne room, on the table was a map detailing Selania and the immediate area around the city wall. Randalene and Urthrad entered the city and walked straight towards Celestia. Commander Drake was outside the city wall carving logs into large pikes to form spiked walls, several dragonkin soldiers were taking the logs and burying them a few feet into the ground at an angle to create channels between various walls of these pikes. Dragonnoth hovered over a large clearing to the west of Commander Drake, carrying a large group of quarried stone in a large vine basket. As Dragonnoth lowered the basket onto the ground the vines began to disappear. Several guards began loading the stones onto carts to move them closer to the trebuchets, which were set up around the fields outside Selania, as Dragonnoth let the last of his vine basket disappear, he then turned and moved himself over the city wall, before landing near Celestia at the war table. The sky had begun to turn orange as the sun descended upon the horizon.

"We should have more than enough ammunition for the trebuchets my Lady," said Dragonnoth.
"Very good, thank you Dragonnoth," replied Celestia, "how are the defences looking?"
"The dragonkins are making swift progress on the pike walls to create channels to funnel the demons into our forces, the humans in the quarries are carving additional boulders for the trebuchets," answered Dragonnoth, "the miners have sent a large shipment of metal ores consisting of thirteen wagons, they should be here within the hour."
"Excellent," responded Celestia, "and what of the troops?"
"My men have readied the cannons and explosives which can be fired from ballista's if need be, the men which I sent to help gather materials report that we have found strong veins of a wide variety of metals," answered Urthrad, "so we should be more than capable of making some high quality mithril armour, assuming that the elven blacksmiths can handle the number of weapons and armour needed."
"That should not be a problem, Cirilla has also made an amazing start to the forging process, having brought all the raw materials she had in her shop, the rest of my smiths are awaiting the materials but that matter has been addressed already," replied

Randalene, "the rest of my men have managed to position and set up the glaive throwers, and have begun providing medical aid both in healing any wounded here and gathering materials for potions and concoctions."

"And with regards to your explosives King Urthrad," stated Celestia, "how much is ready and what is the potential for making more?"

"Currently we have made over two hundred explosives in varying designs, that is about four hundred and fifty pounds of explosive powder," quoted Urthrad, "we have the resources to make a much larger variety and quantity of explosives, however I would urge you to be cautious on how we proceed from here, each explosive can have an explosion of up to ten metres in radius, housing too much of it in any location is unbelievably hazardous."

"I understand the risk Urthrad, but we should at least be ready to make more," replied Celestia, "what is the chances of having men to make more during the battle if need be?"

"That will not be a problem lass," responded Urthrad, "my engineers who fire the cannons are more than capable of creating more at such a time, and they will undoubtedly be doing so once the battle starts even without being ordered to do so."

"Excellent, well then, we just need to focus on getting the defences, weapons and armour ready, once that is done, we will be ready for the demons," sighed Celestia.

Celestia looked over the map and began moving several markers, to represent the layout of the defences and the troop movements. As Celestia focused on the map, Randalene and Urthrad began talking between them. Dragonnoth walked a little away from the war table before leaping into the air and gliding over the fields outside Selania, as he gazed down, he examined the placements of the different artillery and siege weapons. As Dragonnoth began banking around to the right, he looked to the horizon to notice a small swarm of figures flying just above the tree line. Dragonnoth let out a roar, as he did Commander Drake looked up and noticed that Dragonnoth had begun hovering, Commander Drake soared into the sky heading towards Dragonnoth.

"Dragonnoth, what is wrong?" asked Commander Drake.
"We have company, but I cannot distinguish whether they are friend or foe," answered Dragonnoth.
"How many can you count?" queried Commander Drake.
"There are two at the front flying side by side, with an additional thirty-six flying in formation behind them," responded Dragonnoth.
"Thirty-six in formation, that is the same number of phoenix troops which accompanied Amelia and Fiona to Qurendia, stand down Dragonnoth, they are definitely friends," replied Commander Drake.
"But where is Silus?" asked Dragonnoth, "I know that my brother is not amongst them."

"That I cannot answer, come on, let us go and inform Lady Celestia and see what she says," answered Commander Drake.

"As you wish," responded Dragonnoth.

Commander Drake and Dragonnoth turned and flew back towards the city, as they crossed over the city wall they landed, Commander Drake ran to Celestia's side while Dragonnoth took a few steps.

"What is it you two?" asked Celestia.

"We have a large group heading in from the west, my belief is that, it is those we sent to Qurendia," answered Commander Drake.

"Excellent, then Silus can finally put this battle plan to judgement," replied Celestia.

"Silus is not among those returning," interrupted Dragonnoth abruptly.

"Are you sure?" queried Celestia, "I counted two at the head of the group and thirty-six flying in formation behind them, and I can say for certainty that Silus is not among them."

"Curious," replied Celestia, "I wonder what has happened?"

Celestia turned to look west, as she did, she looked up to notice that Fiona was heading straight for the city accompanied by a woman who resembled Amelia. As the two women landed, the phoenix soldiers turned and landed outside the city walls.

"I swear to you Celestia, he is changing, for better or for worse I cannot judge, but he is definitely changing!" shouted Fiona angrily as she approached the war table.

"No need to shout Fiona I am right here, now take a breath and explain what is going on," replied Celestia as she looked up to Samantha, "you look like her, but the main difference is your eye colour."

"Yeah people used to always say that," responded Samantha, "it is a pleasure to meet you again, Lady Celestia, I am Samantha Phoenix."

"Samantha, is that really you... my how you have grown since I last saw you, I am just surprised how alike you are your sister look," chuckled Celestia, "now, Fiona, would you care to explain what has got you so riled up?"

"It is Silus, he used to always be so punctual to anyone of royalty, but now he has become rather unpleasant and irritable," explained Fiona.

"What do you mean?" asked Celestia.

"He has just been constantly stating plans rather than his usual listen to opinions and move on, he just says what he expects people to do, and does not listen to the advice and opinions of others," answered Fiona.

"I partially agree with Fiona, however I believe I know what has Silus so worked up," replied Samantha.

"What?" said Fiona in disbelief, "you knew what has been bothering him, but did not bother mentioning it until now?"

"I may have said something as a jest to Amelia but it obviously affected her, and now Silus is possibly upset about that, and is trying to prove to Amelia that he will always be there for her, no matter what any of us say," explained Samantha, "Silus and Amelia were talking this morning, I could see through the window how upset Amelia was, I also noticed Silus trying his best to conceal his anger that I could have said something to upset Amelia this badly."

Commander Drake quickly looked around to notice that there was a dark swirling cloud a few miles to the north west, before turning back to face the war table.

"Speaking of Amelia, where is she?" asked Commander Drake.
"Where do you think?" questioned Fiona, "she is with Silus, Silus seems to be heading to meet with Shiento."
"Why would he do that?" queried Randalene, "or is he trying to end this war by himself?"
"Hardly," scoffed Fiona.
"Silus explained that when Shiento appeared in the Dark Forest after the battle, the two first fought, then when Silus realised his fatigue, Shiento invited him to talk with him at their family home," explained Samantha.
"I was with Silus when this scrap and conversation took place Lady Celestia," interrupted Randalene, "I can confirm that Shiento did say he wanted to talk with Silus, something about Shiento wanting Silus to know his role in his victory."
"Sounds like something that Shiento would say, he is arrogant and believes he can do anything," replied

Celestia, "so it seems fitting that he would try to unnerve Silus in some way, but why did he take Amelia with him?"

"My guess, those two made some sort of agreement or pact, that they would never allow themselves to be separated by anyone," answered Samantha.

"So what needs to be done here?" asked Fiona.

"Not much at the minute, we are still awaiting a large shipment of materials for the blacksmiths, so they can get to work on armours, weapons and artillery ammunition," answered Fiona.

Fiona sighed before walking towards the city gates, Commander Drake went to follow Fiona but Celestia held up her left hand to tell him to stop.

"Commander Drake, how well would you say our preparations are going?" asked Celestia, "and I want your honest opinion."

"I would say we are proceeding quickly with the defences, however I cannot say that our defences will effectively keep the demons back for long," answered Commander Drake, "if Silus were here, I imagine him recommending magical traps to be planted on the edge of the fields, so that when the demons break free of the forests to the south, they would walk into a gauntlet of magical counter measures."

"Alright, well then let us try and get a head start on that," replied Celestia, "just ensure that everyone is aware of those traps, we do not want any accidents."

"As you wish my Lady," responded Commander Drake.

"Send Fiona with the men you send out to do that," ordered Celestia, "she needs time and space to clear her head."
"Of course," replied Commander Drake.

Commander Drake bowed to Celestia before turning to walk around the table to head for the city gates. Celestia, Randalene, Urthrad, Dragonnoth and Samantha continued discussing the defence plans for the outskirts of Selania.

~

To the far north of the Qurendian mountain region, Silus and Amelia were flying through a gorge area where the river had eroded deep into the rock below. As they came to a large clearing, Silus lead Amelia higher to clear the mountain region. As Silus turned to head east, Amelia flew beside him.

"So, what exactly is the plan for this meeting with Shiento?" asked Amelia.
"There is not a plan, we will play it by ear from here," answered Silus, "if he or Lady Drask draw weapons, then we draw our weapons."
"Are you expecting Shiento to simply talk?" queried Amelia.
"I cannot answer that with any certainty," responded Silus, "are you sure you want to stick with me for this bit, I mean it could lead to a nasty fight."
"I would rather be in a fight then have to listen to my sister or Fiona criticising either of us, besides if I am

with you, I know that nothing bad could possibly happen to me, not as long as you are by my side," explained Amelia.

"You sure you are not over-estimating my abilities?" questioned Silus.

"From what I have seen of your fighting ability, you have just been getting more and more serious in your fights, each battle you show off a new spell or ability, so I think you just do not like the idea of publishing your full power to just anyone," explained Amelia, "besides, someone should bear witness to a possible confrontation between you and Shiento."

"If you say so my love," replied Silus, "there it is."

Amelia looked ahead of them to see a large plateau, part of the plateau had been cleared of rubble, and some structures look like they had been restored or removed. As they flew closer, Silus could see Shiento knelt on both of his knees with his hands placed on his thighs. As Silus and Amelia swooped down to get ready for landing, Amelia spotted Lady Drask standing in the shadow of a reconstructed building on the far side of the plateau.

"Here we go," said Silus.

Silus landed on the plateau just in front of the sanctuary building on the western side of the plateau, Amelia landed a few paces behind Silus and to his right. As the two let their wings fold into their backs, Lady Drask began to walk from the building that she had been leaning against, Lady Drask stopped when she was standing next to Shiento.

"You are early boy," spat Lady Drask, "you still have another day to get here."
"I am not here to talk with you Isabel, now back off," replied Silus.
"Why you," grunted Lady Drask as she stepped forward and raised her right hand as if about to conjure a weapon.

Amelia stood ready to conjure her phoenix sabre, until Silus held up his right hand telling her to stop. Shiento growled deeply and Lady Drask stood up straight before taking three steps back and kneeling on the ground behind Shiento.

"And so here we are, two brothers born in this very place, now reunited at the pinnacle of the greatest war ever waged in the history of the world," smirked Shiento still with his eyes closed.
"Can we hurry this up, I grow tired of these small-scale battles and I am beyond sick of this war," replied Silus.
"But you live only for war, you have spent most of your life seeking battles to fight," said Shiento as he opened his eyes, "so why not end it here."

To Be Continued...

"I must admit, the tension that ran between him and Shiento scared me, but I knew that so long as Silus stood firm, he would never lose, the pinnacle of the war at our doorsteps, all we had to do was walk out and meet it head on, and through it all, he stood strong, never letting his past slow him down, nor allowing his emotions to cloud the future, this tale has a few more twists and turns, but that will have to wait for another day."

~ Amelia Phoenix ~

Printed in Great Britain
by Amazon

67477198R00213